# Unglued:

# The Book of Strafe

## By

## Bill Wetmore

# Dedication

For Yuriko Tsutsumi.

# Acknowledgments

Special thanks to Cynthia Tyler for her tireless efforts making this readable, to Karen Holtman for her invaluable feedback and advice, and to Kenneth Young, Gayle Loos Shumway, and Weeden Wetmore for their unwavering support.

# About the Author

Bill Wetmore grew up in New Jersey and Connecticut but has lived in Northern California for the past 45 years. In addition to *The Autobiography of Charlie Lord*, Wetmore is the author of *The Exodus of Charlie Lord, Unglued: The Book of Strafe*, and a collection of love poems, *Imaginary Love*. Currently, he is working on a collection of short stories.

Wetmore's work explores the search for meaning, love, and significance in modern life. His characters navigate those worlds of hilarious absurdity and heart-breaking poignancy that not only border each other but often occupy the same space.

# Table of Contents

# Chapter 1 Strafe

Call me Strafe. My full name is Peter Caldwell Strafe, I don't even like saying the name. When I was in high school and college my really close friends called me "Jap" because I'm half-Japanese, but everyone else called me "Strafe" except for my parents. My dad calls me Pete, and my mom calls me Peter. It's a name I hate. Other than Richard, Peter is the worst thing you can name a kid. You might as well just name him "Penis" which is basically what all the kids called me when I was in grammar school. By the time I got to high school, I would only answer to "Strafe". If a teacher tried calling me Peter, they were swiftly corrected. Once, a high school biology teacher asked me what I had against my given name. I looked at her and asked how would she like it if her parents named her "Pussy.".

"I see your point," she said.

When I was at Renfield College in Stoker, Connecticut, I switched my major like four times. I started in pre-med, but after a year of organic chemistry, I decided that maybe I would switch to pre-law. I spent my sophomore year reading philosophical works by Plato and Immanuel Kant. Boring. Next, I decided to become a teacher. I took classes in early education and child development. By the end of my junior year, I decided that I hated kids, so teaching was out.

My father sat me down after my junior year and talked to me about my inability to follow through on any of the decisions I'd made about the direction of my life after college.

"I don't understand you, Pete. You're a bright kid, but you need to develop some stick-to-it-ness for lack of a better term. Your brother has stick-to-it-ness. That's why he's a lawyer."

"Stick-to-it-ness?" I asked. "You mean like perseverance?"

"Exactly," my father said. "Perseverance and gumption. Perseverance, gumption, and a little bit of grit. A little bit of grit and a whole lot of backbone. A little bit of grit and a whole lot of backbone mixed in with some gumption and perseverance is your recipe for success, Pete. Find your path and stick to it no matter what!"

1

"Till death do you part. That kind of thing, right, Dad?"

"Absolutely, Pete. Treat your future like a marriage. That's the key to any endeavor."

"Thanks for the talk, Dad. It's really helped me clarify a lot of things about my future."

"I'm glad I could help, Pete."

"By the way, Dad. How's your divorce going with Mom?"

I ended up with a Bachelor of Arts in English literature. I spent my entire senior year and a summer session before and after it reading books by a bunch of writers who were only slightly less boring than Nietzsche and Wittgenstein. The only writer I really enjoyed reading was Mark Twain. Actually, I liked *The Adventures of Huckleberry Finn*. Everything else he wrote was boring, too. When I wasn't reading *Moby Dick* and "Young Goodman Brown" I hung out in the dorm with my buddies, drinking beer and smoking pot. At least I'd stuck to that all my years in college.

The only other thing I stuck to in college was playing rugby. I was the blindside flanker, which meant I needed to stop any players breaking out of the scrum down the narrow side of the field. I was a good tackler and liked to hit opposing players low. As a result, I got my fair share of concussions when my head came in contact with the knees of the guys I was tackling. Altogether, I probably had close to twenty concussions playing rugby, but other than having a few problems with my memory and sometimes getting confused, the concussions weren't a big deal. I'd be foggy for a little bit, but I'd keep playing until the game ended.

After games, we'd go to the campus pub and have contests to see who could drink the most beer or drink beer the fastest. I was pretty good, but Quint Jones, the loosehead prop, was the undisputed champ. He was the biggest player on the team. Someone had gouged out one of his eyes in a game his sophomore year. After a few beers, he liked to take out his fake eye and put it in your glass, whether he liked you or not.

"Here's looking at you!" he'd shout.

2

Anyone who refused to drink when Quint's fake eye was in his glass would have to fight him. Since he was the biggest guy on the team, no one would fight him but me. He'd toss his eye into my beer, and I'd launch myself at him like a missile. I always managed to get in a couple of punches before he'd hit me about three or four times in the head with his gigantic fists, and I'd have another concussion. After I woke up, we'd shake hands like nothing had happened, but I never did drink a single beer contaminated by the loosehead prop's eyeball.

Other than smoking pot in my dorm and drinking beer with the rugby team, I didn't do a lot of socializing. I had headaches from all my concussions and liked sleeping as much as possible. Bright light bothered me, so I spent a lot of time hanging around my room with the curtains drawn. I'd lie in bed and fall asleep listening to soothing music like Jimi Hendrix or The Who on the stereo record player I'd bought for five bucks at a yard sale. The speakers hardly buzzed at all. The only bad thing about the stereo was that when you came to the end of a record, the tonearm wouldn't automatically lift up and shut the turntable off. The record would keep spinning, and the needle would keep playing the amplified silence in the grooves at the record's end. Most mornings, I'd wake up and the record would still be circling around and around.

I had new roommates every year. Most of them didn't like it that I kept the room dark all the time, or that I slept until the afternoon, or that I kept Buffy, the psychedelic toad, in a terrarium on my desk. I had bought Buffy in my sophomore year from a pharmacy major who was graduating. People would pay me up to five dollars to lick Buffy because she exuded a toxin that produced hallucinations that were like taking acid, only the trip was a lot shorter. I made people sign a waiver that basically said licking the toad could possibly kill them, but I had no shortage of customers. Word got around campus that I had a psychedelic toad, and people would knock on my door at all hours for the opportunity to lick him or her, as the case might be.

The only roommate I had who didn't seem to mind living in the same room with me was a guy named Willy Wetmore. He was the kind of guy who laughed at stuff no one else found even remotely funny. I was taller than him and outweighed him by twenty pounds, but he was a

3

hotshot on the Renfield wrestling team. I'd watched him get in fights with people twice his size and walk away without a scratch, while the other guy would be lying on the ground in a puddle of his own puke. You don't want to get in fights with someone like that. He didn't just want to beat you. He wanted to humiliate you.

Willy wasn't a toad licker, but he liked getting high after wrestling practice. We'd smoke pot together, and Willy would tell me about his plans after he'd graduated.

"I'm going to LA," he'd say. "I'm going to write for TV shows. My uncle works at a studio in Burbank, so I've already got a foot in the door."

He had an internship at a local advertising agency that wrote ad copy for car dealerships and plumbing companies. Whenever we watched the Whalers play hockey on the TV down in the dorm lounge, Wetmore would wait for the commercials to come on and tell anyone who'd listen how he'd make the commercial better.

"I know what I'm talking about," he'd say. "I got paid ten dollars for writing the jingle for Peter Piper Plumbing:

*'If your toilet's clogged, don't worry*

*Call Peter Piper, they will hurry*

*We will handle all your gripes*

*And quickly fix your pickled pipes!'*"

I wasn't sure how writing jingles for a plumbing company translated into writing for TV shows in Hollywood, but I didn't say anything to him. I'd discovered that artistic types are probably the most thin-skinned people on earth, so it wasn't worth taking the risk of upsetting him. All in all, I'd much rather have someone hit me in the head and give me a concussion than work me over so thoroughly that I'd be left lying in a puddle of my own vomit.

I enjoyed talking to Willy, but sometimes the conversations left me confused, and not just because of my concussions. Once, just before graduation, Willy and I were hanging around our dorm room getting stoned. Willy had sold me an ounce of pot and then felt obligated to

4

help me smoke it. We got good and high, then Willy asked me what I was going to do after college.

"I want a dog," I said.

"Pet ownership is an unadmirable trait of the bourgeoisie," Willy said. "You can't have Marxism without the end of pet ownership."

"What about Buffy?" I asked.

"You are exploiting the sweat of that toad's secretions. Do you enjoy exploiting toads?"

"In general? Or are we just talking about Buffy?"

"The forest is the tree," said Willy.

"Well, I like that people give me five dollars to lick my toad, and all I have to do is feed her bugs."

"Charging money for toad licking is counter-revolutionary," Wetmore said. "For the sake of social justice, you should share your toad with the masses for free."

"You sell pot," I said. "You charge me twenty dollars for an ounce! Why not give it away?"

"What are you, crazy?" asked Willy. "You need to understand that what you believe and say is more important than what you do. Your word carries more weight than your actions. Words are mightier than swords. Never forget that. God, I'm higher than fuck!"

"Well, I'm giving Buffy away when I graduate," I said. "Matt Tsoukias is going to take her off my hands. He's a psychology major."

"He's a psychopath," said Willy. "Have you ever listened to him talk about how he hates his mother? Plus, he doesn't shower. I'd never lick a toad owned by someone like him. Why would you leave Buffy with him?"

"Because he's giving me fifty bucks," I said. "Money talks."

"It's counter-revolutionary to listen," said Willy. "Anyways, I need to write a jingle for Nutmeg Used Cars. I'm supposed to get fifteen dollars if they like it."

"Isn't that counter-revolutionary?" I asked.

"Obviously you haven't listened to a single thing I've said."

"Well, it sounds like it's hypocritical."

"After the revolution, people like me will be in charge of deciding what is hypocritical and what isn't. You have to realize that anything that advances the cause of equality, justice, and revolution is acceptable. At some point, the hypocrisy of the proletariat will wither away by itself."

"Then what?" I asked.

"Then what, what?"

"What happens after the hypocrisy of the proletariat withers away?"

"I don't know," said Willy.

"What do you mean you don't know, Willy? You just spent twenty minutes convincing me that being counter-revolutionary is bad!"

"You believed that? I don't believe any of that. I was just pulling your leg. I'm an anarchist. I pretty much just believe in sex and chaos. Politics is just for people who are too stupid or ugly to get laid on their own."

Willy stopped talking and went to his desk. He began writing a jingle for Nutmeg Used Cars. After about two minutes, he was done writing.

"Listen to this," he said.

*'Need a car or need a truck*

*But have no money*

*Then you're in luck*

*Nutmeg Used Cars will finance your ride*

*With no cash down*

*You'll drive off in pride*

*We're number one, we'll show you why!*

*Some restrictions do apply.*

6

"Wow," I said. "That's pretty good. You just whipped that out in like nothing flat! I'm going to learn to do that as good as you!"

Willy looked at me. "I like you, Strafe. You're naive and pretentious at the same time. I'm going to write a book about you someday. You'll be the kind of narrator that the reader will love because of your naiveté and laugh at for your pretentiousness."

"What do you mean?" I asked. "I'm not any more naive or pretentious than anyone else."

"Exactly," said Willy.

"Exactly? Why Exactly?"

"You're Everyman," said Willie. "You are Everyman."

# Chapter 2 Glue

After I graduated from Renfield College, I went home to Majestic, New Jersey. I moved down into the basement and spent a few months doing nothing but watching TV and flipping through the pages of Playboy. The basement was crowded with broken toys, useless furniture, and worthless appliances. I made a path through all the junk and moved a set of dumbbells off a mattress in the corner so I could take their place. The dumbbells weighed almost as much as I did and made a big depression in the mattress that my head fit in nicely when I slept. All in all, I felt pretty comfortable in the basement full of crap that didn't work.

My mother had a job at night as the hostess in one of those Japanese restaurants where the chefs strutted around like gunslingers in a Western. They wore their knives in holsters and pulled them out to do fancy tricks, slicing carrots, shrimp, strips of beef, and chicken. They would take an onion and slice it in half, pour some kind of oil on it, and the thing would flame up and burn like a little volcano. That always brought down the house. Not that I wanted to do that for a living, myself, but I could appreciate true artistry. Anyways, my mom didn't usually get home until after one in the morning, and since I usually didn't get out of bed until after she'd left for work, I hardly ever saw her at all and generally had the place all to myself.

My father had moved out of the house and moved into an apartment with a woman who was closer to my age than she was to his. He stopped by every so often when my mom wasn't around. We'd go to dinner, and he'd ask me how my job search was going.

"Not so good, Dad. No one is hiring," I lied. Truth be told, I hadn't gone out of the house once to look for a job. I hadn't even opened the paper to look at the "Help Wanted" listings.

"I hear the movie theater is hiring," my father said. "I was talking to the manager of the theater last night, and he said they needed another usher."

"You mean I get to wear a red monkey suit and sweep up popcorn and used condoms in the balcony?" I said.

"That's not funny, Pete. I don't think you take your future very seriously."

"Sorry, Dad, but I'm waiting for the right job to come along. You know, something I can put my backbone into. Something that requires grit and perseverance and gumption."

This comment went a long way toward cheering my father up. The waiter came by, and my father ordered a couple of imported beers for us. The waiter brought them, and I drank mine in about fifteen seconds, then I spent the next fifteen minutes peeling the label off my bottle while my father drank his and waxed poetic about how work was important for building character.

"Your older brother has character, Pete. All of his hard work has helped him build and develop tremendous character. It wouldn't surprise me if he ended up a judge or senator someday. Would it surprise you?"

"No," I said.

I liked my brother. He was definitely going places, and I refused to hold it against him. He was several years older and had always been kind to me. He had taken me to the movies when I was a kid and taught me to skate. It was easy for me to forgive him for being the kind of person who might end up a judge or senator.

"So, Pete, what's it going to be? Are you going to have character or *be* a character?"

My father drove me home. That night, I lay in bed and stared up at the basement ceiling. I thought about my life. I wasn't sure I wanted to hang around in my mom's basement for the rest of my life, not that I wanted to wake up one day and be a judge or a senator.

"But it would be nice to have a dog," I said out loud. "In order to have a dog, I need a place to live. This means I need to make money, which means I need a job." This sounded good, even though I'd seen plenty of homeless people wandering the streets with a dog walking beside them. Nevertheless, I resolved to find employment.

9

The next day, I dressed in my best pair of sky-blue jeans, a yellow polyester polo shirt, and a pair of fake leather cowboy boots that I'd purchased for $2 in a thrift store. I probably went to fifteen different places. Most of them weren't hiring, but I did manage to get five applications and complete three of them. I had discovered that the less likely you were to want a particular position, the more paperwork they wanted you to fill out in order to be considered for it, so I only filled out the applications that were three pages or fewer. Anything more than three pages, I could tell, was going to be a waste of everyone's time.

The last place I went to that day was a factory set in a long line of ramshackle buildings in the next town over from Majestic. It was the American Starch and Adhesives Company. I had passed by this place a million times while growing up, but had no idea what they did there. I went through a door with a sign outside that said OFFICE. A skinny older woman with cat-eye frame glasses and a hairdo that looked like a beehive sat behind a typewriter, smoking a cigarette. Actually, she had two or three cigarettes burning in a clay ashtray at the same time. The ashtray looked like it had been made from the handprint of a five-year-old, just like the one I'd made for my dad when I was in kindergarten. When I entered the office, the woman took the cigarette out of her mouth and set it to smolder next to the other cigarettes in the child's hand.

"Can I he'p you?" the woman said. She had a Southern accent.

"Do you have an application I can fill out?" I said. "For a job."

"When can you start?" the woman asked. She scratched her head, and the whole beehive moved.

"You don't need me to fill out an application?" I asked. This seemed too good to be true.

"Oh, heavens no, honey. We had a couple more injuries last night. We always need more workers!"

Miss Beehive took down my name and address and sent me down the hall for a physical with the company doctor. He, too, was smoking a cigarette when I went into his office. He never took it out of his mouth when he gave me my physical. An ash fell off the cigarette and nearly landed on my tongue when he was looking in my mouth. Another ash almost fell down my pants while he felt my testicles to see if I had a hernia. I passed the exam with flying colors. The next evening, I began working the midnight shift at The American Starch and Adhesive Company, but no one who worked there called it that. Everyone just called it "The Glue Factory."

I got to the factory early on my first night on the job. The midnight shifts actually ran from 11 p.m. to 7 a.m. so I got there about 10:45 and filled out some papers in the foreman's office saying that I wouldn't sue the company if I fell into one of the huge vats for making glue and got mangled by the giant mixer blades or got cancer somewhere down the line from the hundreds of different carcinogenic agents used in the manufacturing of glue. When I finished signing the liability waivers, the foreman, Virgil, took me on a quick tour of the plant. He was a little guy, not much taller than 5'2" in his boots. He walked like his feet hurt. Outside his office was a sign with a changeable set of numbers indicating how many days the factory had gone without a lost time accident. That number stood at 0. The place smelled terrible. Everything was covered in a sticky, slimy mess; in some places, the goo was several inches thick on the floor.

The glue factory was actually made up of four or five different departments. Virgil walked me through each of them. There was a refinery for processing starch and cellulose before it could be turned into any one of the seventy different adhesives made at American Starch. They made stuff like glue for model airplanes and cars in the Solvent Department. That department was referred to as "the loony bin" because the fumes down in Solvent tended to make the workers goofy. They were supposed to wear respirators in Solvent, but hardly anyone did. The respirators were bulky and poorly made. They didn't work half the time, so people just stopped putting them on. Over in Solid Adhesives, aka SAD, was where adhesives were made from a boiling mixture of petrochemical resins and waxes. After the mix had been filtered, it was put in pans and chilled. Then it was cut into 2-½" cubes in a cutter built especially for that purpose. The resin cutter had a safety switch that prevented people from sticking their hands under the blades to remove pieces of sticky resin that were gumming up the machine, but the workers always disabled the safety switch and stuck their hands into the cutter to clear the blades. There was a resin cutter in Glue, too. More than one person down in SAD and Glue had their fingers taken off by the cutter, right in their work gloves.

"Don't stick your hands in anything you're not supposed to," said Virgil.

We completed circling the plant and went back to Virgil's office.

"You're gonna work here in the Glue Department," he said.

"We make a little of everything down here. We make solid adhesives, we make solvent-based glue, water-based glue, food-grade adhesives, glue with latex in it, glue for cigarette paper, and a different glue for the filters. Glue for beer bottles and another for whiskey bottles. We make library paste and bookbinding glue, rubber cement, and glue for wood. Wallpaper glue and linoleum glue. Bumper sticker glue and cardboard glue. Fabric glue, jelly gums, spray adhesives, glue sticks, mucilage, super glue, craft glue, gum arabic, epoxy."

We left the office and walked onto the floor of the glue department. Virgil led me past a row of six or seven big wooden tanks that had been built before WWII. We turned a corner and went down an aisle past another half dozen tanks.

"I'm gonna put you with Tuttle tonight. He'll show you the ropes," Virgil said.

He had to practically shout to be heard over the din of the pump motors, fans, pressure washers, and the huge belts being used to turn the giant rotating mixing blades inside the tanks.

"You guys will be cleaning up a blow job."

"A blow job?" I said. "Whaddaya mean?"

"It's a mistake," said Virgil. "All mistakes are called blow jobs here. Tank 9-1/2 is our smallest tank. That's where you'll be working. We use that tank to make experimental batches. They're nearly all blow jobs in Tank 9-1/2. We pretty much know in advance that anything going into that tank will come out as a blow job."

"Why aren't they just called mistakes?" I asked.

"I don't know," Virgil said. "I've been here for twenty-five years, and no one's questioned it until now. Kinda makes you think, though, doesn't it?"

"About what?" I asked.

"What about what?" said Virgil.

"Kinda makes me think about what?" I asked. "You said it kinda makes you think?"

Virgil looked at me and shook his head.

"I have no idea what you're thinking about, kid."

We came to the tank marked 9-1/2. A guy was standing there holding a panel of cheesecloth the size of a bed sheet over a 30-gallon drum. The far end of the cheesecloth had been tied to the tank, just below a metal gate in it that acted as a valve. A sticky mess of beige glue full of pasty lumps sat inside the cheesecloth and dripped slowly into the drum. The man's pants, shirt, hands, and arms were covered with the same stuff that was inside the cheesecloth. Virgil introduced me to this specimen. He had to shout over the noise of the factory.

"Hey, Tuttle!" Virgil shouted. "This here's Pete."

"Strafe," I said.

"Pete's gonna be working with you tonight. I need you to show him the ropes."

Tuttle grunted, and Virgil shuffled off. He walked like a hundred-mile-per-hour wind was blowing only at his ankles, impeding him from moving forward. It was truly weird. I'd never seen anything like it.

I looked at Tuttle. He was a scrawny guy in his forties with a bunch of crude tattoos all over him. Daggers and spiderwebs, mostly. He had some words tattooed on his neck. "Born to Lose." I hadn't even said two words to Tuttle before he started filling me in on the sorry details of his life. He was originally from the Bronx and had recently been released from Rahway where he'd served three years for assault with a deadly weapon. While he was in prison, his wife had run off with another man.

13

"That bitch gonna pay if I ever see her again," Tuttle said flatly. "That bitch gonna pay."

After ten minutes or so, Tuttle stopped talking. We stood there in the roaring silence of the factory. A few minutes went by, then Tuttle motioned for me to take the ends of the cheesecloth from him. I took the cheesecloth from his hands, and Tuttle reached into the sticky beige mass in the center of it and began to squeeze the lumps in it with his fingers.

"Thick stuff," Tuttle said. "Maybe if I squeeze it, it'll filter quicker."

He fell silent again and went back to squeezing the lumpy mess in front of him. As far as I could tell, squeezing the glue had no effect on the speed with which it filtered into the drum. After about 45 minutes, we'd managed to fill about ¼ of the drum with filtered glue.

"Thick stuff," Tuttle said.

A bell sounded in the distance.

"Break time," said Tuttle.

We walked down to the locker room and tried to clean up. I had a little bit of the sticky latex-based glue on my hands, and it was nearly impossible for me to get it off. Soap and water did nothing. Mostly, I just had to keep rubbing my hands together to get the latex to loosen. After I'd scraped most of it off, I walked outside. The rest of the midnight shift was sitting on benches outside facing Front Street. There were about seven or eight of us. Everyone was smoking a cigarette. Most of the men were around the same age as Tuttle or older, and like Tuttle, they were all covered in glue. Not so bad as him, but it was remarkable how filthy they were.

"You the new guy?" One of the older workers said.

I looked at him. He was black and had white hair. He sat next to two other black men who were about as old as he was.

"Yeah, I'm Strafe," I said.

Then we all fell silent and watched a car drive past us like it was the most interesting thing in the world. After a few more minutes of silence, the bell sounded in the factory.

14

"Break time's over," someone said. We filed back into the glue department and went back to work.

I worked with Tuttle until about 3 a.m. In three hours, we'd managed to fill three-quarters of the drum. Virgil came by and inspected our work.

"That's all you got done?" he asked. "What've you guys been doing all night?"

"Thick stuff," said Tuttle.

Virgil told me to follow him. I walked behind him and marveled at how the man was able to walk with feet that seemed to move independently of his legs. He brought me to an area filled with three enormous tanks that held 15,000 gallons of glue each. One of the younger guys was putting micron filters into a filter basket that would be placed inside a pump that was bigger than me.

"Graupner, this is Pete."

"Strafe," I said.

"Pete's gonna be working with you for the rest of the night. Show him the ropes."

Virgil left. Somehow, his feet managed to stay with him.

Graupner stopped working on the filter and looked at me.

"You get high?" he asked.

"Sure," I said.

Graupner reached into his pocket and pulled out a joint.

"Follow me," he said.

I followed him up a flight of stairs and onto the roof of the Glue Department. Then we went up a ladder until we reached the deck of a water tower overlooking the entire factory. Little vents of steam were rising up from various spots around the factory. Over at Solvents, there was a little blue flame venting from a chimney stack.

"They're burning off gas down there," Graupner said.

The night was cool, and there was hardly any noise from the fans and pumps up by the water tower. Graupner lit the joint and took a couple of puffs, then he handed it to me. It was crappy pot, full of stems and seeds that crackled and popped as we smoked it. We passed the joint back and forth several times. Then we went back downstairs.

Virgil had given us an easy job. We needed to pump 3500 gallons of glue into a tank truck parked inside the front entrance to the plant, out on a concrete pad. The big fiberglass tank we were pumping from was full of glue that had already been filtered once, and the clean material would fly right through the micron filter into the tank truck.

"This is the best job to do stoned," said Graupner. "It's so easy that an idiot could do it."

The fiberglass tank was translucent, and we could stand on the floor and actually watch the level of the glue drop in the tank. We were able to tell how much glue we had pumped into the tank truck by a measuring gauge on the side of the fiberglass tank. Plus, we had a sheet of paper that told us exactly how many inches of glue to put in the truck before turning the pump off, closing all the valves, unhooking the hoses, and sealing the lid on top of the truck. However, since we were both stoned, it really didn't occur to us that maybe the truck didn't hold 3500 gallons. Maybe it only held 3000 gallons.

By the time we had pumped 3200 gallons into the tank truck, the driver came running into the plant.

"Hey, you got glue running down Front Street!" he hollered.

Sure enough, we had tried to put 3500 gallons into a 3000-gallon truck. My first night there, and I had a fairly impressive "blow job."

Virgil came by.

"What happened here?" he asked.

"Wrong spec sheet," said Graupner. "Staging gave the wrong specs."

"Hose it down the sewer," said Virgil.

We spent the final hour hosing the glue down the Plainfield sewer. Fortunately, it was thin and kind of watery to begin with, not like the batch in tank 9-½, so washing it down the sewer took hardly any time

16

at all. Then it was seven o'clock in the morning, and our shift was over. I went down to the locker room, showered, and changed into my street clothes. I went outside, and the sun was bright and the autumn sky clear. The street was still wet and clean from all the water we'd used to wash our spilled chemical stew into the municipal sewer system. Birds were singing. I went to the strip bar down the street with Graupner to celebrate my first night in the Glue Department. It felt good to be employed. No doubt, I was going to stick around there for a while.

# Chapter 3 Bern

With the rate differential for working the midnight shift, I was making close to $4.50/hr. That wasn't a lot of money, but back in the late 70s, it wasn't horrible. Plus, I had nearly zero expenses. My mom wasn't charging me rent to hole up in the basement, so I seemed to have plenty of money to spend on stereo equipment, bikes, burgers at Friendly's, and beer at Coconuts, the topless bar down the street from the factory.

My father had given me one of his old cars, a 1968 Bel Air that was white and rusted. It had a three-speed manual transmission, and the gear shift was mounted on the steering column. The only real problem was that the car wouldn't shift into reverse, so I had to make sure that whenever I parked, I wouldn't have to back out of the parking space. Also, the floorboard had a hole in it, so if you went over a puddle too fast, water would shoot up through the hole and hit you in the face. Other than that, it was pretty reliable. It got about fifteen miles per gallon and only went through a quart of oil every three or four days. It had a huge back seat, which was good if I ever wanted to take a girl parking somewhere, though I currently didn't have any real prospects in that department.

I had dated a few women in college, but none of the relationships had lasted too long. I had a penchant for being attracted to the wrong women, ones that expected me to pay for everything when we went out on a date, or be interested in having me listen to them talk about their feelings. They might as well have tried talking to me about theoretical physics. What I really wanted was a girl who was interested in smoking pot and going to basketball games with me. The Brooklyn Pistols were planning on moving to a new stadium in the Meadowlands, and while their stadium was being built, they were playing in the University of New Jersey's gym. The college was located across the river in New Brunswick, but the gym was located in Majestic, about five miles from my house. Tickets were cheap, and you could get a beer in the stands for about a buck. Even so, hardly anyone ever went to the games. The Celtics would come into town, and only about 2000 people would show up.

In an attempt to increase attendance, the Pistols were always holding promotions of some sort or another. Around Thanksgiving, they held a turkey race at halftime. They called three people down from the stands, and each of them was assigned a turkey. The turkeys were supposed to race from one end of the court to the other. The person whose turkey won would receive a free turkey dinner for four people with mashed potatoes, gravy, cranberry sauce, and pumpkin pie. Unfortunately, no one told the turkeys they were supposed to race, so they just spent about ten minutes wandering around the court and crapping on the floor, which got a bigger ovation than the Pistols did during the pre-game introductions. Another night, they gave away Frisbees with the team logo on them: A .45 caliber handgun firing a bullet. In the third quarter, with the Pistols down by 23 points to the Knicks, and the sparse crowd sufficiently lubricated with Blue Ribbon, someone tossed a Frisbee from the stands onto the court. The game was stopped while the Frisbee was retrieved and deposited in a waste basket behind the scorer's table. The game restarted, and after the Pistols gave up back-to-back turnovers leading to baskets by the Knicks, someone else tossed a Frisbee onto the court. This one was followed by another, then another, then three more. Suddenly, the entire arena was filled with flying disks, and the entire court was covered. It took about twenty minutes for the Frisbees to get swept up and for the game to restart.

My favorite promotion was $.10 beer night. The Pistols ran that promotion a few weeks after the turkeys had crapped all over the court at halftime. For the entire game, a twelve-ounce plastic cupful of draft was only ten cents. People were buying six beers at a time and returning to their seats with them. A fistfight broke out between a couple of fans in the fourth quarter with about six minutes left to play. The fight swiftly spread through that entire section of the arena. Suddenly, the whole place erupted in one giant brawl. The players on the court stopped playing and watched the pandemonium in the stands. The game was called, and even though there were only six minutes to go, the win was awarded to the visiting Newport News Submariners, who were behind by four points when the game was suspended. The fistfights continued with renewed vigor in the stands and afterward in the parking lot. Needless to say, the Pistols never tried that promotion again.

I went to work after that game. I'd probably had about six or seven beers in the stands, and was pretty hammered, but no one cared. Most of the other guys working the midnight shift showed up drunk, too. Everyone just sort of slopped around in the glue for a few hours until they sobered up. I punched in and went over to the draw supervisor for my work assignment. The draw supervisor was named Lenny. He was a skinny guy with Popeye-like arms and one eye that looked at the wall while he was talking to you. He handed me a sheet.

"Tank 21," was all he said. He was as drunk as me.

I had to pump 4000 gallons of white glue into a railcar out on the train tracks behind the factory. Tank cars came into the factory loaded with latex and emulsifiers used for stabilizing the glues that we made and making them smooth and homogenous. After the tank cars were washed out with steam and water, they were filled up with finished products like bumper sticker glue and sent back out into the world. We used an industrial filter pump called the Bern to move the glue from the tanks inside the factory to the railcar. The Bern was a filter pump made by a company in Bern, Switzerland. It was stamped with the city of its origin, so we just called it the Bern. The Bern could pump 300 gallons per minute if you opened up the tank valve completely and just let the stuff fly through it, but at that speed, the organdy filter inside of it would break apart in just a couple of minutes, and you'd have to replace it. It was better to open the valve on the tank just a little bit and run about 50-60 gallons per minute through the pump. Then you'd only have to change the organdy bag inside the filter basket once or twice.

It took me a while to hook a hose from the Bern to a line that ran along the ceiling and led outside to the railcar. The fitting on the hose was covered in goopy, snot-like glue, plus the fitting was a bit warped. Whenever someone had trouble attaching a hose to a line, they usually just took a metal pipe or a hammer and forced the hose onto the line with brute force. While I was doing this, Jimmy Gresham was driving a little electric motor barrel truck and clearing full barrels from near my area. Jimmy was one of the few guys on the midnight shift who didn't drink. He noticed me staggering around while I was trying to hammer the hose from the pump onto the line that led outside. He stopped the barrel truck and got off it to watch me. Then he stood around laughing while I tripped over the hose that led from the tank to the pump. I almost fell but caught myself just in time. My hand sank into a big sticky clump of glue and debris in the concrete gutter running under the tank.

"This what you learned in college," Jimmy laughed. "How to get drunk and fall down like a jackass?"

"Fuck you, Jimmy. I didn't fall."

"Fuck who?" Jimmy said. I looked at him. He was still laughing, fortunately. He was someone you didn't want to fight. He was 6'3" or 6'4". He weighed about 285 lbs and was built like an NFL defensive lineman.

I wiped the gluey mess in my hand onto the back of my pants while Jimmy watched. He shook his head, then got back on his barrel truck. He picked up a couple of barrels with the truck. It had prongs on the front of it, especially designed for picking up and moving full barrels around. He dropped these barrels by a scale. When he finished picking up all the barrels near my tank he would spend the remainder of the night walking in a circle with his hand truck, weighing the barrels, stenciling the weight onto their heads, then putting them on wooden pallets so that Red, the forklift driver, could take them to the warehouse and stack them on top of each other. It was like watching someone in Dante's Inferno, doomed for Eternity to push objects around in an endless circle. I'd read that poem in college and had nearly enjoyed it. Jimmy drove back over and picked up another couple of barrels, then drove back to the scale with them. For the life of me, I couldn't see how anyone could do Jimmy's job sober.

When I was done hooking up all the hoses, I opened the Bern up and put an organdy filter bag inside the filter basket. Then I tightened down the hinged cast iron lid over the basket with steel nuts and bolts. I opened the valve on the tank and turned on the pump. I watched Jimmy drive back over to pick up more barrels. When I looked back at the Bern, I noticed that the pressure gauge on it had pegged at over 250 psi. It occurred to me that I may have forgotten to open a valve on the

21

line leading out to the railcar. A sound, like that of a mortar landing in a minefield, came from the motor of the filter pump, then the Bern shuddered and literally blew apart. The heavy cast iron lid holding down the filter basket blew off its hinges and flipped over the head of Jimmy, just missing him. What didn't miss him was a volcanic eruption of white craft glue, which shot out of a crack in the side of the Bern. It coated Jimmy from head to foot. The glue had actually shot up to the ceiling and was beginning to drip back down in long white stalactites.

I expected Jimmy to come after me with a box cutter for getting him coated with glue, but he just laughed and shrugged his shoulders. Then he went down to the locker room to shower and change. Virgil came by and looked at the destroyed filter pump. He looked up at the ceiling and watched the stalactites grow longer and longer.

"What happened here, Pete?" Virgil asked.

I wasn't going to correct him about my name this time, that's for sure.

"Someone on the second shift left the valve on the line closed," I said.

"Bunch of assholes," said Virgil.

"Yeah," I said. "Fucking assholes."

"Well, clean it up, Pete. We'll have maintenance look at that pump tomorrow."

Virgil walked away, and I spent the better part of an hour hosing the glue off the floor, the tanks, the walls, and the pump. Most of it came off, except for a few milky white icicles dripping from the ceiling. Graupner came over. He was high. He looked at the glue dripping from the ceiling.

"Yeah," he said. "Yeah, way to go, man! Christmas is just around the corner, too. We needed some decorations in here!"

The break bell sounded, and I turned off the hose. No one had gotten injured, and I hadn't gotten fired. I went down to the vending machine and got a cup of coffee with creamer and sugar. I was starting to sober up and had a headache. I went outside. It was a week and a half or so until Christmas, and the air was cold and crisp. Overhead, you could see a few cold stars burning in the winter sky. I bummed a cigarette from Jimmy. He had showered and put on some clean overalls he'd kept in his locker. Neither of us mentioned what had taken place. I was just glad that the cast iron lid of the Bern had missed him, otherwise, someone on the second shift would've really been in trouble.

I drank my coffee in silence. I looked down at the cigarette. American Starch had made the glue that held this particular brand of cigarettes together. I smoked it down to the filter then flicked the butt into the street. The bell ending break sounded in the factory and echoed down Front Street. I got up from the bench, and some long white strands of glue kept me tethered to the bench as I walked away. I looked up at the sky before ducking back inside. Hopefully, it will snow sometime between now and the holidays. I was looking forward to a white Christmas.

# Chapter 4 Blow Job

It snowed about five days before Christmas, but it wasn't one of those snowfalls with big white flakes that piled up and you could make snowballs and snowmen out of it or fall on your back in it and make an angel by spreading your arms and legs. It was snow mixed with rain, making a slushy mess that froze the next day and turned black on the roadsides from the exhaust of cars and trucks. It looked like the floor in the Glue Department.

The factory was closed for Christmas and New Year's Day, but we still had to work the days in between. Many workers took vacation days between the holidays so they could have nearly ten days off, and the factory operated with a skeleton crew. In an effort to meet customer orders, the supervisors went around and asked everybody if they wanted to work overtime. Most of the other workers passed, preferring to spend their time with their families, but I took as much overtime as I could. When you worked overtime, you were paid over $6.00/hour. I even worked double shifts. When you worked a double, you got paid almost $9.00/hour for the last four hours you worked on the shift. I liked making as much money as I could. The problem with working sixteen hours in a row was that you had a tendency to make more mistakes the more hours you worked.

The other problem was that working overtime required you to work the day shift. I hated working days. There were nearly as many supervisors and managers, and foremen, walking around the floor as there were "process helpers," which was what us donkeys making the glue and putting it into barrels were called. Someone was always looking over your shoulder and asking *how come you were doing a particular thing the way you were doing it,* or *why weren't you doing something the way they thought it should be done.* It was like having a girlfriend all over again, which was one reason I wanted a dog. I never had a dog that ever bugged me about what I was doing. As long as I fed them and rubbed them behind their ears, they seemed perfectly happy.

I worked a double shift on New Year's Eve. There was a rush order that needed to be completed before the factory closed the next day. The first shift production supervisor came over and waved a blue sheet at me.

"Upstairs," he said. "Tank 7."

On the way upstairs, I stopped on the bench between the two floors. The bench was a narrow platform between the two rows of smaller wooden tanks. The bench was where the chemical operators could walk around and open lids on all the tanks and monitor the glue as it was mixing and make corrections, like adding water to thin the mix or acid to correct the pH. There were two chemical operators on duty, Jesús De Jesús and Buda Wladyslaw. De Jesús was from Colombia. He'd left Bogotá in the 1960s after a prolonged period of political turmoil between different political factions had left over 200,000 Colombians dead. He'd been a doctor in Bogotá, but the only job he could find after emigrating to the United States was a job as a chemical operator at American Starch. I didn't have much use for him. He never smiled. When he looked at you, it was over the tops of his glasses, and he had a habit of walking away from you without answering when you had a question about when to add a particular ingredient to a batch you happened to be working on.

De Jesús ignored me when I walked onto the bench. That was fine by me. I'd come to see Buda Wladyslaw, anyway. Wladyslaw was from Krakow and had come to America after the war. He'd spent several years as a POW in Auschwitz and managed to survive the horrors of the death camp. In spite of his brush with death, or maybe because of it, Buda was always genuinely happy to see me. He always shook my left hand with his left when I saw him. The resin cutter had claimed the three fingers on his right hand between the pinky and thumb.

"I'm working on Tank 7, today," I said. "Any shortcuts I can take to get it done quicker? I want to finish it and go hide until it's time to go home."

Buda smiled and shook his head.

"Ah, Rocky," he said. "No, no shortcut on this one. This is a big account, so follow the directions on the sheet."

25

Buda nodded at the blue sheet in my hand and took a sip of coffee from a paper cup. He held the cup in his right hand, his thumb on the top and his pinky on the bottom. He was the only one who could call me something other than Strafe and I'd let it slide. He'd told me that my first name meant "rock," so he always called me Rocky.

I left the bench and went upstairs to the chute for Tank 7. The area by the chute had been stocked with everything I needed to make the glue. Four or five pallets of fifty-pound bags of tapioca starch and dextrin or maltodextrin, some bags of sodium nitrate, and seven or eight drums of emulsifier. There was a water hose with a gauge on it for measuring the three thousand gallons of water I needed to add to the tank before dumping in the rest of the ingredients.

It took about twenty minutes for the tank to fill with the proper amount of water. While the tank filled, I looked at the blue paper. First, I had to dump the starch and dextrin down the chute to the tank, then I needed to wait half an hour before adding the sodium nitrate and the fifty-five-gallon drums of emulsifier used for stabilizing the glue. This was pretty simple. If I'd been working the midnight shift, I probably would've gone up to the water tower deck and gotten high, but I wasn't going to chance it on the day shift. Someone was sure to see me during the daytime.

While the tank filled with water, the Turks came over to talk to me. Their names were Cenkghis Uk and Guney Cenk. They said they were cousins, but since they called everybody "cousin" it was impossible to tell if they were related or not. Cenkghis had been in the United States for four or five years, and his English was pretty good, but whenever he spoke to me, he'd stand about six inches away. Guney had only been in America for six months and could barely speak English. He had gotten the job because Cenkghis was a good worker, but Guney was constantly screwing up batches because he didn't understand the directions on the production sheets.

Cenkghis walked up to me and stood about six inches away. I backed away from him, but he kept walking toward me, closing the distance.

26

"Hey, cousin," Cenkghis said after backing me into a pallet of tapioca, "I know you know English good, cuz. You teach my cousin Guney read English? Bosses say Guney learn English or fire him."

"I'll think about it," I said.

"Tenk you, cousin. Tenk you!"

"No problem," I said.

Cenkghis and Guney left, and I went over to the tank and looked at the water gauge. I only had about one hundred gallons left to go. When I'd put in enough water, I started cutting open bags of starch and dumping the contents down the chute. I worked quickly. The faster I got done, the faster I'd be able to wander around with a broom and dustpan looking like I was busy. I'd figured out pretty quick that the bosses would ignore you if you looked like you were doing something, even if all you were doing was wandering around.

It only took me about an hour to dump nearly two hundred bags down the chute. While the starches dissolved and mixed in with the water, I wandered over to the lab where the department chemist checked all the finished batches for purity before signing off on them. The chemist was an attractive, dark-haired woman in her late twenties or early thirties. Her name was Sonia. She'd done her graduate work at Princeton and was boiling something in a flask. I sat down at the lab table, put my elbows on the tabletop, and put my chin in my hands. I was trying to look casual.

"Whatcha doing, Sonia?" I asked. "Whatcha working on?"

Sonia looked at me over the tops of her safety glasses, the way that Jesús always did.

"I'm making a cup of green tea," she said.

She turned away from me and started flipping through some papers on her desk.

"Good," I said. "Good, good. Lots of antioxidants in green tea. Did you know they neutralize free radicals and prevent cell damage that can lead to cancer and premature aging? I learned that from taking organic chemistry in college. Pre-Med. Did you know that about green tea?"

27

"Uh-huh," said Sonia.

She walked over to her desk, sat down, and began adding figures on a calculator.

"You know what else has antioxidants?" I asked.

"What?" said Sonia without looking at me.

"Cannabis…," I said. "I bet that's something you didn't know."

"You don't say," she said.

She looked at the calculator tape and transferred the final number on it to a piece of paper hanging on a clipboard over her desk.

"Yep…! I do say, indeed! You ever get your antioxidants that way?"

"What way?" she asked.

She still hadn't looked at me since telling me she was making a cup of tea.

"You know!" I said. "The herb."

"The herb?"

"Mary Jane! Bambalachacha! Tweedy tea!"

Sonia hung the clipboard back over her desk and took off her safety glasses. She turned in her chair and looked at me.

"Do you actually need something here?" she asked. "If you're done wasting my time and yours, then you should get back out on the floor. I've got actual work I need to do."

She put her glasses back on and went back to the stack of papers on her desk. I could tell she was starting to soften toward me. The last time I'd visited the lab, she'd thrown me out after about half a minute.

I went back to the tank and looked at the clock on the wall. There were still another ten minutes to go before I could start dumping the stabilizers into the tank. While I waited, I ate the egg and sausage sandwich I'd bought at the truck parked outside the factory in between the midnight and first shift. It was kind of smashed up from being in my pocket, but when I unwrapped it and took a bite, it was fine. It wasn't entirely cold, either. It sure beat the crappy bean and cheese turritos out of the vending machines down by the break room. When I finished the sandwich, I threw the wrapper into the stack of empty starch and dextrin bags. It was time to dump the rest of the ingredients into the tank.

I maneuvered the drums one by one over to the tank with the help of a hand barrel truck. I opened both bungs at the top of one of the drums and tipped it over into the chute. The drum hit the chute with a thunk, then its contents swiftly poured out down the chute. As soon as the drum was empty, I pushed the next drum over to the tank and repeated the process. Then I dumped all of the drums but one. I looked at the clock. I'd be done for the day before the first break had even rolled around. Then it would be broom and dustpan time. I rolled the last drum in place before the tank and opened up the bungs. Then I tipped the drum over. It hit the chute with a satisfying thunk, and the liquid inside the barrel began emptying into the tank.

The last drum wasn't even one quarter empty when I noticed that a foul-smelling mist had begun rising from the tank. When the drum was empty, I pulled it up. The material code on this drum was different than the other four of five drums I had dumped in the tank. Although the barrels all looked the same, this one was marked 731-24. The other drums had been marked 708-04. I looked at the blue sheet. All the drums on the sheet were coded 708-04. I looked at the tank. The mist was still rising, and the smell was getting worse. I decided to go down on the bench and see Buda.

Buda was rinsing out an empty tank with steam and water.

"Hey, Buda," I said. "I think I dumped the wrong stuff in tank 7."

"You think, Rocky? Or you do? Big difference."

"Well..., I'm pretty sure I dumped a drum of 731-24 in the tank instead of 708-04."

"Oh, oh...," he said. Jesús De Jesús was listening to my conversation with Buda. He ran up the stairs and looked at the drum. Then he came back down the stairs and made a phone call. For the next fifteen minutes, every chemical operator, supervisor, shift foreman, and department manager would run up to the tank, look at the drum, then disappear. Even Sonia came out of the lab and looked at the drum. The union rep came up the stairs, and after looking at the drum, he came down on the bench and looked at me.

"You're fucked, kid," was all he said.

The bell sounded for break time, and I went down to the lunchroom. I sat down at a table with some of the other process helpers. Eddie Wiggins looked at me. He'd stay over from the midnight shift to work overtime, too.

"Word's out," Wiggins said. "You got a big blow job!"

"I don't know," I said. "I heard they can rework some of these batches."

"Word is that this one ain't reworkable," said Wiggins.

"I heard the same thing," said Krajewski. "The word is that this is one major blow job. Word is you're fucked."

"That's the word," said Wiggins. "You done be fucked, Strafe."

"I heard several words to that effect," said Grover Cleveland Winkler. "Not those exact words, mind you, but words to the effect that i.e., you're pretty well screwed."

"Whaddaya think they'll do?" I asked. "You think they'll fire me?"

"Don' know," Wiggins said. "But you done be fucked. That must be certain."

"I wouldn't want to be in your shoes," said Krajewski.

"Hell no," said Grover Cleveland Winkler. "Anyone in your shoes is in for a major screwing. The bigger the blow job, the bigger the screwing. I'm not certain as to what the consequences of your blow job will be, but there will be consequences and ramifications. 'They that sow the wind, shall reap the whirlwind!' I repeat, i.e., you're pretty well screwed.

"Damn!" said Wiggins.

The bell sounded, ending break, and we all got up and walked back to the office. The plant manager was waiting at the end of the ramp for me when I got back to the glue department. He was a graduate from Penn State and had a degree in Chemical Engineering. His name was Tom Swift, just like the character in the kids' books. Everyone called him "Swifty," even though he insisted on being called Thomas.

"Hey, Strafe, come into my office," Swifty said.

He opened the office door for me and followed me in. Swifty sat down at his desk, and I sat down in front of him.

"So, tell me what happened."

"Well, Swifty…," I began.

"Call me Thomas," said Swifty.

"Ok, Thomas. I dumped the wrong stuff in Tank 7. There were a couple of pallets with drums on them, and I dumped one drum with 731-24 into the tank instead of a drum of 708-04."

"Uh-huh," said Swifty. "Do you know that you dumped solvent into that tank? Trichlorethylene, to be exact. A degreaser. Believe me when I say it's bad stuff."

"No, I didn't know that."

"Do you know what you were making in Tank 7?"

"No, Swifty…, I mean, no, Thomas."

"You were making cigarette glue. We ship that glue to Paulson-Marlowe so they can glue their cigarettes together. They're one of our best accounts. What you made was poison. If we ship this to them, people will be dying of cancer a whole lot sooner than just smoking cigarettes made with regular glue."

"Are you going to fire me?" I asked.

"Fire you? Hell no! That's a $35,000 mistake you just made. You're gonna make up for that mistake by working here for the rest of your life! That's the biggest blow job in company history! Congratulations. We're shorthanded as it is, and so far as I can tell, you're a decent worker. Virgil tells me good things about you. Just don't do it again. Read the damn sheet before you dump something in a tank. Now get out of my office and go back to work."

I thanked Swifty and then went back onto the floor of the glue department. I was still employed! I got a dustpan and a broom and went upstairs to sweep up around Tank 7. When I was done sweeping up, I spent the rest of the day walking swiftly around Glue, pretending I was on my way somewhere to do something. Everywhere I went, people called after me.

"Blow job! You had a giant blow job!"

"Hey, Strafe, I heard you have the biggest blow job in company history!"

Word had gotten around. I had a huge blow job, but I hadn't gotten screwed. The day shift ended, and I put the broom and dustpan back in the shed with all the other janitorial supplies, then I went down to the locker room. There were only 9 more hours left in 1977, and I was in the record books of a company that had been around since the 1930s. That was something to be proud of, I told myself. I showered and changed, then went home. I planned on going down to Coconuts later in the evening to celebrate the beginning of 1978 and watch the dancers strip and hang from a pole. Blow job or no blow job, I resolved to ask Sonia out in the coming year.

# Chapter 5 The Stars

I met a girl that night at Coconuts. She wasn't a stripper from the bar either. All the strippers had been given the night off to spend with their boyfriends or pimps and what have you because it was New Year's Eve, and the bar had hired some Irish band to play music for the night.

I suppose the band was pretty good in spite of only playing Irish music with fiddles and banjos and a little handheld drum that this fat guy with a big bushy beard was beating with a drumstick that looked like a dildo. I sat down and ordered a beer, then I looked around. The bar was full of a different sort of crowd that night; not as many factory workers getting drunk and swinging pool sticks at each other. This crowd was made up of people who wore loafers and sweaters instead of steel-toe boots, safety vests, and hard hats. There were even a few women there whom I'd never seen before. The women who regularly drank at Coconuts had scraggly hair and were always trying to get you to buy them a drink or give them money for a cab ride somewhere. The women in Coconuts that night looked like they had jobs and actual places to live. One of them was about my age. She was really pretty, had long wavy hair, wore a denim dress, and ankle boots that looked like they were real leather, not like my fake leather cowboy boots. I studied her for a few minutes. She was sipping at a glass of white wine that didn't even have an ice cube. It looked like she might have expensive tastes. She'd probably be high maintenance. I decided to check out the rest of the women.

Most of them were sitting there with guys wearing khaki pants and wool flannel shirts. It was generally hard to compete with a guy wearing a wool flannel shirt when you're wearing a holey t-shirt with a picture of the Grateful Dead on it and a fake leather jacket. I decided to give these women a pass. Then I saw her. She was standing on the other side of the bar and had a couple of Cosmos in front of her. She was taller than just about everyone else in the bar and solid, with long auburn hair that fell down below her shoulders. She wore a waist-length vest covered in spangles and rhinestones that caught the light from the disco ball overhead and sparkled like the sky at midnight when you were up on the deck of the water tower getting high and

33

chanced to look up at the sky above you. Plus, she had little pale blue stars tattooed on her face and neck, and the backs of her hands. I wondered whether there were more stars tattooed under her shirt and pants.

I picked up my beer and walked across the bar to where she was standing.

"Hey," I said.

"Hey, yourself," she said back.

"I'm Strafe," I said. "I saw you standing here by yourself and figured you might want company."

"Suit yourself," the woman said.

The singer for the Irish band stepped to the microphone.

"We're going to play a traditional Irish tune, now. 'The Wind that Shakes the Barley.'"

"I'd buy you a drink, but I already see you got a couple of Cosmos you're working on. I've never seen you here before. You live around here?"

"Naw," she said. "I'm from down the shore. Neptune. Neptune City. Over by Asbury Park."

"Bruce Springsteen," I said. "The Boss."

"The Boss," she said.

"What's your name?" I asked. "You look like a Mary."

The band had finished playing their song and started playing one called 'Johnny I Hardly Knew Ye.'

"Sorry," she said. "I forgot my manners. I'm Stella."

Stella extended her hand to me. Instead of shaking it, I brought it up to my lips like I was going to kiss the back of it, only I kissed the back of my hand instead. I'd done that before and always got a big laugh.

"Stella's my stage name," she said.

"Oh, your stage name! You must be an actress."

"No," she said.

"A stripper?" I asked.

"Not really," she said.

"I give up," I said. "What do you do on stage?"

Stella hesitated for a second, then finished the first Cosmo and took a quick sip of the second.

"Well, if you must know, I'm a professional cake jumper. I jump out cf cakes for a living. I jump cakes," she said. "That's why I'm up here tonight. At midnight, I'm gonna jump from a cake at the VFW in Majestic. Wanna come?"

I had tried to get a drink at the VFW a few months back and had gotten tossed since I'd never even served in the military. I mentioned that to Stella.

"We'll just tell them you're my manager," she said.

"Ok," I said. "I like the way you think, Stella."

Stella looked at me and took another sip of her drink.

"Anyone ever tell you that you remind me of my father?" Stella asked.

"No," I said. "Is that a good thing?"

"Well, the truth is that just about everyone reminds me of my father. So, there's that."

"Nearly everyone reminds me of my father, too," I said.

We both stopped talking and listened to the music. The singer had this clear, sweet tenor that seemed to be at odds with the subject matter of the song. I listened to the lyrics:

*Ye haven't an arm, ye haven't a leg, hurroo, hurroo*

*Ye haven't an arm, ye haven't a leg, hurroo, hurroo*

*Ye haven't an arm, ye haven't a leg*

*Ye're an armless, boneless, chickenless egg*

*Ye'll have to put with a bowl out to beg*

*Oh, Johnny, I hardly knew ye.*

It wasn't exactly the kind of song I wanted to be listening to on New Year's Eve.

"Hey, Stella, let's get out of here," I said. We can go to my place for a bit before you have to cake jump."

"OK," said Stella, "but you have to drive. I had to take a bus from Neptune to get here."

"A bus? How were you planning on getting home?"

"Oh, some guy always gives me a ride back home. I never have to worry about that," she said.

"Maybe I can take you home after your gig," I said. "If you wouldn't mind."

Stella pushed her hair back, and I could see the little blue stars on her neck and shoulders.

"Sure," she said. "Any port in a storm and all that."

We walked out of Coconuts and down the ice-covered street to my car. She was taller than me by at least five inches, and that was without the spangled high-heeled shoes she would don later when she jumped out of the cake at the VFW.

I had parked my car on the street and some asshole had parked in front of me. Stella had to help me roll my car backward because the car wouldn't shift into reverse. I opened the passenger door for her, and she got into the car.

"Such a gentleman," she said. I started the car and warmed up the engine. You could smell the exhaust from the engine burning oil. I put the car in gear and pulled away from the curb.

"We're off!" cried Stella.

We got to my house, and Stella looked around when we got inside.

"You live here alone?" she asked.

"No, it's my mom's place, but she's working tonight. She probably won't be back until 2 am."

"You're lucky," Stella said. "Both my parents are dead. My dad died when I was a kid."

"Too bad," I said.

"He was a mortician," she said, "but he was terrible at it. He never got the skin tones right. Plus, there were incidents?"

"Incidents?"

"Accidents. Once he worked on someone but forgot to put in some spring or other in their back. In the middle of the funeral, the corpse just sat up in the coffin on account of the spring being missing. You should've seen the screaming."

"That's terrible," I said. "If he was such a lousy mortician, why did he do it?"

"He loved it," said Stella. "Why do you think?"

I showed Stella my room down in the basement. She was impressed. I had a bunch of black light posters on the walls. I put in my black light bulb and turned it on. Suddenly, the room was alive with neon phosphorescent colors. Even Stella's tattoos glowed and burned bright blue. She took off her blouse and bra. Then she took off her pants and underwear. Her entire body was covered with stars glowing under the black light.

"The artist used special ink," Stella said. Stella tugged at my clothes, and in a few minutes, we lay writhing on my bed. I hadn't been with a woman in like forever, so it was over nearly as soon as it had begun.

"Wow!" I said. "That was really great!"

"You're sweet," said Stella. We lay in the darkness, and Stella told me about herself. Her real name was Gwendolyn. A former boyfriend had paid for the tattoos. Stella propped herself on her elbow, and I studied her teeth glowing in the ultraviolet rays of the light bulb while she spoke.

"He said it was a metaphor or something. Maybe he meant meteor," she said. "Anyways, it took forever to get them. Then after all the tattoos were finished, he up and dropped me. He said that seeing the

37

tattoos destroyed the metaphor for him or something. Do you think he meant meteor?"

"I was an English major in college," I said. "He probably meant metaphor, but what do I know?"

We lay there for an hour or so without talking. Every so often, she would kiss me, and I would kiss her back. They were long, slow kisses. She slid her tongue into my mouth, and I slid my tongue into hers. I put my hand along the stars spangled across her belly. I traced the outline of a glowing star on her hip with the tips of my fingers.

"That's Betelgeuse," she said.

"I don't know the stars," I said.

Stella took my hand and moved it from Betelgeuse to a group of seven or eight other stars tattooed around it.

"Betelgeuse is a star in the constellation Orion," she said. "The Hunter."

"I can't tell one star from the next," I said.

Stella kissed me.

"Let me teach you," she said.

Stella got out of bed, and the stars on her back shifted as she moved. She rummaged in her purse for a minute, then came back to bed. She reached for my hand and brought it to a star near her breast.

"This is Sirius," Stella said.

"Serious?" I asked.

"The Dog Star…, the brightest star in the sky."

Stella moved my hand to a group of stars near her navel.

"This is a constellation," she said. "Ursa Major. The Big Dipper."

She grabbed my other hand and put a pen in it.

"Now," she said. "You're gonna connect the stars."

For the next hour or so, I connected the stars on Stella's body. I made a scorpion, a whale, a dragon, and a crab. I made twins, a ram, a scale, and a virgin. This last constellation wholly encircled Stella's pubic bone. When I had finished connecting all the stars, it was time for her to go and jump out of a cake.

The truth be told, Stella's cake jumping seemed anti-climactic after we'd spent the last few hours together. Midnight came, and they wheeled out this giant cake. Everyone sang "Auld Lang Syne," then Stella burst out of the cake wearing a skimpy outfit and holding sparklers. The stars were definitely a nice touch. I had helped her wash the pen marks off her body, and you could barely see them. After her performance, some old guy in an army cap gave Stella a wad of cash, and then we left.

I drove down to Neptune with Stella cuddled up next to me on the Bel Air's big front seat. We stopped in Asbury Park long enough to look at the waves lapping up on the shore, and out over the ocean, a cold ribbon of stars ran all the way to the horizon. I dropped her off at her place, then I drove home. We never saw each other again. The headlights on the freeway were bright yet finite, and above me, in the clear dark expanse of sky, I followed a river of nearly imperceptible stars back to my house.

# Chapter 6 Hot Melt

I went to watch the Pistols play the 76ers in early January of 1978. Erving scored about 50 points and had a spectacular dunk that started with him leaping from near the free-throw line. The stands were packed with all of 1800 fans. It was pretty pathetic. I only had a few beers that night and was pretty sober when I showed up at work that evening. We'd had a big order from a soup company headquartered in New Jersey that had production locations all across the country. They needed glue to hold the labels onto their metal soup cans. The Solid Adhesives Department normally handled big orders for "Hot Melt", but they needed some help filling this particular order because of its size. Since there was one ancient hot melt tank in the glue department, workers were assigned to make, filter, cut, and package the hot melt around the clock for several months running.

Hot melt was made from various petrochemical resins and waxes heated to a boil in this particular metal tank that had been around since the 1930s. The safety protocols for handling hot melt seemed to date from the 1930s, as well, which meant there pretty much weren't any. The day shift usually made this stuff. Second shift sometimes "drew it off" (i.e., filtered it through organdy or cheesecloth bags into metal pans), but mostly that job fell to us on the midnight shift. If you were lucky enough to get assigned a tankful of hot melt to "draw off," your main job was essentially to make sure the organdy or cheesecloth bag you were filtering the hot melt through didn't suddenly break (which invariably happened) and splash boiling wax and oils onto you. This in itself was quite a feat since hardly anyone working the midnight shift was sober.

Also, the fumes from this stuff were thick and noxious. To keep from breathing them, we tied cheesecloth around our noses and mouths. To protect ourselves from getting burned from this crazy mixture, we were required to wear green cotton aprons, the kind you find in kitchens everywhere, a pair of insulated gloves, and some green sleeves that went over your forearms up to the elbow. These were made of the same heavy-duty cotton as the aprons.

I didn't particularly care for working with hot melt, mostly because that tank was highly visible. It was right up by Gresham's scale and was the first thing you saw when you came up the forklift ramp and turned the corner into Glue. You couldn't hide out when you were working on that tank. Plus, the work was hot and nasty and probably the most dangerous thing to work on in the entire department. I'd only been there for a few months and had already witnessed at least a half-dozen accidents. Most were pretty minor. A bag would break, and "Hot Melt" would end up on someone's pants. There'd be burns. That had happened to me in my first week in Glue. I had tied an organdy bag to the long metal pipe that I had screwed into the swing fitting by the tank valve. The swing fitting allowed you to move the pipe with the organdy back and forth between a pair of metal buckets. As soon as one bucket filled, you swung the bag over the next bucket by hand. It was during one of those moments while I was swinging the organdy bag from one bucket to the next that the organdy broke, and a little bit of the hot melt caught my left pant leg on the inside of my thigh. Even through my pants, it burned. Later, during break time, I went into the locker room and looked at the burn. It was an angry-looking blistered red welt the size of a half dollar.

Fortunately, it wasn't my turn to work hot melt that evening. Wall-eyed Lenny, the draw supervisor, gave that tank to Willie Thibodeaux. Willie was the white-haired black man I'd met my first night at the factory, the one who'd asked my name. He was from Baton Rouge, Louisiana, and was easy-going and gregarious. He liked to tell stories about life in the Red Stick, about how he'd eaten possum pie and turtle eggs, rattlesnake, and grilled raccoon.

"A man will eats mos' anythang if he be hongry 'nuff," said Willie. "Plus, it were mos'ly delicious!"

Willie had joined the Marines and served in Korea. He had survived the Battle of the Chosin Reservoir, where he'd earned a Silver Star for valor in combat. He'd suffered frostbite as one of the "Chosin Frozen" and lost a couple of toes on each foot.

"Ain't nobody don' know how important your toes be fo' walkin' 'til somebody done lop 'em off," said Willie.

41

After Korea, Willie left the Marines and traveled around the country picking up odd jobs here and there. He liked liquor and women and spent time in jail on numerous occasions on account of both these subjects of desire.

"Booze an' pussy," Willie said one night while we were sitting outside on Front Street watching the cars pass during break. "If yo' evah wants to set a trap fo' ol' Willie, that's what yo' baits it wid."

Willie, like just about everyone working that night, was drunk. Lenny gave him the draw sheet, and Willie eyeballed it.

"Goddamn, Lenny, can't yo gimme no sweet li'l jelly gum tonight? Dis goddamn hot melt is like workin' in hell."

"Tank 19," growled Lenny. He pointed to the hot melt tank, and Willie trudged over to the equipment locker to get a pair of insulated gloves, an apron, and protective sleeves.

Lenny glared at me with his good eye. His other eye looked at Gresham weighing drums on his scale.

"Any special requests from you, too?" Lenny asked. "Maybe you'd like a pillow and blanket so you can take a nap up by the sugar shack?"

That wasn't such a bad idea. The sugar shack was where they kept the glucose tank locked up so people wouldn't steal it in five-gallon buckets and take it home to pour on their pancakes. It was out of the way, and you could hide up there all night and nobody would know. I decided against antagonizing Lenny and his Popeye-sized forearms by making any requests.

"Here's an easy job for you," Lenny said. "Tank 6. That's the jelly gum that other fuck-up wanted." He jerked a thumb over his shoulder at Willie. "Don't milk it all night. We got a tank truck coming in at three, and I need you to load it when it comes in."

I plucked the blue sheet from Lenny's hand and sauntered over to the tank. Graupner was standing by the pressure washer near Tank 8, staring at a pair of rubber-coated work gloves lying on the ground.

"Graupner, what're up to?" I asked.

42

"Fuck me," Graupner said. "I dropped acid a couple of hours ago, and I can't tell if there are hands in those gloves."

I looked at the gloves and kicked at one of them.

"They're empty," I said.

Graupner grunted and wandered over to Lenny to get his work assignment. I stared after him. Personally, I drew the line at getting high while working. I'd dropped acid a couple of times in college and couldn't imagine doing anything while tripping except drinking beer and watching baseball.

I put my tool bag down by the tank, then I went down to the stencil machine down by the resin cutter and cut out a stencil on a sheet of cardboard. The stencil included the batch number of the material I was working on and the tare weight of the empty barrel. The batch number and the weight of the empty barrel got stenciled on the head of the barrel after you filled and sealed it. Then you marked the drum with a number in crayon, indicating which barrel got filled first, second, third, etc. I finished cutting out my stencil and went back up to the tank. I found a pump with a boom holding an overhead filter basket, and put a cheesecloth filter bag in the basket, then I reached into the bag I used to carry my tools and fished out a donut shaped metal ring that I put into the mouth of the basket to hold the filter bag in place. I positioned the funnel of the pump under the gate of the tank and took my hammer and banged on the handle of the metal gate acting as the tank valve, and the jelly gum oozed out of the tank into the funnel. I turned on the pump, and in a few seconds, the filter basket was coated in a viscous brownish goo that began filling the poly bag inside the barrel I had placed beneath it. I was in business!

While the first barrel filled, I rolled an empty barrel over. I pulled an ink pad with orange ink out of my bag and a roller, and stenciled the batch number and the empty barrel weight on the head of the drum. The tare weight never changed. It was always 50 pounds. I opened the barrel up and put a poly bag inside the drum. Then I rolled that barrel over to the pump and positioned it next to the first barrel, that now ⅔ full. When the glue in the drum reached two or three inches from the top of the barrel, I loosened the boom holding the filter basket and tipped the second barrel over toward the first so I wouldn't spill any glue on the ground. Then I swung the boom over to that drum. Tightening the boom, I covered the jelly gum in the barrel with a plastic poly circle, put the head on it, and tightened the metal hoop, the ring seal, holding the head onto the barrel. Then I put a metal wire tie through the ring seal and twisted it so the head wouldn't come off the drum. I marked the drum #1 with a black crayon, then I rolled it out of the way with a hand barrel truck. I grabbed another empty barrel, stenciled it, took the head off, filled it with a poly bag, and rolled it over to the pump. Barrel #2 was ¾ full by this time. When it was full, I swung the boom over to the third barrel, tightened the boom down, and sealed the drum as I had done earlier. Then I grabbed another empty drum and repeated the process.

The tank only held about twenty barrels of glue. The full barrels were ultimately destined for a brewery in Milwaukee to hold the labels on bottles of lager and ale. Most of the other workers stretched this job out for four to six hours, but I liked filling the barrels as swiftly as possible. Even with downtime to stop the pump and change the cheesecloth bag inside the filter basket when the bag got dirty, I liked finishing drawing off the tank by the time the first break rolled around at 1 am. Then I'd screw around for the next couple hours until the tank truck came in.

Break time came, and I went down to the break room down by the front entrance. It was too cold to sit outside so we all sat in the break room and swapped lies about all the women we were screwing. John Motley was originally from Detroit where he claimed to have been a pimp.

"I had me a whole stable," Motley said. "A whole muthafucking stable. I could take my pick anytime I wanted. Black ones, white ones, yellow ones, purple ones, ones from Venus, and another two or three from Mars."

"You're talking out of Uranus," said Klein. We all laughed at that like a pack of hyenas. The only one who didn't laugh was Jerry Hrabowski. Jerry was a born-again Christian. He sat by himself reading a Bible. He'd served nine years in Ossining--Sing Sing--for manslaughter. He'd gotten drunk as a teenager and killed someone while driving on the New York Thruway. He was pretty damaged, and all of us left him

44

alone. He and Jimmy Gresham were the only ones on the midnight shift who never showed up drunk. In Jimmy's case, it was a personal choice. He'd watch his father get drunk and abuse his mother. In Jerry's case, it was a court-mandated condition of his parole, though it would've been difficult to imagine him ever drinking again given the circumstances of his life.

Willie had started sobering up and wasn't feeling too good. He sat across the table from me with his head on his arms.

"Goddamn," he said. Jesus Christ."

"You OK, Willie?"

"Jesus Christ. Goddamn."

"Maybe you should sit over there with Jerry," said Klein. "You two can be the amen corner."

"Good Lord! Jesus Christ!" moaned Willie. "I need me a goddamn drink."

The break ended, and we all got up and shuffled back to Glue. Virgil caught me at the base of the ramp and walked up to the weigh station with me.

"Management's got their eye on you, Pete." This time, I ignored him by using my real name. No matter how many times I told him to call me Strafe, he never did.

"Yeah, I know. I had that big screw up in Tank 7."

"Peanuts, kid. Don't worry about it. They're looking at you for a supervisor position. After a few years, you can be a foreman, then somewhere down the line, you'll get promoted to the front office. The company will send you to school and pay for you to get a Chemical Engineering degree. They take care of their own around here."

"I don't know," I said. "I'm not sure I want to be telling other people what to do."

"Supervisors start off at twenty-five grand a year," said Virgil. "Where else are you gonna find a job making that kind of money around here?"

"That's pretty good," I said.

"Damn right!" said Virgil. "Just keep your nose clean. Keep your nose clean and pressed to the grindstone. Keep your nose to the grindstone and your shoulder to the wheel. Next thing you know, you'll look behind you and you'll be amazed at how far you've come."

"Nose clean and face to the grindstone," I said.

"Think about it," said Virgil. He left, and I watched him wobble away back towards the glue office. I liked the idea of making three times more money than I was currently making, but I wasn't sure I was management material, though I'd probably have a better chance with Sonia if I had an engineering degree. Of course, I'd have to take all those chemistry classes to get one of those, and that didn't sound appealing in the least. There had to be an easier way to get into Sonia's pants. Maybe I could invent something, like a pen that doubled as a pH monitor, which would make Sonia's job easier. The next time I saw her, I'd casually mention I was working on an invention that had the potential to revolutionize lab work everywhere. That was only one of my ideas. I liked getting high and coming up with different inventions. Unfortunately, I never wrote any of them down and had forgotten most of them when I woke up the next morning.

I was interrupted by my thoughts of management, Sonia, and inventions by a low moan that was coming from over near the weigh station. I picked up my tool bag by Tank 7, then headed over to where the noise was coming from. By now, the moans had become a full-throated scream. I came around the corner to the main aisle and saw Willie. He was crying, shaking, and screaming. He'd tripped and fallen into one of the rectangular cooling pans full of hot melt, and the burning glue had poured down into one of his sleeves. He had hot melt on the side of his face and neck and on the back of his shirt. Lenny had dragged him to the safety shower next to the tank and had pulled the chain to the water tank. Water was pouring over Willie, whose screams were now a wild, uncontrollable wail that continued for ten minutes until the ambulance arrived. The rest of us gathered around the weigh scale until the paramedics arrived and took Willie to the hospital in an ambulance.

After the paramedics left, Lenny came over to us.

46

"Stop looking at each other like baboons and get back to work," Lenny said. Lenny handed me the sheet for the hot melt tank.

"Finish that tank up, then load the tank truck when it comes in," he said.

I went down to the equipment locker by the cutter and stencil machine and put on some protective gear. On my way back up the ramp, I vowed never to eat another can of soup, no matter how long I lived.

# Chapter 7 Zen

After my shift ended, I normally went down to Coconuts and had a couple of beers before going home and going to bed. My mom was normally still asleep when I got back to the house, and I'd go down to my room and fall asleep while listening to a Grateful Dead or Allman Brothers album. The record would still be spinning on my stereo when I woke up sometime in the afternoon, the needle running around and around in the grooves at the center of the disk. Sometimes I felt like that was my life. Not that it was a bad thing.

I would get out of bed about 4 p.m., then spend the next few hours getting high and watching TV. My mother was normally gone by three, and I liked the solitude. Sometimes I'd go back up to Coconuts before my shift and spend a couple of hours drinking beer and watching the ball game on the TV over the bar when I wasn't staring at the strippers. I'd stopped throwing my money at them after a few weeks working at the factory. No matter how much money you gave them, it never led to anything. They all had boyfriends, and the bar only hired them, so you'd hang around longer drinking up your paycheck.

Some afternoons, I'd go to a park in Majestic on the banks of the Raritan River and just sit on a bench enjoying the warmth of the sun. There were lots of cherry trees in the park, and I liked watching the blossoms bloom or fall and drift from the trees a few weeks later. Every so often, a co-ed from across the river at UNJ would walk past, and I would mentally undress her. On rare occasions, one might be sitting on a park bench reading a book, and I'd sit down beside them.

"Whatcha reading?" I would ask.

Most of the time, they would just ignore me, and I'd move on to another bench, but on a couple of occasions, they actually talked to me. One of them was reading a book titled *The Lesbian Nation: The Feminist Solution*.

"The author claims that women should make a total break from men and male-dominated capitalist institutions," the woman said. "I happen to agree."

That was obviously a pretty short conversation. Another time, I sat down on a bench next to a gorgeous girl wearing a pair of patched jeans and a macrame vest. She handed me her book when I asked what she was reading. It was titled *Zen and the Art of Motorcycle Maintenance*. I turned the book in my hands.

"What's it about?" I asked.

"It's about values," the woman said.

"Maybe you should give me your phone number and we can talk about values, sometime," I said. "I was an English major in college."

I didn't feel too bad that she didn't give me her phone number. When she stood up from the bench, I noticed that she had thick legs and a large butt. I wouldn't have asked for her number if I'd noticed that first thing. Still, I went to the library and checked the book out and tried reading it, but it was too convoluted for me to really understand. I decided to read a little bit about Zen Buddhism. Maybe if I knew what Zen was about, I'd understand the book better. I checked out some books about Zen and read them every morning before going to sleep. I didn't understand any of it. There was stuff about finding your original face and the sound one hand clapping made. It made my head hurt thinking about some of what I'd read, still, I figured it would be good to learn more about it, just in case I ever ran into another chick in the park, I could casually drop that I was studying Zen and knew the sound of one hand clapping. I began practicing meditation.

Mostly, I did this at work while I was sitting on top of a tank truck loading it with glue. I'd sit on top of the truck with my legs crossed and my eyes closed and ponder Zen koans and riddles about monks carrying girls across muddy roads or the Buddha being three pounds of flax. The first time I tried meditating on top of the tank truck, I fell asleep and almost fell off. After that, I hooked myself with a safety harness to the top of the truck, even though the rope attached to the harness was way too long. If I fell off the truck wearing the harness, I probably would've broken my legs or my neck. I guess I could've fixed the rope, but it didn't really occur to me to do that. When you're sitting on top of a tank truck, you can only be enlightened about so many things.

One night, while I was putting 2500 gallons of glue in a tank truck that held 2500 gallons of glue, I was meditating on this Zen riddle:

A blind man is visiting a friend. As he's leaving, he's given a paper lantern with a candle inside.

"I don't need a candle. Light and dark are all the same to me."

"Just so," his friend replies. "This lantern is so that other people won't run into you in the dark."

As the blind man is walking, someone bumps into him. The blind man shouts at the other person.

"Hey, watch where you're going! Don't you see my lantern?" The other man pauses, then answers calmly.

"Brother, your candle has gone out."

I couldn't make heads or tails of this story. The bell for break sounded, and I was about to climb the ladder off the truck when I heard a noise by the side of it. I shined my flashlight over the side of the truck and saw an enormous rat by the truck's rear wheel, right at the base of the ladder. It was as big as most house cats. As long as the rat was there, there was no way I was climbing down the ladder. I spent my entire break on top of the tank truck. When the rat finally wandered off into the night, I put my flashlight in my back pocket and climbed down. I went over to the pump and turned it off, even though I had five or six hundred gallons left to put in the truck. Then I went and took the break I'd missed. I wasn't going to let the rat prevent me from sitting down in the break room for fifteen minutes.

The break room was empty. I went outside and looked to see if anyone was sitting there, but the benches were deserted. I looked at the sky. A mass of storm clouds rolled ominously above me; the undersides of the clouds were a sick-looking yellow color from the lights of Dunellen, Plainfield, and Majestic. For the briefest of moments, I thought about Stella. I had really enjoyed being with her, I'd even learned something, but I'd also realized that I could never choose to fully love someone like her. I mean, once you dig beneath the surface of someone like Stella, you discover that the outside pretty much matches their insides. That's refreshing, because you rarely find people who are the same inside and outside, but after a while, they get boring. I like it better when people are different on the surface than they are deep down inside themselves. That way, they'll always surprise you. I was about to go back inside and finish loading the truck when something hit me in the leg, and then a man walked right into me. It startled the hell out of me.

"Shit," I yelled. "What the hell, man!"

I looked at the person who'd run into me. He held a cane in his right hand.

"I'm sorry, sir, but I didn't see you. I'm blind."

"Yeah. I see that now," I said. I reached into my back pocket and pulled out my flashlight. I turned it on and put it into his hand.

"Here," I said. "that's my flashlight you're holding."

"Oh, I don't need a flashlight, I'm perfectly fine in the dark," the man said.

"The light ain't for you, ya dummy! It's so everyone else will see you coming and get out of the way!"

"I see!" the man said. He paused for a few seconds. "That's a joke," he said. "Aren't you going to laugh?"

"Yeah, yeah. Hilarious," I said. "You're a regular Robin Williams."

"Who?"

"You know, that guy on TV. Mork from Ork."

"I'm afraid I don't watch TV." the man said. "I'm blind."

"Oh, yeah."

"Well, it was really nice running into you," the blind man said.

"Yeah, I get the joke," I said.

The blind man waved the flashlight and started walking down the street.

"Change the batteries when you notice the flashlight getting dim," I shouted.

"How would I know?" he hollered back. "I'm blind."

51

"Ask someone, ya dummy!"

I went back inside the building and slowly wandered back to Glue. I hoped the rat wasn't around. I'd made the mistake of giving that blind guy my flashlight. If the rat was back, I could've used the flashlight as a club if need be. There's generous, and then there's stupid. I stopped by my tool bag inside the doorway leading to the truck outside on the concrete pad. I fished out my hammer and stuck it in my back pocket. I was prepared now if I ran into anything else in the dark.

# Chapter 8 Mom

The weekend came, and I hung around Saturday afternoon watching the Indy 500 race on TV. It was Memorial Day weekend, and nothing much else was on TV in the afternoon. The Mets weren't playing until later in the evening. Doc Gooden was scheduled to pitch. The Yankees were playing a doubleheader against the Orioles, but I hated the Yankees. If the Red Chinese had formed a team and played the Yanks, I would've been rooting for the Godless Reds, so I watched a bunch of guys drive around the track for three or four hours even though I couldn't care less about it. After a couple of hours, I went outside and checked on the pot plant I was growing in the backyard. My mother had thought it was a weed, and I had to stop her from digging it up.

"Leave it alone, Ma!" I hollered. "That's my plant!"

"Your plant, Peter? What kind of plant is this?" My mother had been in the country for nearly thirty years and still couldn't speak English in complete sentences.

"That? Oh, that's an Egyptian tomato plant," I said.

"That doesn't look like a tomato plant, Peter. You sure that is an Egyptian tomato?"

"That's what the guy at the store said," I said.

My mother walked away from the pot plant, muttering something in Japanese to herself. I had no idea what she was saying. My brother and I had never been taught Japanese when we were growing up. My father's parents refused to let her teach us anything but English, and my mother had gone along with them. She was new to the country and did whatever they told her to do.

I watered my plant, then put some Miracle Gro on it. The leaves were big and green, but I didn't see any buds on it yet. I pulled off a bunch of the leaves at the bottom of the plant and noticed that some of them had little bug holes. I went back into the house and rummaged under the sink. Then I came back out with the pump sprayer with the can of Black Flag Bug and Insect Killer attached to it. I soaked the plant with

53

bug spray and went back to the house. Come October, I was hoping to have a fine crop of tomatoes.

I didn't have to work that night and decided to go to the Pink Pony nightclub in Majestic on the way to Edison. It was called a nightclub, but it was really just a bigger strip joint than Coconuts. The girls at the Pink Pony were better looking, though, and more daring than the ones at Coconuts. I'd been there around Christmas, and one of the girls had an act that included candy canes. She'd put them down her G-string, then throw them out to the perverts hanging around the bar. It was a pretty great act. No one cared that she had tiny breasts.

I got to the nightclub, and there was a kid in the parking lot with a flashlight directing cars. I stopped and rolled down the window.

"Hey, kid, where can I park so I don't have to shift in reverse?" I asked. "You got a spot where I can just drive forward when I'm leaving here?"

The kid directed me to a spot near a gap in the fence on the back side of the lot.

"Perfect," I said. I gave him a buck, then pulled into the spot. When I got my next paycheck, I was planning to get my transmission fixed so I could shift the Bel Air into reverse, but even if I didn't, it was okay. Indy cars didn't go in reverse either, and nobody said anything about that.

The action at the Pink Pony was pretty sparse that night. Everyone must have gotten too drunk at the family bar-b-que, or were still getting drunk at the family bar-b-que. The crowd was about half the size of what it normally was, and none of the dancers had an act as remotely interesting as the girl with the candy canes. I left early and drove around until about midnight. I stopped at a couple of bars hoping to run into someone I knew. Sometimes you'd find someone who was on their way to a party, and you'd tag along. The next thing you knew, you'd be making out with some chick in the spare bedroom without even knowing their name, but that night I didn't run across anyone. I went home and fell asleep about 1 a.m. and slept until about noon the next day.

When I got up, I got dressed and went upstairs. My mom was in the kitchen drinking a cup of coffee with sweetened condensed milk and sugar. She'd made the coffee in the electric percolator, and it was dark and rich. She wasn't much of a cook, but she knew how to make coffee. I poured some into an expensive China teacup with a chip in it, then hung around listening to my mom gossip about the other people working at the restaurant. She'd been telling me about them for ten years, and I still couldn't tell who was who.

"You remember Ilene," she said.

"Ilene?" I asked.

"No, Ilene," my mom said.

"Right. Irene," I said.

"Yes, Ilene. She has daughter your age, Peter. Not married. Went college. Amherst."

"So?"

"So Ilene want you meet daughter. Come by tonight."

"Tonight!" I said. "Jesus, ma. I don't want to date no Japanese girl! I'm not dating anyone who reminds me of you!"

"She all American girl, not Japanese. Ilene bookkeeper at restaurant. Not waitress. Husband American, too. Daughter pretty girl. I think you like, Peter. And what you not like about Japanese girl?"

"What time are they coming?" I asked.

"Six clock," my mom said. "I take you shopping. Buy you nice pants."

We went down to Tepper's in Plainfield, and my mother made me try on several pairs of pants and a couple of pullover polo shirts. I wanted to get the orange shirt with the lizard on it, but my mom didn't like it.

"Make your face look fat!" she said. I let her buy me the purple one and a pair of khaki pants with pleats on the front of them. They actually looked pretty good with my cowboy boots.

"I'm only doing this to make you happy, ma," I said when we got back to the house.

55

"Very pretty girl," my mother said.

I went downstairs and took a nap. When I woke up, it was nearly five. I went upstairs and showered but didn't shave. I'd been growing a beard for the past week, and it was just beginning to come in. The hair on my head was dark brown, but the hair on my chin and jawline was bright red, the kind of beard you'd see on a Viking or Scottish giant, only it was a whole lot wispier because of me being half Japanese. My mom's side of the family didn't grow much facial hair. I'd seen a picture of her brother, and he'd had a ratty-looking moustache when he was about my age. I just hoped my facial hair filled in a whole lot better than his.

I doused myself with about half a bottle of Old Spice, then I got dressed in my new clothes.

"You handsome guy!" my mom said. I went out back and had a smoke. When I came back in my mom was on the phone in the kitchen, talking excitedly in Japanese to one of her friends on the phone. The call must've lasted for fifteen minutes. Every few seconds, my mom would nod her head vigorously and practically shout into the phone.

"*Hai! Hai! Hontodesuka! So…, so…, so…, ah so!*"

My mom hung up, and I asked her what she and her friend were talking about.

"Oh, that Hideko. Only call to say 'harro.'"

"She only called to say 'hello?' Jesus, ma. You guys talked for fifteen minutes!"

"Take longer to say harro in Japanese than English," my mother said.

"See, that's why I won't date anyone who reminds me of you, ma."

The doorbell rang. Irene and her daughter had arrived. My mother went to the door and opened it. She invited them to come in, and the mother entered first. She was a short, rotund woman, and my heart sank. I'd learned long ago that if you ever wanted to see what a girl would look like down the line, you look at her mother first. My mom had bought me the purple shirt and khaki pants for nothing. Then the girl stepped through the doorway into the living room. My mom hadn't been kidding. She was beautiful. She had long wavy hair and wore a simple black shirt, a denim skirt that came down below her knees, and a pair of leather ankle boots. She was the girl I'd seen on New Year's Eve listening to Irish music in Coconuts the night I'd met Stella. She was the girl I'd rejected because she was drinking white wine without an ice cube. She looked at me and smiled, and every thought I'd ever had about asking out Sonia completely vanished.

# Chapter 9 Mandy

Irene's daughter was named Mandy. Actually, her real name was Amanda, but Mandy was the name I called her. She wasn't particularly fond of Mandy, kind of like I wasn't fond of people calling me Peter or Pete, but over time, she got used to it. She had gotten a degree in Art at Amherst with an emphasis on sculpture. When she was in college, she'd designed a bronze piece for a local church that they'd actually commissioned her to create, but after she graduated, she'd only been able to find a job selling paint, ink, and paper in an art supply store.

Mandy took me to see her sculpture. I picked her up and we drove over to the church together.

"My family's been coming to this church since I was little," she said. "I used to think that whenever people said the Lord's Prayer, they weren't saying 'Our Father, who art in heaven', they were really saying 'Our Father's heart's in heaven'. I liked my understanding better than the real words. I've always known that God is love."

"I don't necessarily believe or not believe in God," I said, "but I'm all about love. I mean as a concept, yeah."

The church was one of those modern-looking ones, the kind that had giant curved wooden beams that ran the entire length of the church, so it looked like a ship or a whale. Mandy's sculpture was sitting in an open courtyard. It was a pair of hands that were cupped together, palms up. The hands were starting to turn green. Inside the hands was a bronze globe of the Earth that was turning green, too. The sculpture was almost as tall as I was.

"What do you think?" Mandy said.

"How come the fingers are so long?" I asked. "Why didn't you make them look like real fingers?"

"I wanted them to symbolize that God's reach is longer than we imagine," said Mandy. I wanted to roll my eyes, but since it was our first date, I figured I better not.

"I like the globe," I said. "I think you did a really good job with South America and Europe, but I'm kind of disappointed I can't see all the way around the world to the other side. I've always liked Australia. I bet you didn't know that if you turn Australia upside down, it kind of looks like the US pretty much. Yeah, it looks like the US, but without Florida. Without Florida and a little bit missing from the State of Texas."

Mandy laughed and clapped her hands together.

"You say exactly what's on your mind, don't you?" she said. "You're kind of unfiltered."

"Well, funny you say that," I said. "I work in a factory filtering glue into barrels. Unfiltered glue is pretty much a mess. If you didn't filter it, nobody would buy it."

"Really!" Mandy said. Her blue eyes sparkled as though she were laughing.

"They want me to be a supervisor," I said. "They want to pay to send me back to school to get an Engineering degree."

"Why don't you do it?" Mandy asked. "If someone wanted to pay to send me back to college, I'd do it in a second!"

"I don't know," I said. "It's kind of a crazy place. Everyone's drunk. People are getting hurt all the time. Every other night, there's another quote-unquote blow job, which just means a mistake that seems to cost the company a fortune. It's pretty entertaining, but I'm not sure I want to work there forever."

"Well, Strafe, what else do you want to do?"

"I don't know," I said. "I got a degree in English, so there's not much you can really do with it. I don't even like reading. What I do know is I don't want to live in my mom's basement forever."

"I'm tired of living at my mom's, too," Mandy said. "My mom's been trying to get rid of me. That's why she keeps introducing me to guys from the restaurant. Mostly, they're cooks or waiters and busboys. We've nothing in common, and the dates never go anywhere."

"Do you like dogs?" I asked. "I want to have my own place so I can get a dog."

"Sure," said Mandy. "Everyone likes dogs."

"I'm not so sure I like them," I said. "I just want one."

We went to Friendly's for clam strips and pie, only Mandy didn't have any clam strips. She was the kind of vegetarian who wouldn't eat an egg or fish, just cheese. She didn't eat the pie either, just had a cup of hot water that she put her own tea bag into from out of her purse. She was a cheap date. I was liking her better and better.

While Mandy was soaking her tea bag, I told her all about myself. I gave her the long version, so it took me like five minutes to tell her about my favorite food, my favorite color, my favorite basketball team, and my favorite thing to do with my clothes on. Mandy blushed when I said, "My favorite thing to do with my clothes on is watch TV." Mandy took the tea bag out of the hot water, squeezed the juice out of it, then wrapped it in a napkin and stuck it back in her purse. She was turning out to be too good to be true.

"Do you like going to museums?" Mandy asked.

"Sure," I said. I'd been to the Museum of Natural History in the City about six or seven times. I liked the dinosaurs and the room with all the planets in it. They had this scale that you'd jump on, and it would give you your weight if you were on Jupiter. If you were 150 pounds on Earth, you'd be about three hundred and fifty pounds on Jupiter and less than sixty pounds on Mars. That kind of stuff was actually pretty interesting to me.

"Maybe we can go to MoMA," Mandy said. "Or take a day trip up to the Cloisters on the Hudson."

"I've never been to those museums," I said. "What kind of dinosaurs do they have?"

"Dinosaurs? I've never seen any dinosaurs there, Strafe. Those are art museums. Have you ever been to an art museum?"

"Sure," I said. "All the time."

Actually, the only art museum I'd ever been to was in a building that curled around and around like a snail when I was in middle school. We'd gone there on a school field trip, but had to leave early because there was a painting of a woman without clothes on. The next thing you know, we were all on the bus heading back to Majestic. I didn't remember too much about the museum except one guy wearing all white who was standing in front of a painting that was all white, too. If you looked at him quick, all you could see was his head and his hands. That was interesting as hell.

"I can't wait for you to see Van Gogh's Starry Night at MoMA," Mandy said. "I think you'll fall in love with it the way I did."

"No problem," I said. I thought about Stella.

"Maybe we can go sometime."

"I'm free next week," Mandy said. "What's your schedule like?"

I looked at her. She had these calm blue eyes that seemed to take everything in. I looked away.

"Ok," I said. "We can leave in the morning anytime next week after I get off work if you're OK with driving. I'll take a nap on the way there."

After Friendly's, I dropped her off at her mom's place. I was pretty much a perfect gentleman, too. I hardly made any sexual innuendos or dropped any hints about getting into her pants, which certainly wasn't like me. Part of me felt a bit like a phony for behaving differently around her than normal, but part of me felt good, too, like there was something in front of me worth pursuing. Even if I had to be different in order to catch Mandy, there was something in me that saw the value in it.

I got home about eight o'clock and spent a couple of hours before work trying to write a love poem for Mandy, but I didn't get very far, though I did end up with a poem called Bug:

Bug

I

Fly

Including the title, the poem was only seven letters long. I was pretty happy about that. Then I tried writing another poem, even shorter than that one. I wrote a poem called Me:

Me

I

Shy

It wasn't as good as the first poem, and anyone who knew me knew that I wasn't particularly shy, but for only six letters, including the title, it wasn't horrible. I figured that maybe I'd submit it to the local paper and have them print it on the page next to the comics. That would pretty much ensure that a lot of people would read it. If you want to catch people's attention, the funny pages were a good place to start. Everyone I knew read the funny pages, even my mom did, and she didn't understand a thing she read. I had to explain the "Family Circus" to her just about every Sunday.

I made a few attempts to write a poem that only had five letters, but couldn't really come up with anything except a four-letter poem without a title:

We

Be

The only title I could come up with that made any sense was "Us," but that meant the shortest I could get it was six letters. I put it aside and figured I'd work on it later. By now, it was time to go to work, so I drove over to the factory. I put on my glue pants in the locker room. Wiggins was in the locker room, too. He'd done time for petty theft and had taken me under his wing, so to speak, and was always giving me helpful hints. He was a black guy with processed hair and a thin little moustache that made him look like Nat King Cole with bad teeth.

"Hey, Strafe," he said as I was putting on my pants and T-shirt, "if you ever are in the Big House and someone puts an apple on your bed, don't take it."

"How come?" I asked.

"That means you his girlfrien'," Wiggins said.

"I'll remember that," I said.

I finished dressing and went over to the urinal in between the locker room and the showers. Smitty, the shithouse attendant, had been busy at the stencil machine. He'd cut out a bunch of signs and had stenciled "NO LICE HERE" above the urinals. He'd stenciled a sign over the exit to the locker room, too:

KEEP THIS OPEN DOOR CLOSED

Smitty called himself the Locker Room Chief though everyone else called him Shitty Smitty. I suppose if I had his job, I'd call myself the Locker Room Chief, too. When I'd finished at the urinal, I washed my hands in the big roundabout sink while reading a sign that the Chief had stenciled on the wall.

DON'T DROP THE SOAP

Like Wiggins, Smitty had also done time and was just trying to pass on the wisdom gained from his time behind bars. I dried my hands and walked out of the locker room and up the long ramp leading into Glue. I went over to the time clock outside Virgil's office. As I was punching in, I realized that this was the first night I'd ever shown up at the factory completely sober. I couldn't remember the last time I'd gone a whole twenty-four hours without a beer or a shot of cheap bourbon or tequila. I hadn't even thought about it until that very moment. I went over to Gresham's scale and hung around until Lenny handed me my blue draw sheet.

"Tank 10," he growled.

I looked at the sheet. It was a fairly easy job. I had to filter seven hundred and fifty gallons into a metal tote bin of a perfumed glue going to Omlever for their line of feminine hygiene products. The glue would be used to adhere a gauze pad to a plastic set of "wings." After putting cheesecloth in the filter basket and positioning the pump under the tank, you basically just had to turn the pump on and watch the tank fill up. You probably had to change the filter two or three times, but that was no big deal. I'd be done by the first break if the glue was pretty clean, by the second break at the latest if the glue was dirty and the filter had to be changed every ten or fifteen minutes.

63

The best part about this job was that you didn't have to run around stenciling drums, opening them up, and putting poly bags in them. You just had to stand there and make sure the cheesecloth filter didn't break. Omlever had their own QC department, and if the glue didn't meet their spec, they'd send it back, so you just had to make sure you changed the filter in the basket before it broke and contaminated the whole tote.

In spite of how easy this job was, a lot of guys in the department didn't want to have anything to do with a perfume batch. Whenever you worked on a batch scented with perfume, you'd end up leaving the factory smelling like you'd spent the night in a whorehouse. Larry Edgerton was one of the guys who would refuse to work on one of these batches. He'd been an accountant but had lost just about every job he'd ever had due to alcoholism. He'd sober up for a year or so, then go on a bender. He'd recently lost a job at DuPont and was working in Glue until someone hired him as an accountant, again. Larry came over to me while I was filling the stainless-steel tote.

"Last time I worked on one of these perfume batches, my wife accused me of cheating on her," Larry said. "She ragged on me for three days."

"You told me you were cheating on her," I said. "Aren't you?"

"Sure, I am, but so long as I don't smell like I'm cheating on her, everything's good."

Wiggins had come over to us and listened in on the conversation.

"Does your wife know you're seeing someone else?" I asked.

"Of course," said Larry. "She always knows, but just so long as I don't flaunt it in her face by coming home from work and smelling like menstrual pads, everything's fine."

"That's right," Wiggins said. "I told my wife I quit drinking, but she knows I'm lying. Just so long as I don't smell like gin, then we good. Ain't that right? That's why I switched to vodka and grain alcohol."

"I didn't have anything to drink, tonight," I said. "Not a drop."

"Damn!" said Wiggins. "Look at you! Yo' girlfrien' must've told you she'd drop yo' ass if you didn't quit. Din't she? I bet she did!"

64

"My old lady's always after me to quit," Larry said. "Rag, rag, rag. Maybe if she stopped ragging, I'd stop cheating on her."

"You ever think of quitting for good, Larry?"

"Cheating or drinking?" Larry asked.

"Drinking," I said. Larry frowned.

"I went to some meetings, but those are for people who've got a problem with alcohol. I don't have a drinking problem. I've got a wife problem."

"Damn!" said Wiggins. "Ain't that the truth!"

Wiggins and Larry wandered off together. Larry had been bringing vodka onto the floor in a pocket flask, and I knew that they were going upstairs to drink by the sugar shack. I turned off the pump and spent five minutes changing the cheesecloth bag inside the filter basket. The old bag was full of oval-shaped balls of starch that hadn't dissolved. The batch was dirtier than normal. I put the basket with the new filter back onto the pump, then I looked at the clock over the forklift ramp leading out of the department. Wiggins and Larry Edgerton were walking down the ramp toward the locker room. It was break time. I thought about Mandy and wished that I could call her, but she wasn't the type of girl you could call at 1 a.m. just to say, "Hi." Maybe if you were suicidal or something, which wasn't the case with me. I thought about my poem, and an idea came to me. I pulled my black crayon out of my pocket and wrote out a poem on a napkin in the lunchroom:

I

Be

Me

Including the title, it was five letters. I re-read it about fifteen times. It was maybe the definitive statement about existentialism ever written. It was existential and very Zen. The meditation stuff was working after all. I'd like to see someone beat that. Even if they did manage to write a shorter poem, I'd come up with another winner with the same title:

I

## My!

That one was only three letters plus the exclamation point. I couldn't wait to send that one to the local paper. I sorta wished Mandy was the type of girl that I could wake up in the middle of the night and read her poetry. The only one I knew who was probably still awake was Stella, but I wasn't gonna call her. She was probably entertaining some old guy who'd driven her home after she'd jumped out of a cake at the American Legion or International Order of Odd Fellows. Larry came over and sat down across from me. Vodka's not supposed to have any smell, but you could tell that he'd been drinking from the smell of his sweat. He smelled sour and toxic, like nail polish remover mixed with fruit juice.

"What you writing, kid? A love letter?"

"Naw," I said. "Some poetry."

"Let me see it," he said. "I've been known to write a limerick or two in my time. Mostly they begin 'There once was a girl from Nantucket'."

I handed Larry my napkin, and he read my poem while stroking his chin.

"I don't get it," he said. He re-read it three or four times. "It rhymes, though, so I guess it's a poem."

"I was an English major in college," I said.

"No kidding," he said.

"Yeah, I didn't read much poetry except stuff by a bunch of English guys from Wales and Ireland, but I read enough to know that you need to follow certain grammatical rules like rhyming even when writing poetry."

"Keep it up, kid. Someday, when you're a famous poet, I'll buy one of your books and say, 'I remember him when he was working in a glue factory'."

The break ended, and Larry and Wiggins walked up the ramp together. I walked back with Graupner. He looked at my face.

"Your beard's red," he said. "It's either red or the drugs I'm eating are fucking with my vision."

"No, your vision's OK. My beard's red."

"Wow! You're a ginger motherfucker," he said. "I wish I had a red beard. The last time I grew one, it was blue."

I looked at Graupner to see if he was joking, but he was completely serious.

"Graupner, are you fucked up right now?"

"Not really," he said, "but I wouldn't swear to it, Strafe. Wanna grab a beer after work?"

"Naw," I said. "I've got some stuff I need to do."

"No problem, Strafe. Maybe I'll just grab Willie and buy him a drink."

"Willie? Willie hasn't been back to work since he fell in the hot melt."

"Really? Weird. I thought I saw him earlier tonight."

"Maybe you just need to go home after work and go to bed."

"Sleep? Shit! I'll sleep when I'm dead. That's my motto as of right now."

"Just be careful driving home," I said. "You don't want to get in an accident."

Graupner went over to the weigh scale to get another work assignment from Lenny, and I went back to Tank 10. I only had about a quarter of the metal tote left to fill, then I'd spend the rest of the night on the bench talking with Buda as long as De Jesús wasn't around. I'd learned that De Jesús was a rat who'd turn you into the bosses if you bent the rules and he didn't like it, then you'd spend the rest of the night drawing hot melt or running it through the crusher upstairs after it had been frozen. You had to break up the frozen hot melt with a hammer before throwing the pieces into the crusher, and you'd get covered with resin dust everywhere. It would get in your nose and beard and turn into a sticky mess as soon as it reached room temperature.

67

"Fuck Jesús," I said out loud. Then I opened the gate on Tank 10 and let the smell of perfumed glue intoxicate me.

# Chapter 10 Buda

I finished up Tank 10, then went up on the bench to see Buda Wladyslaw. Buda was wearing safety goggles, a respirator, and long rubberized gloves that came up to his elbows. He was looking at a lab sheet. When he saw me, he held up his hand, warning me not to come near him. He picked up a plastic bucket of hydrochloric acid and poured some carefully into a measuring beaker made of glass. When he was done adding the acid to one of the tanks, he put the bucket away and rinsed out the beaker carefully for about three minutes with cold running water in a little plastic sink. He looked at the lab sheet again. He picked up a plastic jugful of citric acid and poured about a cup into another glass beaker, and added that to another tank. When he was done making the adjustments, he removed his goggles and the respirator and smiled.

"Ah, Rocky. You hiding from boss? No?"

"Pretty much," I said. "That prick Jesús isn't around, is he?"

"No, no. Mr De Jesús not here. Working second shift, now."

"Good!" I said. "I got put on hot melt the last time that prick told the day foreman I was hiding out on the bench. I still got the burn mark on my arm from brushing up against that metal pipe coming from the tank."

"Now it's the fault of Jesús you got burned?"

"Screw him," I said. "Virgil says that management is looking at me for a supervisor position."

Buda nodded his head. He picked up a plastic bottle marked CORROSIVE in big red letters. He turned the bottle around and studied the skull and crossbones on the label. Then he put it down and looked at me.

"What I'm asking, Buda, is what do you think? You think it's worth it for me to become a supervisor?"

"Me, Rocky? Question is what you tink," Buda said. "Is the job right for you?"

"I don't know," I said. "It's more money."

"Money not everytink," said Buda. "Company gave me big money when resin cutter took my fingers, even though my own stupidity. I'd rather have fingers instead of money. They make me a chemical operator, too! Nice job! Easy money! Rather have fingers back. You need ask yourself, 'What fingers does Rocky have to lose?' Because I tell you sometink, as somebody spent time in death camp, everybody got fingers to lose. Sometimes they start with fingers and take whole arm or leg. Maybe life, too. Question is, is Rocky willing to lose one, two, three fingers or maybe an arm or an eye? Give your life for blow jobs and batches of cigarette glue? Only one can answer a big question like that is Rocky."

Buda put his goggles and respirator back on and picked up the bottle marked CORROSIVE, again. He poured some into a beaker and added it to a tank of jelly gum. He put the bottle on a shelf with the skull and crossbones facing me, then he reached up and turned the bottle so the front label was visible. He reached across one of the tanks to a lever and pulled on it. Overhead, a belt shifted and started turning a wheel above a tank full of water. The blades inside the tank started spinning around and around in the water, sloshing the liquid clockwise swiftly.

"What is life of Rocky worth?" Buda asked.

The bell sounded for the 5 a.m. break, and I headed outside to sit on the bench, smoke cigarettes, and watch the traffic move slowly past. The sky was still dark, but the air was warm and moist. It would probably be hot and humid when I got up in the afternoon. At least it was cool down in my basement. I looked forward to sleeping during the heat of the day while the record on my stereo spun around and around and around, the needle wearing itself out on grooves with nothing on them.

Everyone got done with their work assignments early, and we hung around down by the time clock for ten minutes, waiting for seven o'clock to roll around so we could punch out. Graupner and Wiggins sat on a pallet filled with leaking five-gallon metal buckets of some material used to improve the adherent properties of varnish. The buckets were stamped with the same kind of skull and crossbones as the plastic bottles marked CORROSIVE up on the bench. I glanced at the warning label on the back of one of the buckets.

"Warning! Exposure to tin oxide can cause nausea, vomiting, abdominal cramping, diarrhea, fatigue, headache, bronchitis, pneumonitis, and metal fume fever. In case of skin contact, flush the affected area for half an hour with cold water and seek medical assistance. In case of contact with clothing, remove clothing immediately, destroy clothing, and seek medical assistance."

"Guys," I said. "You might want to get off those buckets and read this label." The hands on the time clock hit seven, and everyone surged toward the clock with their timecards in hand. Graupner and Wiggins hopped off the buckets of tin oxide. Their pants were wet from the leaking buckets.

"Graupner! Wiggins! You better read the warning label!" I said. "That stuff on your pants is really bad!"

"Can't be any worse than the rest o' the chemicals in this place," said Wiggins. "None this stuff'll kill you short term. They just put them warning labels on cause some rats got fed this stuff in a lab somewhere for three months an' got sick. Me an' Graupner, we'll be okay. We ain't rats!"

I punched out, then went down to the locker room and showered in cold water for fifteen minutes. The Locker Room Chief had been busy in the shower room, too:

SHAVE YOUR JUNK AT HOME

I dried off and dressed swiftly. I'd gotten paid and wanted to take my car to the service station around the corner from my house to have them look at the transmission. I parked the Bel Air and hung around in the office of the service station until a technician came out and filled out a ticket.

"Prolly just the linkage," he said. "Hopefully. If it ain't the linkage, then we're looking at a rebuild, maybe. Maybe a rebuild an' a new differential. Differential an' maybe a flywheel. Flywheel, torque converter, an' maybe the clutch plate. Clutch plate an' input shaft,

71

output shaft bearing an' pinion bearing. That's an expensive repair, maybe, if it ain't the linkage, but it's prolly the linkage."

"Jesus," I said. "How much for the repair if it's not the linkage?" I asked.

"Hard to say," the technician said. He wiped his nose on his sleeve. "Depends on what we find when we open 'er up. We'll let you know as soon as we know, if not sooner."

I walked home after grabbing one of my Zen books from the front seat of the car. On the way, I passed a coffee shop next to a pizza parlor. I decided to get a cup of coffee and read some of my book before going to bed. I went into the coffee shop and grabbed one of the little circular red leather seats at the counter. I ordered a cup of coffee and started reading a chapter in the book about the Eightfold Path. The waitress brought the coffee, and I took a sip. The coffee was old and bitter. I put three or four teaspoons of sugar into it. It was just a sweeter version of awful. As I sat drinking my lousy coffee, I felt something hit me in the leg. I looked up and saw that it was a blind man who'd run into me on the sidewalk outside of Glue back in January. He was wearing a three-piece linen suit even though it was nearly summer, and the weather was hot and sticky. He looked a bit like a traveling salesman, the kind you saw pitching non-stick irons or tangleless fishing lines on late-night TV. On his head was a Panama fedora with a blue striped band about it. He was pretty well dressed for a blind guy. I mean, most blind guys I knew always wore mismatched socks or brown belts with black shoes. Stuff like that. Granted, I'd really only known one blind guy in my life. He'd lived in my dorm in college. He was probably the worst dresser of anyone I'd ever met and would even get mad at you for offering gentle suggestions on how he could improve his appearance by pressing his pants or wearing a shirt without a big ink stain on the pocket. I've learned that most people don't want constructive criticism, but that doesn't stop me from offering it. I think it's one of my better traits. Anyway, the blind guy in the coffee shop kept sweeping his cane around like a bug's antenna. He hit me in the leg again.

"Hey," I said. "I know you. I'm the guy who gave you the flashlight!"

"Oh, yeah! Hello! I recognize your voice!"

"No kidding. The seat's open next to me. Sit down and take a load off your feet. I'm Strafe," I said.

"Strafe…, good to put a name with a face. That's a joke," he said. "My name's Parker."

Parker folded up his cane and put it in his coat pocket, then he did something weird. He reached over and grabbed my face with both his hands and felt it all over. After he'd finished feeling my face, he sat down next to me.

"Native American?" he asked.

"Half Japanese," I said.

"Interesting," he grunted.

"Well, how's life?" I asked. "What've you been up to?"

"Oh, you know. Traveling around, here and there. A little of this and a little of that. Wine, women, and song."

"No kidding," I said.

"Certainly," said Parker. "Let me tell you a story."

"Go right ahead," I said. "I've got time."

"So, several months ago, I'm sitting right here, where I'm sitting now, but instead of you, there was an attractive woman sitting there. Her perfume was like Lily of the Valley."

"How could you tell she was attractive?" I asked.

"I felt her face, just like I did yours," Parker said. "Most people don't mind. Either that or they're too polite to say anything. Anyways, she was an attractive gal, about your age, I guess, but when I was feeling her face, I noticed something strange. She had these little bumps under her chin, and another few bumps on her neck and by her ear. She noticed my fingers lingering over the bumps. 'It's some kind of rash,' she says. 'I've had this rash all over me the past couple of days. I don't know what it is.' Well, I knew what it was. I read Braille, and the bumps on her neck, chin, and ear were perfectly readable verses from the Song of Solomon, King James Version."

73

"Get out!" I said.

"As God is my witness," Parker said. "'Let him kiss me with the kisses of his mouth! For thy love is better than wine....,' That's what the bumps under her chin read! I was amazed, as was she! Behind her ear, the bumps spelled out 'Behold, thou art fair, my love; behold, thou art fair, thou hast doves' eyes within thy locks.' I read her arms and neck right here in the coffee shop. She asked me to put my hands in her blouse and read the bumps on her breasts, but I refused even though she begged!"

"I don't believe it," I said.

"You don't have to believe it, but may God strike me down if I'm telling you anything less than the truth. Finally, the woman invited me to her home here in Majestic. She was the wife of a prominent businessman whom she suspected of having an affair. Reluctantly, I accompanied her to her car, and on the ride to her house, she drew my hand to the inside of her thigh and made me read aloud the words written in her flesh. Once we reached her place, she closed the drapes and undressed quickly. She made me read aloud each verse written on her back, her hips, and her belly, her body quivering under my touch, 'The joints of thy thighs are like jewels, the work of the hands of a cunning craftsman. Thy navel is like a round goblet, which wanteth not liquor: thy belly is like a heap of wheat set about with lilies.'"

The blind man took off his Panama hat and slowly turned it in his hands.

"I put my hand on the mound of her sex, and then she kissed me and drew me to her bed. Two hours later, she drove me back to this coffee shop and dropped me at the door. 'You were sent by God,' she said. And maybe I was. She kissed me on the lips, then sent me away, and though I've returned to this humble coffee shop every day since then, she's not returned. If she had, her lavish perfume would tell me of her presence."

Parker stood up and reached into his pocket. He unfolded his cane and tapped it on the floor in front of him.

"Adieu, my friend. To God," he said. Then he left.

The waitress came by and refilled my cup with bad coffee.

"Several months my ass," she said. "He's been telling that same bullshit story to everyone in here for the past five years. I don't believe it for a second."

I thought about telling the waitress about Stella and her little blue star tattoos, but decided against it. The most unbelievable stuff is often the truest, even if it never happened. I paid for my coffee and Parker's and threw some change on the counter for a tip. Then I walked down the street to my house. It was already getting hot and muggy. I opened the door. I went downstairs to the basement and put on a record by Crosby, Stills, and Nash. I drifted off to sleep while "Helplessly Hoping" echoed around the basement walls. Then I slept the sleep of the gullible, the guileless, and the weary.

# Chapter 11 Dog

I slept pretty poorly that morning. Every half an hour or so, I'd wake up from some miserable dream or other where I was either running down an alley somewhere that led nowhere or standing on a hillside looking out over a valley full of burning brush. It was a relief when I woke up and saw that it was a little after two-thirty in the afternoon. I'd slept for nearly six hours, and that was enough. I got out of bed and went upstairs in my boxer shorts. The house was hot and humid, a typical June afternoon in the Garden State. With any luck, we'd get a thunderstorm in the evening before I went to work, and the factory would be tolerable.

My mom was in the dining room having a cup of coffee before she left for the restaurant.

"Ilene's daughter call you," my mom said. "We have long talk. Very nice girl don't you think, Peter? She tell me you going to New York next week. To art museum. I didn't know you like art, Peter? How come I don't know you like painting?"

I was about to say something really clever and sarcastic like I normally did when my mother mentioned anything about me and my life, but I didn't, even though I wanted to.

"Bet you didn't know I write poems, too," I said.

"Really?" my mom said.

"Absolutely! I'm gonna send them to The Majestic Times Herald Picayune to see if they'll publish them."

"Oh, that's so wonderful, Peter!"

"It is wonderful," I said. "The factory is thinking about making me a supervisor. They're even talking about sending me back to school to get a degree in Chemical Engineering."

"Really, Peter. Such good news!"

"Tell me about it," I said. "If I become a supervisor, I'll make about three times what I'm making now to start. In a couple of years, I'll get promoted to foreman, according to Virgil, anyway."

"I'm going to call Ilene and tell her good news!" my mother said.

"Irene? Mandy's mom?"

"No! I said Ilene! That her American name. She Japanese friend. Japanese name Setsuko. She work with me at restaurant. Waitress, Peter. I tell you about her all the time."

"Oh, yeah. Ilene. How could I forget?"

"Ilene has not very pretty daughter. Nice girl, but not very pretty."

I went upstairs to shower and clean the glue out of my beard while my mother called Ilene and began a long, frenetic conversation full of staccato exclamations in Japanese. After I finished showering, I went back down to the basement. My mom was still on the phone with her friend Ilene, saying *"hai," "so," "uwa,"* and *"honto"* every three seconds. I didn't have to understand any Japanese to get the gist. It was all pretty much just filler, the way everyone kind of says "yeah," "right," "no kidding," or "wow" with someone else on the phone while waiting for their turn to speak. I got dressed in my khaki pants and purple shirt and walked down to the service station. The same guy I'd spoken to earlier was behind the desk. He had grease and oil all over him and was sweating a river all over a stack of papers on the counter in front of him. The whole front of his shirt was drenched in car grime and sweat. He would've fit right in at the glue factory.

"I was just 'bout to call you," he said. "I told you it was prolly the linkage, an' the good news is that the linkage was shot to shit if you'll pardon my French. Shot to shit an' hell an' back. We got that fixed up an' checked the oil. Down a quart an' a quarter, so took care of that. Looked at the brakes an' the radiator cap. Kicked the tires an' weegeed the windows. Diddled the rotor an' kadiddled the carb. Gapped the plugs an' plugged the gaps. Solenoid, check. Battery, check, alternator, check, heater hose, check, thermostat, check, timing, check, fan belt, check, U-joint, check, drive shaft, check, fuel filter, check, exhaust manifold, check, compression, check, high beams, check, brake lights, check, mirrors, check. Air conditioner? You don't have none, so couldn't check that, but I whizzed in the radiator just to top 'er off! Got her running like a gyroscope on a string! That'll be $922.50."

"What?" I gasped. "I don't have that kind of money!"

"Just pulling your chain, buddy! Gimme $22.50 folding money or write me a check an' away you go!" I looked at the man's shirt. He had an oval patch over his left breast with the name "Ralph" embroidered in red thread.

"That's great," I said. "Had me scared there for a minute, Ralph."

"Oh, I'm not Ralph," he said. "He died a while back. My name's "Carroll," but never much cared for that name, so here I am, sweating in a dead man's shirt!"

I gave Ralph twenty-five bucks and told him to keep the change. I was happy. I didn't even care much that someone had backed into my car while it was at the shop and dented the front bumper.

"Oh, that'll prolly just buff right out," Carroll/Ralph said.

I grabbed my keys and was about to leave when a dog came around the counter and looked at me. It was pretty ugly. It had long, stiff, wiry hair that sort of made your skin crawl when you pet it. Plus, it had a whole mess of long, dirty hair around its muzzle.

"Wanna dog?" Ralph/Carroll asked. "Got all her shots. Rabies, distemper, heartworm, parvo. I'll throw in two cans of dog food an' you can take 'er free!"

"She's pretty ugly," I said.

"I admit she's a bit of an eyesore, but shave 'er down a bit an' give 'er a bath. She'll grow on you. I'd keep 'er myself, but I'm 'lergic to cats. Had a snake once. Boa constrictor. Six feet long an' scared the wife. Let me tell you! Had to get rid of it when it tried eating the baby."

I was exhausted when I finally left the shop with the dog under my arm. Carroll had worn me out. I put the dog on the front seat and drove back home. My mother was just leaving the house for work when I pulled into the driveway. I got out of the car, and she looked at the dog.

"What that?"

"It's a dog," I said.

"I know is dog," she said. "What dog?"

"My dog," I said. "The guy at the gas station gave me two cans of dog food, too."

"Your dog, Peter? Who is take care dog when you always work? Huh? Can't leave dog all day alone in basement! Who clean up dog mess? You?"

"The dog'll be fine," I said. "I mostly work the midnight shift, and you get home around one in the morning. She can sleep at night, and I'll be around to take care of her during the day."

"Who watch her while you sleep? Me?"

"Sure," I said. "You can watch her until I get up."

"I'm not watching dog." My mom looked at the dog again and patted her on the head.

"Not very pretty," she said. "Remind me of Japanese friend Ilene's daughter. Nice girl, but very ugly for Japanese."

"Good thing you didn't set me up with her," I said.

"Why I set you up with ugly girl?" my mother asked. "Why I want ugly grandchildren?"

My mother said goodbye, then got in her car and backed out of the double driveway. She drove a lemon-yellow Mazda that nearly got hit by a Cadillac as she was backing out. The stereotype about Asian drivers being terrible was certainly true when it came to my mom. How she had managed to drive to Union and back every night without getting killed was a mystery to me.

I took the dog in the house and went down into the basement. I put the dog on my bed.

"This is where we sleep," I said. I went up to the kitchen with one of the cans of dog food, and the animal followed me up the stairs. I opened the can and emptied it into a saucepan. Then I put the pan on the floor

The dog ate the food in like thirty seconds, then licked the pan for about two minutes after the food was gone. When she'd finished, she sat down and looked at me. The mess of beard and whiskers around her face was covered in dog food. I took a dishrag and wiped the food off her face, then I took her downstairs and watched TV. She fell asleep on my lap for about an hour. Then she got up, jumped off my lap, and peed on the rug.

I took her out back and let her wander around. The backyard was completely surrounded by a wooden fence, so she couldn't get out. While she was exploring the backyard, I went into the kitchen and called Mandy.

"Hello," she said.

"I got a dog," I said. "The guy at the gas station gave me a dog."

"How exciting," said Mandy. "You told me you wanted one."

"I did. I got one. I wrote some poems, too. I'll read them to you when we go to New York."

"Sure, I'd like that! What day do you want to go?"

"Tuesday," I said. "I'll pick you up around nine. I'll read you my poems, and then I'll take a nap if you don't mind driving."

"I don't have a problem with driving," Mandy said.

"Good. Just so long as you're a better driver than my mom, which won't be hard. Trust me on that one."

"Strafe! That's a terrible thing to say!"

"I know," I said. "The truth is a cruel mistress."

I looked out the window in the door that led out to the back yard. My dog was dragging a leafy bush around the grass.

"I'll call you later, Mandy. The dog got into something."

I hung up without saying goodbye. I ran outside, which was dumb in itself. No amount of hurrying was going to reverse time and return my pot plant to the soil. There'd be no Egyptian tomatoes this year. I grabbed the pot plant out of the dog's mouth and tossed it away. The dog ran after the bush and dragged it back to me. I threw the bush away again, and the dog went and fetched it back. It's hard to stay mad at a dog for very long. They're always doing something to piss you off, and then they do something that makes you glad you were around to see it. Even an ugly dog can make you happy. An ugly girl can probably make you happy, too, but I'd like to see one fetch a stick for half an hour. Ain't gonna happen.

I took the carpet out back and washed it with Ajax, then hosed it down for five or six minutes. When I was done washing it, I hung it on the clothesline to dry. It wasn't like the rug was new or anything. It wasn't even made in America, just some cheap two- hundred-year-old crap rug made in Pakistan or Iran. It wasn't even that attractive to begin with, in spite of what my mother thought. She used to have it in the living room, and everyone who came over would ooh and ahh over it like it was some holy relic.

"Oh, Hatsuko! What a beautiful Persian rug," they'd say, though I knew it was a lie just to make my mom feel better about having a ratty old rug.

"Oh, Hatsu! The Persian rug ties the whole room together." I thought about doing my mom a favor and taking it to the dump.

I took the dog inside and put her on my bed. She curled up and fell asleep. While she slept, I spent about two hours writing. I had this idea for a play. There's this man who only eats peanut butter and jelly sandwiches. He sits alone in his room, eating peanut butter and jelly. A woman comes over and tries to get him to eat bologna, but he refuses to eat it and sends her away. Someone else comes by and tries to get him to eat Lobster Newburg, but he refuses to eat the lobster and sends that person away, too. The play ends with the man getting a dog and giving it his last peanut butter and jelly sandwich, so that he goes hungry. I wrote about ten pages by hand, then the phone rang, and I went upstairs. The dog followed me. I was hoping that Mandy had called me back, but it was only my dad.

"Pete, what are you doing?" he asked.

"I got a dog," I said.

81

"A dog? Great! What kind of dog?

"An ugly one," I said, "but it fetches sticks like crazy."

"Is it a Lab or a Shepherd, or a Boxer? What kind is it?"

"I don't know," I said. "I didn't ask. That guy at the service station gave her to me along with a couple of cans of dog food."

"Crazy Carroll? The mechanic?"

"That's the one?"

"Great mechanic, but a bit of an odd duck. He's got a boa constrictor."

"He had to get rid of it. It tried to eat his baby."

"Wow!" said my father. "Speaking of eating, want to go to Hojo's for dinner?"

"Howard Johnson's? Sure. I'll meet you over there."

"See you in about half an hour?"

"Sounds good, Dad."

I left the dog sleeping on the bed and drove over to Hojo's. I liked going there for fried shrimp. Actually, I really liked their tartar sauce. You could have just served me an order of tartar sauce on a dish, and I would have been happy.

My father was sitting in a booth, drinking a beer, when I got there. I sat down across from him, and he reached across the table and shook my hand. We weren't the kind of people who hugged each other. He looked really good. Like he was happier than I could ever remember seeing him.

"You've gotta red beard!" My father said.

"So, I've been told. When the left side comes in a little better, I'll get a pair of scissors and even it out."

The waiter came and took our order. My dad ordered a steak. I ordered the tartar sauce with a side of fried shrimp. The waiter didn't smile when I said that, but that's only because he was being professional. While we waited for our meal, we talked about this and that.

"Job's going well?"

"Yeah, they're talking about making me a supervisor. Even sending me back to school for a Chemical Engineering degree."

"Good!" my father said. "I knew you had it in you!"

"I've been writing poetry, too."

"Really?" my father said. "Are you gonna send it out to get published? Literary journals? Poetry magazines? That kind of thing?"

"I was thinking about The Majestic Times Herald Picayune first, then maybe branching out later. I'm writing a play, too."

"Impressive, Pete. A poet and a playwright! You've been industrious."

"I'll let you read the play when I'm done with it."

"Excellent!"

The meal came, and I ate my dinner really quick, which was how I'd always eaten. All my life, my mom and dad were constantly telling me to slow down when I was eating, but I've never been able to do it. I don't necessarily eat a lot. I just shovel it down really quick, then wait for everyone to catch up, like ten minutes later. In some ways, I kind of wish that eating too quickly could be one of the fingers that Buda had asked I would be willing to lose, but I don't think it works that way. I looked at my father. I was happy that he was happy, but he'd lost at least a few fingers in the process. He probably thought that I was one of the fingers he'd lost, but that wasn't true.

"You look happy, Dad. I'm happy for you, really," I said while he was eating his steak.

"Well, that was out of the blue," he said, "but I appreciate that. Thanks!"

"I've got a girlfriend, too," I said. "She went to Amherst and has a sculpture at that church that looks like a ship. It's a pair of long-fingered bronze hands holding a bronze globe."

"Wow! A poet and a sculptor."

"We're going to look at paintings in the City on Tuesday," I said. "The museum only has paintings and sculptures. They don't have fossils or exhibits about the planets or the Moon."

"Which one are you going to see?"

"The one called MaMA," I said.

"Oh, MoMA. The Museum of Modern Art. I've been there. It's fantastic. You'll love Van Gogh's Starry Night!"

"Mandy said that, too."

After we left the restaurant, my father shook my hand in the parking lot.

"Keep up the good work," he said.

"Thanks for dinner, Dad. You really look great!" I watched him get in his car and drive off. He really looked less lonely than any time I could ever remember. I got in the Bel Air and drove back home. The dog had torn up the bedding and crapped on the floor.

I cleaned up the crap and poured bleach on the concrete. Then I looked at the bedding. Fortunately, the quilt just had a few little holes chewed in the corner, but I had to throw both sheets away.

"Keep this up and you're gonna have to fetch a lot of sticks," I said.

I went upstairs to the kitchen and dining room. It hadn't rained and the house was still baking even though it was after nine. I wasn't looking forward to going to work. It was always ten to fifteen degrees hotter inside the factory than it was outside, and the second floor was hotter still. I hoped I didn't have to work upstairs, dumping tanks or on the resin cutter. Summer was still officially a week away, and I was already dreading working in the heat. What would it be like working with Glue in the middle of August when temperature and humidity were both over 95 on their respective scales? I wasn't looking forward to summer in Hell.

# Chapter 12 Tuttle

When I got to Glue, the place was buzzing. Kenny Krajewski was pumping latex from a tank truck that had pulled around back to the rear pad alongside the railroad tracks into one of the fiberglass tanks out by the front truck pad, but forgot to open the lid of the tank truck. A vacuum had been created in the tanker, and the aluminum had crumpled. It looked like a giant hand had come down from heaven and squished the truck like it was an empty beer can. About 1500 gallons of latex were running down the tracks. Parts of the truck pad were covered with three to four inches of the stuff, and the entire second shift had been slopping around out back, scooping up the latex by hand into five-gallon buckets.

Wiggins and I went out back before our shift started and watched the second shift wade through the latex in the dark. They were all wearing lights on their hard hats, and the lights bobbed up and down in the dark. While they wandered around scooping up latex, clouds of fireflies hovered about them, flashing their own lights on and off in the warm night air.

"That's way more 'n a blow job," said Wiggins. "That's'n absolute cluster fuck."

"I hate that shit," I said. "You get it on you, and it doesn't come off."

"I wash it off with that 731-24. That solvent you dumped in Tank 7 when you were making that cigarette glue."

"Trichlorethylene? That's a known carcinogen. You don't want to be washing in that!"

"Gits it off'n me! That's all I cares 'bout."

"I read the material data sheets on the stuff after I dumped it in the tank. It fucks up your nervous system, kidneys, blood, liver, respiratory system, heart. Jesus, Wiggins, why mess with that stuff at all?"

"Got me a little side piece," said Wiggins. "She don't want nothin' to do with me if I'm covered in latex, 'cepting one part o' me. I ain' no diff'rent than mos' men. Willin' to die fo' pussy. Listen here, we all

85

got to go sometime. Might as well go in the pursuit of a woman! Men will sigh fo' pussy, cry fo' pussy, lie fo' pussy, die fo' pussy. Prisons be full o' men willing to kill fo' pussy, too! Go to the 'lectric chair and fry fo' pussy! Any man who ever loved a woman knows what I'm talkin' 'bout. An' if you got a woman you ain' willin' to go to the edge o' death fo', well then shame on you!"

Wiggins walked away, and I went over to the weigh scale to wait for the third shift to start, and looked at the thermometer on the wall. It was 110° I hung around at the scale and watched Gresham for a while. Jimmy had come in early and was weighing barrels. He had about forty drums to the right of the scale. He would grab one with his hand truck, roll it onto the scale, weigh the drum, then stencil the gross weight on the head in black between the batch number and drum tare. Then he'd grabbed the drum again with his hand truck and rolled it up a three-foot ramp onto a group of twelve pallets that held four drums each. He'd set the drum on one of the pallets, then grab another drum and start the process all over again. Dante would have placed this punishment in a Circle of Hell devoted to those who committed violence against themselves. If nothing else, it was spiritual suicide.

Tuttle came over. His shirt was open because of the heat, and his chest was lousy with tattoos. He put his tool bag on the weigh scale table, and I looked at the tattoos on his hands. He had a letter tattooed on the back of each of his fingers. The letters on the fingers of his right hand spelled "ANGEL" and the letters on his left hand spelled "DEVIL." The letters were pretty crude looking, like he'd inked them himself, though he'd probably gotten the tattoos in prison.

Tuttle noticed me looking at the letters on his fingers.

"I'm not religious," he said. "But I've known my share of evil in my life, just as I've known my share of love and goodness. I've been a son, a loving husband, and a father, and I've been a thief and a con man, a man given to drunkenness, rage, and violence."

By now, the rest of the midnight shift had gathered around the weigh scale, and all eyes were fixed on Tuttle as he spoke. He took his shirt off and flexed, and the tattoos on his chest and back rippled.

"Behold the man!" he said.

He raised his arms and turned around so that everyone could see his tattoos. He had a pair of praying hands tattooed on his right side under an image of the Virgin Mary. On his right shoulder, there was a picture of Jesus walking on water above a tattoo of the Archangel Michael pinning a winged dragon with a woman's face and torso to the ground with a spear. On the left side of his chest, there was a bloody dagger under an image of Satan sitting on a throne, while all around him, demons were torturing people. His left shoulder had been inked with a picture of a green serpent offering an apple to Eve above a tattoo of Cain murdering his brother Abel. On the right side of his back, there was a large tattoo of three women standing and looking at an open tomb that was empty. Across from this tattoo, on the left side of Tuttle's back, was an equally large one of Christ on the Cross being speared in the side by a Roman soldier. I looked at the soldier holding the spear and noticed that his face looked exactly like Tuttle's.

Lenny came over with a sheaf of blue papers in his hand. He looked at Tuttle and shook his head.

"Put your shirt on, Tuttle. This ain't no sideshow at the carnival. The rest of you baboons are damned lucky you don't have to spend all night outside scooping up latex with five-gallon buckets. We got two dozen tanks that need to be emptied."

Lenny handed out the draw sheets. Tuttle got hot melt, of course, for the sin of being conspicuous. Wiggins got a jelly gum. When Lenny handed him the blue sheet, Wiggins rubbed his hands together like he'd just gotten a Christmas present.

"Oh, I love me some jelly gum!" he said.

Graupner got Tank 27; that one held over one hundred and twenty barrels. It was white craft glue, the same stuff that I'd showered Gresham with six months earlier. It didn't need poly bags, so you could set up ten barrels at a time and run the glue through a high-speed filter pump. A twenty-foot hose on the end of the pump was fitted with a barrel nozzle that you could hook to the side of a drum and just leave it there while the barrel filled up. It took less than a minute to fill a drum with this setup. Graupner would be done emptying the tank in two or three hours, then he'd spend the rest of the evening up on the deck of the water tower.

Lenny gave a latex batch to Larry Edgerton. It was only twenty barrels, but that stuff was always dirty. He'd be lucky to filter four or five drums an hour. He'd be slopping around in glue and water all night. I was the last one to get an assignment.

"Tank 30," Lenny said. "Tank truck." He handed the draw sheet to me, and I looked it over. Four thousand gallons needed to be pumped into a truck due in half an hour. I wandered over to the tank and took my time setting up the filter press. The material in the tank needed to be filtered through a press consisting of six or seven filter plates. Each plate consisted of a square iron frame around a gold mesh filter screen. I had to drape a sheet of cheesecloth over each of the plates, push the plates up against each other, then tighten down these big metal eye bolts that held the press together. You tightened the bolts by running a steel rod through the bolt eyes and using all your strength and weight to screw them down tight. I was sweating up a storm by the time I finished setting up the press. While I waited for the tank truck to arrive, I went up on the bench to look for Buda.

The bench was empty when I climbed the steps, but that was okay. I liked walking around on it and examining the details of its construction. It had been built in the 1930s along with the tanks surrounding it. It had been built by a shipwright, so it resembled a ship in its construction and in its intentional use of space. There were wood cabinets everywhere, and shelves for everything the chemical operators needed to ensure the integrity of the batches. A geared rod, turned by a huge squeaking rubber belt, ran along the ceiling over the length of the bench, then crossed the aisle and ran above the newer tanks, too. From the bench, the chemical operators could throw levers and engage or disengage the mixing blades of a particular tank. It wasn't unusual to have ten or twelve tanks mixing glue all at once. When that happened, the racket was unbelievable. The tanks themselves were originally made of wood, but over the years, they'd become an amalgam of wood and metal. While the outsides of the tanks still outwardly showed their original wooden planks, their insides had been outfitted with steam jackets made of stainless steel to assist in the cooking of the batches. I opened the lid of one of the tanks and watched an adhesive that looked like cake batter getting turned again and again by the blades. While I was watching the glue mix, Jesús De Jesús came down the stairs from the second floor.

"You don't belong here," he said. He had a heavy Colombian accent.

"I'm waiting for Buda," I said.

"Wait down on the floor, chico. This is not a place for children."

I shrugged and was about to leave, but decided to say something.

"What's your problem with me, Jesús? I've never done anything to you. I've never even spoken to you, really, but is it just me you treat like shit, or is it everyone? If it's everyone, then you're just a prick. If it's just me then I'd like to know what I did to deserve being treated like I'm some kind of jackass."

De Jesús stared at me but said nothing. After about fifteen seconds, I turned and walked to the stairs.

"It is not you," Jesús said when I reached the stairs. I turned around and looked at him. "Two years ago, one of the workers was inside Tank 11, cleaning the glue built up on the mixing blades. He was supposed to wear a respirator when in the tank because of the fumes, but he took it off while I was on the bench. He passed out then. I did not find him until half an hour later. By then, it was too late to save him. Since then, I have always been scared someone would come onto the bench and hurt themselves with acid or caustic soda. I apologize for treating you poorly. Just worry about your safety, young man."

"I got it," I said. "I shouldn't be poking around when nobody's here. I guess I'd be concerned too if I were you."

I walked over to Jesús and shook his hand, then I went down on the floor over to my tank. The truck had just pulled onto the concrete pad. Once the truck got situated, I connected the hose from the tank to the valve at the end of the truck. I double checked to make sure all the right valves were opened, then I turned on the pump. I climbed up onto the top of the truck and looked into the hatch. Glue was streaming across the bottom of the tank. I hooked myself onto the top of the truck with a safety harness that was the correct size. If I fell off the truck, I wouldn't hit the pavement but would just dangle about three feet off the ground. Then I sat on the top of the truck with my legs crossed. I closed my eyes and put my hands in my lap, palms up, and focused on my breathing. It was a struggle. I wanted to fall asleep or go away somewhere. One of the things I'd begun noticing was how noisy it was inside my head. There seemed to be an unending stream of conversation taking place inside my skull. My mind was like a little monkey jumping through the trees from one branch to the next. After about twenty minutes of struggling to sit zazen, I opened my eyes. Nothing had changed. I measured the glue in the tank truck. Almost eleven inches. I had another thirty-one to go before the truck was full. I remained seated on the top of the tank truck, but instead of meditating, I just listened to the sound of fork trucks running in the factory, the rubber belt squealing above the bench, the pump on the pressure washer kicking on and off, the hiss of steam being vented from down in Solvents. Everything was what it was. The bell for break sounded, I climbed down off the truck, and turned off the pump. I would clean out the filter plates and put new cheesecloth sheets in the press after the break. Then I walked down past the locker room and went outside. I sat on the bench and took my fifteen-minute break like a man sitting on a bench taking a fifteen-minute break.

Wiggins sat down next to me. Neither of us said anything. The one o'clock break was mostly reserved for self-reflection and penance. Just about everyone was starting to sober up a little, and most of the crew was feeling the need for a drink or snort of something to take the edge off. Tuttle seemed slumped in on himself. Unlike his performance earlier at the weigh scale, where he'd come across as larger than life, he seemed to have reverted to a shrunken, scrawnier version of himself. Wiggins saw me looking at Tuttle and leaned over toward me.

"That speed junkie's wagon be crashing. Innit?"

I looked down Front Street toward Dunellen to the left. There was a wail of distant sirens that seemed to be coming from that direction and growing louder with each passing second. Everyone on the crew began staring toward Dunellen.

"Somethin's goin' on," said Wiggins.

90

He stood up and crouched over with his hands on his knees. Flashing lights had appeared in the distance, and the wailing of sirens was becoming one long continuous blare. The rest of the crew rose to their feet and adopted various postures of wary anticipation. Just in case we needed to run for our lives, we wanted to be sure we could get a running start. Then suddenly it was upon us. A big rig with its headlights and running lights turned off went screaming past us at 90 miles per hour, followed by at least fifteen squad cars with their lights flashing and their sirens going full tilt. There were police cars all the way from Bridgewater-Raritan and South Bound Brook. The last police car passed. It was the fix everyone needed. Adrenaline was pumping through all of our bodies.

"Wow! That muthafucker be bookin'!" said Wiggins.

"Solid!" said Smoky.

"Did you all just see that?" said Graupner. "That trucker had like every cop in the world chasing him!"

"That muthafucker be bookin.' Didja see all them police cars?"

"He be bookin'," said Smoky.

"Solid!" said Wiggins.

Even Tuttle had gotten excited by all the commotion.

"Wonder if he'll get away?" he asked.

"That many police? Oh, they gonna git him a'right. Hope he ain't no black man tryin' to outrun the police like that. They ain't gonna beat no white fellow near as bad as some black dude."

"The screws never laid their hands on me," said Tuttle.

"What's this? 1959 an' we watchin' *Dragnet*? Ain't nobody ever call the police 'screws' now!"

Tuttle sat down on the bench and seemed to shrink into himself again. The bell sounded, ending the break, and we all shuffled into the factory. In a few minutes, I'd be on top of the tank truck listening for the sound of one hand clapping and the faint cry of sirens wailing in the distance.

# Chapter 13 MoMA

Tuesday rolled around, and I drove over to Mandy's after going home and changing into my best pair of blue jeans and a reversible shirt. It was lime green on one side and neon pink on the other. I wore the shirt with the green side out. My $2 fake leather cowboy boots had developed a hole in the left sole. If it hadn't been raining, I would've worn the boots, but I put on a pair of penny loafers. I didn't like those shoes very much, but at least my socks wouldn't get wet.

My mom was awake when I'd gotten changed and gone up to the kitchen for a cup of coffee. My dog was sleeping on the living room sofa. My mother looked at her.

"Terrible dog," she said. "Make mess two times after you leave last night. I have to clean up two messes! How come you don't get dog already trained?"

I sat down on the sofa and ran my hands over the dog. My skin didn't crawl as much when I pet her now. I'd taken her to a pet groomer over in South Plainfield the previous day, and they'd shaved her down to about half the size as when I got her. With all her hair gone, she wasn't horrible to look at.

"Terrible dog," my mother said.

"Terra the Terrible," I said. I liked the name. It seemed to fit. "Stop crapping all over the place, Terra."

She looked up at me and licked my hand. You can't be mad at a dog for longer than thirty seconds. They always have a way of looking at you that makes you have to forgive them, but a cat? No one should ever forgive a cat anything.

I went outside and brought in the newspaper. The paper boy hadn't wrapped it and had just thrown it on the grass. It was a wet mess. I opened it up and looked through the pages to see if there was a story about the big rig that had roared past us last night with half the police in New Jersey chasing him, but there was nothing. I'd have to pick up the Bound Brook paper that came out in the afternoon to find out what that was about. My mother had made coffee, and I put some sweetened condensed milk in it. It was like drinking candy. My mother came over and sat down on the sofa on the other side of the dog, and I read the comics to her. I had to explain Beetle Bailey and Peanuts to her, but I didn't mind. All that meditation I was doing was probably making me a better human, not that I was a total asshole before I'd started looking for my original face while sitting atop a tank truck at three-thirty in the morning. I opened the sports page and looked at the box scores.

"Fuck," I said. The Mets had dropped a game to the Rangers. Dr K, Dwight Gooden, had taken the loss. "Son of a bitch."

"Don't use such bad language," my mother said.

I looked at my watch. I had an el cheapo Timex that I'd bought in a flea market for $.75. The second hand was broken, but the minute and hour hands worked perfectly fine. Nobody really needs a second hand on a watch unless you've got a job defusing bombs or timing horse races where seconds matter. It was about 8:55 and I needed to pick up Mandy.

"Shit, I'm late," I said. "Mandy and I are going to the City."

"Don't use such bad language around Ilene's daughter," my mother said. "She's nice girl."

"Jesus, ma! I'm not gonna use any bad language in front of Mandy! I'm not a complete dope!"

I ran out of the house, leaving my mom and my dog to keep each other occupied. Then I drove over to Mandy's. I was in a hurry and nearly hit the blind guy in the crosswalk outside the coffee shop. Normally, I would've stopped, rolled down the window, and asked if he'd had any more luck finding the lady with the Bible verses on her, but I didn't have time. Not that particular day, anyway. When I pulled up to Mandy's place, I got out of the car and ran around to the passenger side and opened the door. All that Zen stuff was turning me into a gentleman. I went up to the porch and knocked on the door. She opened it, and I looked inside. It was one of those houses that looked light and spacious and everything clean and orderly, not like my place. Our house was dark and cramped and strewn with books and papers all over the place. You could sit anywhere at our house and put your feet on the furniture if you wanted to. I was pretty certain you couldn't put your feet on anything at Mandy's.

I walked Mandy to my car. She was driving, so I climbed into the open passenger door and waited for Mandy to get into the driver's side. Her parents had owned a Volkswagen Bug, so she knew how to operate the clutch, but she had never driven a car with the gear shift on the steering column.

"Three on the tree," I said.

It took her a couple of minutes to get acclimated to the Bel Air's shift pattern, but she picked it up okay, then she pulled away from the curb for the City. While she drove, I pulled out my poems and read each one to her several times, so she really understood them. Then I explained in great detail what I'd been thinking about when I wrote them, and how I had some great ideas to write another fifty poems. None of them was going to be any longer than seven letters, including the titles.

"Most people have short attention spans," I said. "The sooner you make your point, the better."

"I like the one titled 'Bug'," Mandy said.

That was probably my overall masterpiece, so I was happy it was her favorite. Pretty soon, I yawned.

"I'm gonna get a little shut-eye," I said. I fished in my pocket and pulled out a bunch of change that I handed to Mandy.

"For the tolls," I said.

I slept all the way to New York. When I woke up, we were in the middle of the Holland Tunnel. I looked at the Tunnel walls as we drove past. Some of the tiles had fallen off the walls and lay broken on a little walkway between the walls and the road. It wouldn't have surprised me to learn the batch of crappy glue holding the tiles to the wall had been made by the midnight shift at American Starch.

When we got to the museum, Mandy found a place to park close by in one of those attended lots that gouge you for $2 in order to park. I gave the attendant the money.

"Fucking robbery," I said. The attendant shrugged. He probably heard that like twenty times a day.

We walked over to the museum under Mandy's umbrella. She'd brought it so she could walk around in the sculpture garden outside the museum. We wandered around the sculptures for fifteen minutes or so. She really liked this red metal sculpture that had these yellow and blue fins sticking out of it. It looked like something you'd hang over a baby's crib.

"It's a Calder," she said.

"Precisely," I told her.

We went inside and went from room to room. Most of the stuff was forgettable. Landscapes and portraits and whatnot. There was one painting that was completely red. It had different shades of red squares and red circles, and drops of red dripping down into another shade of red. It looked like something you'd see on the side of a tank in the glue factory, the dripping part anyway. We probably made red glue, though I'd never seen any.

After about an hour, we came to a room and Mandy stopped me before I entered it.

"Cover your eyes," she said.

"Ok," I said. "Just make sure I don't bump into anything and break it."

I covered my eyes, and she took my hand in hers and led me into the room. Her hand was cool and soft, not sweaty and sticky like some people's hands. After a little bit, we stopped, and Mandy turned me to the left.

"Ok," she said. "You can take your hands away from your eyes now."

I uncovered my eyes. There was a painting of a scene at night with about ten swirly stars and swirly clouds, a crescent moon, and something that might have been a tree poking up between the stars. There was a building with a steeple in the middle of the painting surrounded by some houses, and in the distance, the hills ranged in shades of pale blue to nearly black. In some ways, the painting seemed large when I looked at everything inside of it, but when you glanced at

95

it casually, it wasn't that big, just about two and a half feet by three feet. I probably stood there for ten minutes looking at Van Gogh. It was probably the only thing I saw in the museum that I really liked, other than this painting of a person driving a car that looked exactly like a photograph of a person driving a car, only the Van Gogh painting didn't look like a photograph. It was way better than the poems I'd written. I knew that much, but I couldn't tell you why. After I'd stood there in silence for a while, Mandy came up beside me and took my hand in hers again.

"When I look at this painting, I feel like I'm looking at someone's soul," Mandy said.

"Precisely," I answered. I meant it, too.

After the museum, we stopped at a street vendor and had a hot dog, some greasy fries, and a soda. Mandy was a vegetarian and didn't eat fried food or sugar, so she just had water. Then she opened her purse and rummaged around in it for a carrot. She was certainly cheap to feed.

We went back over to the lot, and there was a different attendant. I couldn't find the ticket the first guy had given me, so I had to give the new guy another two bucks.

"You guys are robbers," I said. "There goes your tip."

The new guy just shrugged and looked away.

I drove on the way back. It was early afternoon, and the traffic wasn't bad. We got back to Majestic in less than an hour. On the drive, Mandy sat next to me and talked about the sculptures she'd seen and the paintings she liked. She mentioned Picasso and Dali, and Rauschenberg. I didn't remember seeing any of their paintings. I told Mandy about everything I'd been learning about Zen and mindfulness, and how my life was basically perfect now that I'd been studying Zen riddles about the Buddha being dried shit on a stick.

I exhausted that subject in about eight minutes, and we drove in silence. Mandy leaned her head on my shoulder, and I put my arm around her, but I had to take my arm back after about a minute because the exit came up, and I needed to downshift to second. Then we were sitting in front of her house kissing each other for about three seconds until she got out of the car and stood looking at me.

"That was fun," she said. Maybe we can go to the opera sometime."

"Sure," I said. "I'm a big opera fan."

I had never been to the opera or ever heard any records of people singing opera, but that was okay. I thought about what Wiggins had told me about how a man needed to be willing to go to the edge of death when he loved a woman. Opera was close enough.

I got home and went into the living room. My mom had already left for work, and Terra the Terrible was sleeping on the sofa. She raised her head and looked at me when I walked in. Then she lay back down and went to sleep. I walked around the house. She hadn't chewed anything up or crapped on anything, or if she had my mom had cleaned it up. I was still hungry, so I made myself a grilled Spam and Velveeta cheese sandwich on pumpernickel. I sat on the sofa next to the dog while I ate my sandwich. Every so often, I tore off a hunk and fed it to Terra. She liked Spam and Velveeta as much as I did. When I was done with the sandwich and Terra had licked my fingers clean, I went down into the basement and put an old Buffalo Springfield album on my stereo. Terra had followed me down the stairs and jumped on the bed next to me after I'd undressed and climbed under the covers. I would sleep until seven, then get up and watch the Mets play the Rangers before going to work. The rain had cooled everything off, and the factory would be nice and cool when I started my shift. I thought about Mandy while the song "Bluebird" played. When the song ended, I drifted off to sleep while the needle moved along in the record's worn grooves. "For What it's Worth."

# Chapter 14 Jerry

I woke up at about seven o'clock and got out of bed. Terra was upstairs, sitting by the back door. She pawed at it when she saw me, wanting to be let out.

"Good girl," I said. She hadn't crapped anywhere. I let her out. After a few minutes, I let her back in and spent the next couple of hours watching the ballgame on TV. While the game was on, I worked on my play. I finished it in about an hour. It was only about twenty pages long and didn't have a whole lot of dialogue, maybe thirty or forty lines, but it was damn fine dialogue. Poignant and piquant. I re-read the play a couple of times. The ending was as piquant and poignant as the dialogue. The man who refuses to eat anything but peanut butter and jelly sandwiches sits in a chair holding a peanut butter and jelly sandwich in one hand and a dog in the other. Then everything goes dark except this one little spotlight fixed on the sandwich. The light lingers on the sandwich for ten seconds, then everything fades to black. Maybe I'd try to get the local theater group to perform the play sometime. I wondered who I'd call for something like that.

I looked at the clock. It was 8:30. I still had a couple of hours to kill before heading to the factory. I got another piece of paper and started writing a story about a man who photographs a bowl of fruit. Every time he takes a picture, he moves the bowl of fruit very slightly, first in one direction then in another. When he's done taking about a thousand photos over the course of a week, he strings the photos all together in some process I didn't really understand and makes a film of the bowl of fruit. He sits in his room and watches the film while smoking a cigarette. The bowl moves to the right, then to the left like it's dancing, while the fruit in the bowl gets older. The bananas grow brown spots, the apples start wrinkling, and the oranges get all moldy. The story ends with the fruit in the bowl all rotten, while the man just sits quietly smoking his cigarette. There wasn't any dialogue because the man was alone and would be crazy to have a conversation with a bowl of fruit. By the time I finished the story, it was time to go to work.

I left Terra sleeping on the sofa when I left the house. We hadn't made much glue the past couple of days. One of the big bosses above Swifty had walked through the glue department and hadn't been happy.

"The place looks like a shithouse," was what he'd said to Virgil.

We spent the entire week chiseling glue off the floors, getting rid of broken pallets that were scattered all over the place, and clearing out half-empty drums of different chemicals and consolidating them in one or two barrels. That night, they put me with Jerry, the born-again Christian who'd done time for manslaughter. Our job was to take the half-empty butts, which was what you called a drum that wasn't full and turn them into full drums. You had to take the butts down to the barrel refill station between the resin cutter and the stencil machine and put them on a lift that raised and lowered the drum when you pulled a chain. You opened the bungs on the head of the drum, raised it, then pulled another chain that would tip the drum forward. The liquid inside the butt on the lift would pour out into a funnel you'd placed in the open bung of another butt. Sometimes it would take three or four butts to make one full barrel. The empty barrels were taken out by the tank pad and hauled away every couple of weeks.

In theory, this was a pretty easy job. We weren't making or filtering anything, and just so long as you made sure that the ID codes on the heads of all the barrels matched, the job should have been easy. In reality, however, refilling barrels was a pain in the ass. You never seemed to get the drum on the lift to the correct height, and when you tipped the barrel forward, the liquid in it would miss the funnel entirely and land in front of the second drum or behind it. Even if you did manage to hit the funnel, the liquid always flowed unevenly out of the suspended barrel. One second it would be flowing into the funnel, and the next second it would be all over the top of the drum or dripping on the floor. Plus, in order to see how full the drum was that you were filling, you had to open this little bung on top of that barrel and peer down into it as the liquid in it rose. That never seemed to go right either. The liquid always got all over the top of the drums, and you'd have to seal the barrel, then spend half the night standing in water full of chemicals that could probably kill you.

Jerry, the twice-born, didn't talk much. I'd been around Christians before who wouldn't stop yapping about Jesus and how good God had been to them. Fortunately, I was able to reverse the tables and tell Jerry all about Zen and how, if everyone sat in meditation and cleared their minds, the world would be 1000% better.

"When you realize that you're Buddha AND Jesus and they're nothing more than bowls of warm shit, then you've really got it all figured out," I said.

Jerry didn't say anything when I said that. He just kept working, which kind of annoyed me. I'd never really won an argument with a Christian before on account of they didn't really argue fair and always had to say things like "well, the Bible says" or "it's in the Bible", and now I could pull out my own argument ending lines like "well, according to the Eightfold Path" or "the Dhammapada says", but I couldn't get Jerry to argue no matter what I said. I couldn't decide which kind of Christian I disliked more, the ones who wouldn't shut up or the ones who wouldn't talk.

One o'clock came, and we went down to the break room. I sat down at the table with Jerry just in case he wanted to have a conversation with me about why Christianity was better than Zen, but he didn't say anything about that, just offered me his sandwich when he noticed that I hadn't brought my lunch with me, and then his sweatshirt when he noticed I was cold. Then he spent the rest of break telling me about his mom and dad, how they'd come to see him at least once a week when he was doing time in Sing Sing, and that sitting in prison for nine years away from the society of regular people was about the worst punishment you could inflict on a man short of killing or torturing him, and that there were more people rotting in jails and prisons in the US than there were in the rest of the world combined. By the time the break was over, I didn't want to argue with him anymore, which was kind of a pity. I really had thought up some good zingers which I'd just have to practice on some other born-again.

After break ended, we went back down to the barrel refill area and consolidated all the butts of that emulsifier 708-04. Then we consolidated about six butts of 858-47 which got all over the place, but that wasn't so bad. It was just corn oil that was used in making some kinds of wood glues. Barrels of corn oil were all over the factory, mostly because you could pump it on your hands or a rag and get lots of different kinds of glue off of you. A couple of the workers on the second shift had stashed barrels of corn oil in various locations around the department so they would always have it handy. It wouldn't loosen latex, though, and you were just better off not getting anywhere near a latex batch.

By the end of the evening, Jerry and I had cleaned up nearly all the half-empty barrels except the 731-24, the trichlorethylene. Jerry wanted to consolidate three or four butts of it, but I said "No." I'd accidentally dropped my hammer in a batch of glue once that had heavy trichlorethylene in it. I'd taken the drum down to the barrel refill area, but Gresham had the lift machine tied up for the rest of the shift. I had to reach into the 55-gallon drum of glue with my left hand and find my hammer that way. The glue got all the way up to my shoulder and even on the side of my face and beard, but my entire arm was tingling from the trichlorethylene for the rest of the shift, even after I'd washed it all off. I got my hammer back, but I kept a wide berth from that stuff after reading how bad it was for you. It couldn't kill you just by looking at it, but I never wanted to see a barrel of the stuff again if I could help it.

Near the end of the shift, Jerry and I walked up to the weigh scale. It was amazing how much better the place looked. All the broken pallets, empty cardboard boxes, and used up chemical drums had been taken cut back to be hauled away. The broken pail lids that we'd tossed around like Frisbees when we first clocked in and were still drunk had all been gathered up and thrown away along with all the lunch bags and soda cans that we'd just tossed under the tanks when we were finished with them. Even the area around the hot melt tank looked way better. Graupner and Wiggins had taken heavy metal chisels about six feet long and cut down about six inches through the built-up hot melt all the way to the floor. There was still some buildup left for the first shift to handle, but the entire shift was amazed. We all gathered around the hot melt and examined the floor and pointed to the layers of glue they'd cut through, like we were archaeologists on a dig along the Grand Canyon. Wiggins and Graupner strutted around still holding their chisels like they had just harpooned a whale. Only Tuttle stood off by himself. He'd spent the evening alone, scraping the glue off the fittings of all the hoses in the department while the angels and demons inside him battled for supremacy.

The third shift ended, and we punched out. I walked down the ramp to the locker room with Jerry.

"When I was in the joint, I read Alan Watts' book *This is It*," he said. "It's about Zen. You'll probably get something out of it. I certainly did."

I sat at my locker and felt confused. For a Christian, Jerry seemed like a pretty good Buddhist. You didn't run into that every day.

I went home and took Terra for a walk. She liked chasing cars, so I made sure I walked along a busy street so she'd get plenty of exercise. Then I took her home. She was pretty tired after running so much and just lay down on the sofa and fell asleep. I hung around in the kitchen and wrote a story about a man who goes out in the middle of the desert and builds a highway by himself. It takes him years and years, but he finally gets it done. The highway just sort of begins nowhere and ends nowhere. It's got on ramps and off ramps, so that overhead it looks like a four-leaf clover. He even puts a traffic light on it. The last sentence of the story is about the man standing and staring at the traffic light blinking red, yellow, green, red, yellow, green over and over again. It was three pages long. I read the story to myself aloud three or four times. I managed to put in some dialogue this time. The man has a long monologue full of Zen riddles with someone who asks him why he's building a highway that doesn't lead anywhere.

It was definitely the best short story I'd ever read. I decided that I'd mail a copy to my father and let him read it, too. Then I took my dog and went downstairs. I put her on my bed and climbed under the covers, still wearing my clothes. I went to sleep without even putting a record on. I just let the conversation in my head spin me around and around.

# Chapter 15 Honeymoon Glue

Willie came back to work sometime in July or August. He'd had skin grafts on his arm, back, and face where the hot melt had burned him. He looked pretty good considering. The grafts had taken fairly well, but there was plenty of scarring. The grafts were kind of pink. Against his dark skin, they made him look like a black cow with several noses scattered around his body. He'd quit drinking while recuperating in the hospital and had lost some weight or gained some weight or just shifted the weight around in a more healthy fashion and was preaching temperance to anyone who would listen to him. The company had paid all his medical expenses and even kept him on payroll and paid him his base salary every week while he was off. The rumor was that the company had also cut Willie a check to keep him from retaining a lawyer and suing the company for maintaining a hazardous work environment. Wiggins asked him point-blank when we were all on break if the rumor was true.

"They break you off a piece?" Wiggins asked. "I know they done broke you off a piece."

Willie pursed his lips and refused to answer.

"I knew it!" said Wiggins. "You'd say sumpin' if they didn' give you nuthin'! What they do? Make you sign one of them non-disclosures?"

"I cain't say nuffin' 'bout nuffin'," said Willie.

"Damn!" said Wiggins. "What they give you? Fifteen large? Twen'y? Me? They'd have to gimme at least twen'y-five plus lemme take home all the glucose from the sugar shack I wanted! Free glucose and corn oil, plus all the tapioca flour I could fit in my car, so I'd have puddin' for life! Damn! Makes me sorry wasn't my ass fell in the hot melt!"

"Yo' keeps on drinkin' yo' will fall in th' hot melt one o' these days, certain," said Willie.

"Shit!" said Wiggins. "You fell in the hot melt cause you lost them damn toes to fros' bite in Korea and couldn' keep your goddamn balance! Me? I got all my toes! Ain' that right?! I ain' fallin' in no hot melt drunk or sober, less'n I want to."

When the break ended, I went back to work cutting resin and packing it out in cardboard boxes. The second shift had started cutting this batch, and I needed to finish it up. This job probably scared me worse than any other job in Glue. Besides Buda, I knew at least two other people who'd lost fingers in the cutter. One of them, Walter Weidrick on the second shift, had lost three fingers on his left hand in the cutter. He was from a little town on the Danube River outside Budapest, so everyone called him Hungry Walter. He'd come to the United States in 1956, along with 30,000 other refugees after the failed Hungarian Revolution, and had gotten processed through Camp Kilmer on the outskirts of Majestic. He was a big, burly guy who'd been a boxer when he was younger and was always telling me to get a haircut.

"You look like goddamn hippy gypsy," he'd say. "Long hair is only for women! You not woman, are you? Goddamn hippy gypsy with red beard. You need shave too!"

Hungry Walter hardly ever worked the midnight shift, but this was one of those rare occasions when he'd said "yes" when the second shift supervisor had asked if he'd work overtime. He saw me while I was cutting resin as he rode past on an electric pallet jack.

"Hey, you hippy gypsy. Watch your fingers!" he said. He raised his left hand and showed me the stubs where his fingers should have been.

"Look, kiddo, I'm giving you an invisible middle finger!"

Hungry Walter disappeared up the forklift ramp into the glue department. I still had about ten pans of hot melt to cut. It was easy to cut when you first took it out of the freezer, but it was beginning to thaw out now, and the cutter blades were starting to gum up with hunks of warm resin. I had tried to put the resin back in the freezer over by the elevator to the second floor, but there were no empty spaces in it now. Those had been taken by fresh pans of hot melt that had recently come out of the tank.

Every two or three pans I had to stop cutting the hot melt into two-and-one-half-inch cubes and clean off the cutter blades. The only way you could do this was by reaching under the blades with your fingers and pulling off the resin by hand. This was strictly forbidden by company policy, but the supervisors would always look the other way when you did it. If you didn't clean off the blades by hand, you'd never finish cutting the hot melt and get it packed out. You just had to be careful you didn't lean across the lever for lowering the cutter blade while your hand was underneath it, which was how Buda and Hungry Walter had both lost their fingers. I made sure I stayed as far away from the lever as possible while clearing the resin off the blades.

When I finished cutting and packing out the last pan, I took the empty green pans up to the hot melt tank and stacked them into three or four rows of ten pans each. I just hoped I wasn't the next guy who had to either fill those pans or cut the resin in them after they'd been filled. Then I went and grabbed the electric pallet jack that Hungry Walter had been using when he'd gone past. I spent the next hour before the 3 am break riding around the department and going up and down the elevator like I was doing something. The elevator was by Virgil's office. I was just about to go up the elevator for about the third time and ride around on the second floor when the office door opened, and Virgil came out.

"Hey, Pete, what are you working on?"

"I'm just taking this pallet jack down to the recharging station," I said. "The battery's starting to die."

"Good man," said Virgil. "Midnight shift needs a supervisor. The front office has been looking at you. Interested?"

"Probably," I said.

"There are a couple other candidates for the position, but just between you, me, and the shithouse wall, you've got the job if you want it. Just say the word. Just say the word and the position's yours."

"The word," I said.

"What's that?" said Virgil. "I didn't quite catch that."

"The word," I said. "You said 'say the word,' so I said, 'the word.' I was making a joke."

"If you say so," said Virgil. "Swifty likes you. I like you, too. Even that asshole De Jesús likes you. At least he said as much at our last production meeting. Everyone likes you, Pete. Even the guys on the floor like you. You're 'Mr Popular' around here. The company paper is going to put you on the front page as Employee of the Month. You'll have the EOM parking space at the front of the parking lot and get your name on a plaque. Plus, you and a guest of your choice will get a gift certificate for two at the Leaning Tower of Pizza up on Route 22. You're on your way, kid!"

Virgil walked away, and I watched him go. He moved like a shopping cart with four bad wheels. He disappeared up into the bench, and I rode the pallet jack down the forklift ramp to the charging station. After hooking it up to a battery charger, I looked at the clock. It was still five minutes to break time. I got a broom and swept up around the resin cutter. I'd already swept around it after I'd finished cutting and packing out that last batch of hot melt, but so long as I kept looking busy, I was on the fast track to management and a degree in Chemical Engineering. I should've started this Zen stuff years ago, I told myself. I'd probably be the Plant Manager already if I had.

The bell for break sounded, and I went outside and sat on the bench to watch traffic. If we were lucky, there'd be another chase with police cars and maybe a fire truck or two. Willie and Larry Edgerton came outside and walked past me to the far end of the bench. The way Willie was walking it was apparent that his sobriety had come to an abrupt end. Graupner came out of the building and sat next to me.

"I hate cutting that fucking hot melt," I said. "Putting my hand under that damn cutter blade is the scariest thing you can do around here."

"Why you putting your hand under the cutter blade?" Graupner asked. "Just spray it with Insta-Freeze from the supply shed and chip the resin off with a chisel. No one told you that?"

"Hell no! No one tells you anything around here until it's too late. I'm just glad I didn't chop off my fingers!"

"Fuck it," said Graupner. "There's a supervisor position they're trying to fill. Word is you're on the short list."

"I don't know about that," I said.

"Word is that the job is yours if you want it. Word is you just have to say the word and they'll give you a clipboard and a whistle."

"A whistle?" I said. "None of the supervisors have whistles."

"It's a metaphor," said Graupner. "That's a word I never use, but I'm using it now. Just don't be a rat. Just don't rat us out for sleeping or getting high up by the water tower, drinking on the job, stealing glucose from the sugar shack, taking long breaks, playing Frisbee with the five-gallon pail lids, dropping acid, snorting speed, peeing in the hot melt tank while they're cooking up a batch, fucking up in general. Nobody likes a rat."

"You've peed in the hot melt tank?"

"I'm not saying I have or haven't, but it's pretty damn hot standing over the tank, and I wouldn't recommend it. Just don't be a rat."

"Do I look like a rat?" I asked.

"Walk around with a clipboard and a metaphoric whistle and you'll be a rat in no time," Graupner said. "It comes with the territory. Only make sure the rat territory ends at the boundaries of the territory known as Graupner."

The break ended, and I walked up to the weigh scale alone. Lenny came out of a little room just behind the weigh scale and squinted at me with his good eye.

"You done cutting resin?" he asked.

"Cut and packed," I said. "Cut, packed, sealed, stacked. Stacked, racked, and motherfacked."

"Don't start," Lenny said. "I got enough headaches on this shift. I don't need you being a headache, too. You haven't seen that migraine Graupner have you?"

"He's up peeing in the hot melt," I said.

"What?"

"Just kidding. No, I don't know where he is."

"I had a good job for him. Honeymoon glue. Fifty-five-gallon pails coming out of Tank 4. Nothing in it but corn germ meal and water. Everything's all set up and ready to go. Just open the valve, turn on the pump, and let 'er rip. His loss, though. You'll be done in half an hour."

Lenny tossed the blue sheet at me, and I plucked it out of the air. All that meditation had sharpened my reflexes, I told myself. I went over to Tank 4, and Lenny had told the truth. The filter pump had been set up, the buckets had all been stenciled, and a boxful of plastic bucket lids was sitting on a pallet to the right of the tank. I set up a semi-circle of ten buckets, opened the valve on the tank, and picked up the two-inch hose with the barrel nozzle on the end of it. Then I turned on the pump. A thin watery gruel sputtered out of the nozzle and then gathered speed. It was called honeymoon glue due to its resemblance to seminal fluid. I filled the first bucket in about thirty seconds, then began filling the second. Five minutes later, all the buckets were full. I turned off the pump and put plastic lids on all the buckets, then hammered the lids down tight. While I was hammering down the lids, Graupner came over.

"Lenny told me that you told him I was upstairs peeing in the hot melt tank! You're not even a supervisor yet, and you're already ratting me out!"

"I was just joking," I said. "Lenny asked where you were, and I said you were probably peeing in the hot melt tank. I told him I was joking."

"That's not what he told me! He told me that you told him that I was upstairs peeing in the hot melt!"

"So, were you?" I asked.

"Course," he said. "But I didn't expect you to be a fucking rat. Don't expect me to share any more pot with you, either."

Graupner walked away. I finished putting the lids on and then stacked the buckets on the pallet. When the last bucket had been transferred to the pallet, I made another semi-circle of empty buckets, picked up the hose, turned on the pump, and the virgin plastic buckets were swiftly filled with warm honeymoon glue. I finished the tank in about half an hour, then spent a few minutes stripping down the filter pump, hosing it out, and hosing down the floor around the tank where some glue had landed on the floor. I broke down the cardboard box that had held the lids, tore off a big flap of cardboard, then I sat on some empty drums by Tank 8 and pulled the black crayon out of my tool bag. I began writing a poem for Mandy:

Mandy

If you would be wood

I would be wood too

And with words of love

Would glue myself to you

So that none might come

And separate you from me

So would I woo

And stick to thee

I read the poem over and over to myself. I wasn't sure of the last lines, but she'd like it. She hadn't read much poetry and probably never had someone write any poems on her behalf before. This was definitely guaranteed to score major points with her, even if it was longer than seven letters. I folded the cardboard in half and stuck it in my back pocket as far as I could. It stuck up pretty far, though, and poked me in the back when I walked. I sauntered over to the weigh scale. A tank truck had come in, and I needed to fill it with 4500 gallons of perfume glue by the end of the shift. I sat on top of the truck and breathed in the sweet fragrance of perfume and formaldehyde. By the time seven o'clock rolled around, I was slightly goofy from the fumes. On the drive home, I realized I had fallen in love.

# Chapter 16 Opera

A few days later, I got called into Swifty's office when my shift ended. They were interviewing for the midnight shift supervisor position, and he wanted to speak to me. He'd come in early on a Saturday morning expressly for that purpose. He was sitting with his shoes up on his desk when I entered his office. I sat down in the chair opposite him and tried to look supervisorial. Swifty looked at me.

"Something wrong with your eyes," he said. "One of them is only half open."

My supervisorial look hadn't worked.

"Long shift," I said. "I'm a bit tired."

"No doubt," said Swifty. "Look, I'm gonna cut to the chase. The midnight shift needs an actual supervisor besides Lenny. He's got his hands full assigning the workflow. He doesn't have the time to make sure all the guys are giving maximal effort. Virgil's busy with the department reports. The last thing I want him doing is wandering the floor all night, making sure there's no malingering in the department. That's where you would come in. You have any problem working to ensure maximal effort and cut down on malingering and malfeasance?"

"In general, or here in the glue department?"

"In the department, naturally," said Swifty. "What you do on your own time isn't my concern."

"I don't think I'd have a problem cutting those things down," I said. "You don't want people peeing in the hot melt tank or getting drunk on the job."

Swifty took his feet off the desk and leaned across the table.

"People are getting drunk and peeing in the hot melt?" he asked.

"No…, I just meant those as examples of malfeasance and malingering," I said. "If I came across any malingering or malfeasance, such as those examples, I'd nip it in the bud."

"Damn right you would!" said Swifty.

"I've got a couple more guys I'm interviewing for the position," he said, "but just between you, me, the shithouse wall, and the rest of management, we're all pretty well convinced you're the man for the job. Just keep your nose clean for the next week or two, and you'll be walking the floor with a clipboard."

"My nose is clean," I said.

"Good! Just keep it that way," said Swifty. "Close the door on your way out."

When I got home, my mom was still sleeping. Her door was open when I went upstairs to the bathroom. The dog was lying on the bed next to her. I went into the bathroom and looked at my face in the mirror. My beard was looking really good except for a bald patch where I'd had to cut out a piece of latex that wouldn't come off. Mandy and I were going to the opera in the City that evening, and I wanted to look my best. I took a pair of scissors and cut another spot in my beard exactly opposite from the bald spot so that I looked symmetrical. Then I went downstairs and wrote a story titled "An Interesting Story." It was about a factory worker named Charlie Lord who meets a blind guy in a coffee shop who tells him a story about meeting a woman with inexplicable bumps all over her that are actually Bible verses written in Braille. The blind guy reads her bumps, then they go back to her house and have sex. Afterwards, the woman drops the blind guy off and he keeps going back to the coffee shop hoping to smell the woman's perfume, again, but never does. The story ends with Charlie Lord reading a book about Zen Buddhism while the waitress pours him lousy coffee. The story was about three or four pages and mostly all dialogue. It sort of wrote itself since I didn't have to make any of it up except for the name of the factory worker. I just wrote down exactly what happened and finished it in about an hour. When I was done rereading it, I wrote out a copy on a few sheets of lined paper, stuck it in an envelope, and addressed it to my father. I'd been mailing him poems, plays, and short stories that I'd written just about every day for a couple of weeks now, and was looking forward to going to dinner with him and hearing what he had to say after reading them all.

When I was done being a writer, I went downstairs and tried to sleep, but my head seemed to be swarming with about a thousand different

111

stories that I wanted to write about, all the interesting stuff that happened in the glue factory. I got out of bed and went back upstairs. I was going to write a story about the time I dropped my hammer in the batch of glue and had to fish it out by sticking my arm into the barrel all the way up to my shoulder, only I was going to make the hammer an expensive engagement ring that the main character had bought for his girlfriend, and the drum of glue I was going to turn into twenty-five drums that take him all day to go through until he finally finds it only to have the girl tell him "no" after he proposes. The last paragraph of the story would be about the man thinking about all the trichlorethylene he'd now got in his system slowly poisoning him after fishing around in the drums all day, but still glad he'd been willing to go to the edge of death for a woman, even if she didn't want him.

Unfortunately, my mom was awake and sitting in the living room with my dog, so I never did write the story. She and my dog were watching a Japanese monster movie. A man in a latex Godzilla suit was destroying a city made of cardboard and glue. I went to the refrigerator and grabbed a beer, then sat down on the sofa next to her. My mother looked at the beer in my hand.

"You drink beer in the morning?" she said. "Why?"

"Technically, it's my evening," I said. "I just got off work. They interviewed me for the supervisor position."

"Good!" my mom said. "Peter, that so wonderful news! Better money? Yes?"

"About three times more," I said.

We sat and watched Godzilla open its mouth. Radioactive steam came out of it and set fire to a number of cardboard buildings. It was nearly as entertaining as watching people fall into the hot melt at American Starch. When I was done with my beer, I had another, then another. By the time the movie ended, I was pretty drunk. It was the first time I'd gotten hammered in weeks. I looked at the clock. It was ten. I needed to pick Mandy up at five in the evening so we could go to the City. That meant I could sleep until four pm. I went downstairs and put on a record. Keith Jarrett was playing solo piano at a concert in Cologne. It was sort of jazz and sort of something else that I couldn't describe other than to say it reminded me of that painting by Van Gogh, not neat and tidy but large, messy, and brilliant somehow. The notes in the music were like a night sky full of shimmering stars and swirling clouds. I let the music carry me away to the distant blue hills of sleep.

I woke up with a hangover. I got out of bed and went upstairs. My mom had already left for work. There was some coffee left in the percolator that I poured into a pan and heated up on the stove. It tasted metallic and bitter. My mother had left Terra in the backyard. I let her in, and she followed me up the stairs and lay on the floor outside the bathroom while I showered. When I'd finished showering, I went downstairs and dressed in a pair of burgundy polyester dress pants and a burgundy turtleneck. I'd found a pair of Earth shoes my size in a secondhand store and put them on. The forefoot of the shoes was higher than the heels, so it took a little while to get used to walking in them. The first time I'd put them on, I'd almost fallen over backward, but I'd heard the negative heel technology had been invented by some Danish yogi and was really good for improving your posture. The heels were a bit worn, but not alarmingly so. I'd gone over to Solvents and scooped some epoxy out of a drum. Then I slathered it around the heels of the shoes to keep them from wearing out completely.

I put on my corduroy sports coat with the zippered pockets and leather patches on the sleeves and looked at myself in the oven window. Bitchin'! I was about to leave when the phone rang. It was my dad.

"Hi, Pete. How you doing?"

"Good!" I said. "I'm on my way out the door. I'm going to the opera with Mandy."

"I'm impressed," my father said. "You're becoming quite the man of culture."

"They interviewed me for the supervisor position this morning," I said. "They pretty much said the job is mine."

"That's terrific, Pete. I was a little concerned when you first started working there. I'd heard stories about that place, but I'm really happy things are working out. I also wanted to tell you that I've been reading the poems and stories you've been sending me. The poems are okay, but the stories are really something! Let's go to dinner next week and talk? Thursday sounds good?"

"Sure," I said. "Hojo's?"

"If that's where you want to go, it's fine by me. See you at six?"

"Absolutely," I said.

I got to Mandy's a few minutes early and stood around in the living room while waiting for her. Mandy's dad came in from the backyard and shook my hand. He was a little guy with an enormous head. He worked for Honeywell as an efficiency expert. Basically, he walked around with a clipboard and a stopwatch, timing people and making notes about how to cut costs. He was paid more than $80,000 per year to get more work out of guys making five or six dollars per hour. It was a pretty good gig. He offered me a glass of scotch while I was waiting for Mandy, but I turned it down just in case it was a test to see if I'd actually drink, then get behind the wheel of a car and drive his daughter to New York on one of the busiest highways in America. Plus, I hated scotch. It tasted like rubber, dirt, and leather to me, but not in a good way. The taste of it reminded me of hot melt if you poured some in a glass and added ice cubes to it. I suppose anything can become an acquired taste so long as you torture yourself long enough to get over your initial repugnance.

Mandy came downstairs. She looked good. She wore an ankle-length black dress with horizontal white stripes, freshwater pearls, and a pair of open-toe sandals. Naturally, my outfit was more eye-catching than hers, but it was better that way. I'd rather have people notice me than stare at her. I wasn't really a jealous guy, but I didn't like the idea of strangers eyeballing her.

The drive to the City was smooth sailing. Even though Mandy hated the smell of Old Spice, she cuddled up next to me in the car. I hadn't used too much, though, only enough to cover the smell of cigarettes in my hair and beard. While we drove, I handed Mandy the poem I'd written her. I made her read it aloud a couple of times and only had to correct her once about emphasizing the word "wood" in the first line. She cried the second time reading the poem through, and that's when I knew my poem had been a big hit.

114

"Wait'll you read the next one I write for you?" I said. "It'll knock your socks off. Maybe even your dress," I said.

"Well, we'll just have to see about that," Mandy said.

"Yep, we'll see," I said.

We got to the opera house but couldn't find any parking on the street, so we had to park in another one of those rip-off lots where they charged me three dollars. I put the ticket in my wallet this time. I wasn't going to pay another three bucks for parking for just a few hours. The opera was nearly sold out, but we managed to get tickets up in the nosebleed section. Fortunately, Mandy had brought opera glasses that I let her use almost as much as I did.

The opera was one called "Rigoletto." It was really good. I only fell asleep two or three times during the performance, which wasn't all that unusual considering I generally fell asleep listening to music on my stereo every morning after work. I couldn't really follow the story, especially the parts where I was sleeping, but there's a hunchback that sings. After that, it was all a matter of conjecture. Anyway, the opera ends when this skinny lady dies while the hunchback sings. Then we had to clap like forever, sit down, then stand up and clap some more. It was annoying and made me wonder who invented this crap. I decided to write a science fiction story about it.

By now, I was really hungry and wanted to get something substantial somewhere, like a corn dog at a 7-11, but Mandy told me not to stop.

"I've got something in my pocketbook," she said.

"Oh my God," I thought to myself. "She's going to feed me a carrot."

Mandy reached into her bag and pulled out a clear Tupperware container full of something that looked like it came out of a tank at American Starch.

"It's homemade yogurt," she said. "I made it myself. Would you like some?"

"Sure," I said, even though I'm not a big yogurt fan. Mandy put some on a spoon and fed me while I was driving, which was a mistake. The yogurt was warm and didn't have any sugar or honey or fruit or vanilla.

or anything in it to make it edible, so here it was rolling around and around in my mouth. Then I had to swallow it. It made me do one of those whole-body shivers, the kind that starts with your face and goes all the way to your hips. The kind people did and then said "Yuck!" but I didn't say that.

"Yum," I said. "That's really good."

Mandy sat back in her seat and took a bite of her homemade yogurt. She didn't seem to mind that it was horrible. She looked like she'd just taken a bite of the juiciest steak a person could eat.

"It's the perfect food, Strafe. Did you know that? It's full of living bacterial cultures that are good for your gut. The oldest people in the world live in the mountains of Russia and Tibet, and they eat yogurt every day."

"Don't you ever crave a hamburger?" I asked.

"Meat is murder," Mandy said. "Besides, yogurt and tofu have all the protein anyone ever needs."

"Tofu," I asked. "What's that?"

"Fermented soybean cake," Mandy said.

"You make that, too?" I asked.

"No, I buy it at the store, but you have to wash it daily; otherwise, it gets stale. But I do grow my own bean sprouts and wheatgrass. I put the wheatgrass in a juicer, then drink it straight, but it's not very tasty."

"Not as tasty as the yogurt, huh?"

"Not nearly," she said, "but it's really good for your intestinal tract. I'm thinking of having a wheatgrass colonic. Have you ever had a colonic?"

"Like a gin and tonic or something?"

"No," Mandy said. "A colonic is when they irrigate your colon and flush out your system. Did you know that most Americans have 20 pounds of poop trapped in their bodies?"

"I didn't know that," I said.

"Maybe we can go to a spa sometime and get colonics," she said. "You don't want to be full of that much crap all the time."

"Yeah," I said. "A colonic…, sure."

I pulled up to Mandy's house. We hung around in the car and made out for like ten or fifteen minutes, even after all the colonic conversation, then the porch light came on. Her parents must have been watching us make out in front of the house and gotten nervous. Mandy kissed me once more, then got out of the car and went into the house. I hoped I didn't have to have a colonic. A man might need to go to the edge of death for a woman, but some things on the way to the edge, a man should be allowed to dodge.

# Chapter 17 Doggerel

I played hooky from work later that week and stayed up all night writing a story about a woman accused of murdering her sister's boyfriend by stabbing him in the neck. A lawyer from the public defender's office visits her and discovers the woman and her sister are actually conjoined, though they've had a falling out and haven't spoken to one another in years. The lawyer falls in love with the sister of the accused and visits her while she's stuck in jail, even though she hasn't been accused of any crime. The case goes to trial, and the accused is found guilty, but the judge has no choice but to free both women since he cannot imprison an innocent woman along with one who has been found guilty. The lawyer and the innocent sister start dating and eventually consummate their relationship while the guilty sister lies next to them covered with a sheet at the insistence of the lawyer even though the two sisters share a vagina. The story ends with a twist. The real murderer is the sister the lawyer has been sleeping with. When the lawyer questions the one who'd been found guilty as to why she hadn't said anything before, the woman replies, "I'm not a rat." From then on, the lawyer will only make love to the woman who was actually innocent, but is kind of forced to look at the face of his original girlfriend when having sex, for fear she might stab him too.

The story ran about nine or ten pages and was really convoluted and tricky to write, but I got it done and copied it out on some clean sheets of paper for my dad to read when I went to dinner with him. Then my mom came downstairs because it was morning. I drove Terra over to a park and let her fetch sticks and chase geese and ducks for half an hour or so until some lady in the park got mad and said, "All dogs on a leash! All dogs on a leash!"

"Where's yours, lady?" I said and walked away.

Obviously, it wasn't a very Zen thing to do. I would have to meditate more if I wanted to become any more enlightened than I already am. On the drive home, I stopped at the coffee shop and got a bag of donuts. The blind man wasn't around, but there was a very attractive woman about my age wearing some fancy perfume that could have been Lily of the Valley but may just as easily have been jasmine or lavender or narcissus. It smelled better than the menstrual pad glue we made for Omlever, though, that much was certain. I looked at her face, neck, and arms but didn't see anything that looked like Braille, just a few freckles and a mole here or there. One of the moles on her neck had black hairs sprouting from it, but the blind man said he'd read bumps on the woman and hadn't mentioned mole hairs at all. I was about to sit down next to her and ask her if she'd ever had a rash that translated into King James verse, but another woman came into the coffee shop.

"Does anyone own a white Chevrolet?" she said. "If so, there's a dog inside with the windows up."

"That's my dog," I said. "I just came in for a minute."

"You'd be surprised how quickly the inside of a car can become fatally hot for an animal," the woman said.

"She's fine," I said.

I paid for my donuts and left. As I was walking past Mrs Concerned, I heard her muttering under her breath.

"Some people shouldn't be allowed to own pets," she said.

I wanted to respond with something nasty, but remembered the Ten Essential Precepts of Buddhism about cultivating loving kindness and understanding.

"I forgive you for being a rude busybody," I said.

I went out to my car and opened the door. The inside of the car wasn't very hot. Terra wasn't even panting very heavily. The car probably wouldn't have gotten really hot for another five or ten minutes at least. I fed Terra half a plain donut, then rolled down her window so she could stick her head out and smell the wind. When I was a kid, I liked doing that, too. My dad had to always tell me to keep my head in the car so I wouldn't get hit by a car coming in the opposite direction. It's fun to have something in common with your dog.

My mom had just finished perking coffee when I came in with the donuts. She liked maple bars, so I got her three of them. She wrapped two of them in plastic and stuck them in the freezer for later, but I ate all three of mine right then. First, I ate the jelly-filled one, then I ate the bear claw with the sugar glaze on it, and finally I ate the blueberry/apple fritter. I felt a little sick when I finished eating them, but the coffee seemed to help with my nausea. I'd put an extra helping of sweetened condensed milk in it, and it seemed to coat and soothe my stomach. I hung around for a few more minutes and read my mother her horoscope in the paper.

"Ma," I said. "It says here, 'Your communicative ability and alert responsiveness allow you to get along well with others, today.'"

"Really!?" my mother said. "What is meaning, Peter?"

"It means your ability to talk to people and respond to them will help you in getting along with others," I said. "Now I know where I get it from. I get along with just about everyone. So long as they're not an asshole."

"Enough of bad language!" my mother said. "You better not say words like that in front Mandy."

"No, I'm a perfect gentleman with her. We went to the opera in the City last night."

"Oh, the opera!" my mother said. "That must have been expensive!"

"Not too bad. Mandy brought her own yogurt. She makes it herself in the oven out of milk and yogurt yeast. She grows beans and wheat germ, too. She's pretty clever."

"That's so wonderful, Peter. She's such nice girl!"

I thought about telling my mom that Mandy wanted me to have a colonic with her, but I decided not to mention it. I didn't feel like having to explain that one.

I finished my coffee and then went to bed later than usual. It was nearly noon, and I was meeting my father at six for dinner. I'd have to sleep fast. I put on a Rolling Stones album to help me go under: Sticky Fingers. My favorite song on the album was "Can't You Hear Me Knocking." I dropped the record needle on it, jumped into bed, and listened to Keith Richards' guitar kick the song into gear. I grabbed hold of a couple of notes and rode the song swiftly down into darkness.

I overslept and was about fifteen minutes late getting to the restaurant. My father didn't seem to mind. He had my writing in a manila folder in front of him and was rereading the story I'd written about Stella and her blue tattoos. I slid into the seat across from him and handed him the story I'd written in the morning, called The Twins. My father read it right there at the table. While I waited for my father to finish reading, I ordered a beer. The waiter brought a bottle and set it on the table. After a couple of minutes, there was condensation all over the bottle, and the back label slid around when I wiped the condensation off. I hoped I hadn't made that batch.

My dad continued reading my story. He took out his pen and corrected some typos and grammatical mistakes here and there, but when he was done, he took off his glasses and looked at me, and shook his head.

"It's incredible stuff," he said. "Just incredible! Obviously, you need someone to edit these stories of yours, but they're brilliant and funny! How do you come up with the ideas?"

I thought about Stella, but didn't want to tell my dad that I'd had sex with her and connected all the stars on her body in real life down in the basement.

"They just kind of come to me," I said. "I think it's all the Zen meditation stuff I'm doing."

"Well, just keep writing," my dad said. "Maybe you should think about writing a potboiler."

"A potboiler?" I said. "What's a potboiler?"

"You know, a whodunit,"

"A whodunit?"

"That's another word for a mystery," my dad said.

"Yeah, that's what I've been trying to get at! The whole Zen idea of life being a riddle and a mystery."

"No, I meant something more commercial, a spy or detective novel, maybe a western."

"I don't know anything about any of that stuff," I said.

"Well, that's what people want to read. Horror stories, thrillers, sci-fi, romance. You should read some thrillers, Pete. That's what people really want these days."

"Ok," I said. "What did you think of the poetry?" I asked.

"I really don't know much about poetry, but it seems like doggerel. If I were you, I'd stick to fiction."

I didn't know what doggerel was, but it didn't sound good. That was okay, though. I was able to practice Zen non-attachment, so I didn't take my father's words too personally. Maybe I really just needed to focus on writing stories like he said. I tried to imagine what a Zen western, or detective story, looked like and figured I'd try to scratch something out. I'm sure I would surprise myself one way or another.

My father shook my hand out in the parking lot. He looked really peaceful and relaxed, like he'd also been meditating. I asked if he'd been sitting zazen, but he just looked at me like I had two heads, like the two women in my story. I figured I needed to give my brother a call sometime. He was a lawyer and could probably tell me if conjoined twins could actually get away with murder the way mine had. Then I went home and spent the rest of the evening writing Mandy love poems. It may have been doggerel, but it was my doggerel, and Mandy liked it.

# Chapter 18 Crusher

I called my brother in the DA's office on Monday afternoon and asked him if he thought that a conjoined twin who committed murder would be set free because you couldn't imprison the twin who was innocent. My brother laughed.

"Why do you want to know?" he asked. Even though he'd grown up in Jersey, he'd gone to college in Boston and in four years had developed a Boston accent. It sounded good on him, the way a pinstripe suit looked good on some people and terrible on others.

"I wrote a short story about it," I said. "In my story, the judge refuses to send the conjoined twins to jail even though one is found guilty."

"Well, theoretically, I suppose that could happen, but the District Attorney in that county would probably try to get the twins on conspiracy. Be hard to prove, though. It's a head scratchah, that's for certain. Dad told me you were writing stories. He said you were wicked good, but you probably needed to work on dialogue a little. Said you had a girlfriend, too."

"Yeah, I've been dating this vegetarian who went to Amherst. She wants me to get a colonic."

"Love stinks," my brother said.

"Dad told me I should write a potboiler," I said. "A thriller or murder mystery, something like that."

"Get your law degree and go to work for a D.A. You'll have plenty of source material in no time."

"American Starch is making me a supervisor," I said.

"Whoa! That place? I heard there's a class action brewing against them by a lot of formah employees who've been maimed or injured there."

"It's dangerous as fuck," I said. "I know a bunch of guys who've lost fingers. One guy fell into this glue for soup can labels and had to get skin grafts. I was there when it happened."

"Just make sure you don't get hurt," my brother said. "You won't be able to type if you lose your fingahs."

"Have you talked to mom lately?" I asked.

"Yah, a couple times a week. She told me she got a new dog."

"That's my dog!" I said.

"According to her, it's her dog. She told me that she's housebroken it and is teaching it to 'sit' and 'stay.' She says it has a bad habit of chasing cats and begging for food like cake and peanut butter sandwiches. She's trying to break the dog of those habits, too. What kind of idiot feeds a dog cake?"

"Must be a real idiot to do that," I said. "I been practicing Zen meditation, too."

"Zen, huh? How's that going?"

"Pretty good. I've been counting my breaths, erasing dualities, and destroying my ego, though maybe not in that particular order. I've been exploring the idea that objects are events. The idea that maybe man isn't the measure of all things, you know, just trying to see things through the eyeballs of a jellyfish or squid, Stuff like that."

"Take it all with a grain of salt," my brother said. "Just remember: 'Little boys who play with Zen, may not grow up to be big men.' I read that somewhere."

"When I meet the Buddha, I'll be sure to kill him," I said.

"I got to run," my brother said. "I'm due in court on a murdah for hire case. Not as interesting as a conjoined twin being tried for murdah, or killing the Buddha, but pretty damn close. Lots of circumstantial evidence, but I think we'll put this guy away. I'll talk to you latah."

I hung up the receiver and went out back. Terra was sleeping under a rose bush along the fence. She got up and ran over to me when I walked onto the porch.

"You're my dog," I said. "Aren't you?"

I took Terra for a long walk along the Raritan across from UNJ. There were a bunch of co-eds sitting on benches studying or listening to music on their transistor radios, but I didn't pay them too much attention, even though about half of them smiled when they saw my dog and started asking me questions about her. If I ever broke up with Mandy, this would be the first place I'd come with Terra. I'd have a new girl in nothing flat. I let Terra off her leash and let her chase a swan or two in this little man-made pond in the park. No one seemed to care. After a while, Terra got tired and lay at my feet with her tongue lolling out of her mouth. She'd drunk a bunch of water from the river and the pond, and she seemed perfectly content. I was content, too. Mostly. Things were going so well, it was kind of hard to believe. There didn't seem to be any drama or tension in my life, and that was a concern for me. In the past my life was always teetering on the edge of some enormous fuck-up, and I wasn't 100% sure I liked my perfect new life. Where was the balance?

I went home and wrote a story about my first night working in the factory. I left out certain things, like how I went up on the water tower with Graupner to smoke pot, and I changed everyone's name, too. I even changed the name of the factory to the National Milk and Dairy Company. This worker has to filter a really messy cheese by hand with another worker. Then they put him with someone else, not named Graupner, to load a tank truck full of milk, but they end up overflowing the tank truck and have to hose all the milk down into the sewer. The story ends with the main character leaving the factory when his shift is over and going out, ironically for a milkshake instead of a beer. Then I went back and put in some commas and quotation marks. I reread the story a couple of times and was pretty happy with it, even though it lacked a certain something since milk generally doesn't contain chemicals that can kill you unless you're talking about botulism or E. coli. I tried to fit botulism into the story, but it didn't make any sense. Who's going to put contaminated milk into a tank truck? So, I just put the story aside to let it fester for a while.

By now, it was time to go to work. When I got up on the floor, everyone was crowded around a new piece of equipment. They had taken Tank 20, one of the big tanks to the right of the hot melt tank, and outfitted it with its own scale that they'd elevated about a foot off the floor on rubber legs so glue wouldn't get all along the bottom of it. Hungry Walter rolled a barrel onto the scale and took the head off of it. He positioned it under an overhead hose hooked to a pump, then he pressed a green button on a control panel with orange digital numbers on it that all read zero. The pump sputtered to life, and white emulsion began flowing from the overhead hose into the barrel. As the barrel filled, the orange numbers started climbing. Lenny pointed to the rapidly changing numbers.

"Three hundred pounds, three hundred and five pounds, three hundred and ten pounds."

The digital readout hit five hundred and the pump shut off abruptly.

"This is the future of glue!" said Lenny.

"I don't like it!" said Wiggins. "First of all, you can't fill but one barrel at a time. Second of all, when that pump shuts off you gots to move that full drum off'n that scale one foot up in th' air. How you gon' do that? It gon' fly down off'n that scale all by itself? Third of all, it's dumb! I can gets ten barrels filled, sealed, and stenciled all by myself by th' time you git one barrel out'n that piece o' junk."

Lenny squinted at Wiggins with his good eye.

"Tank 20," he said. "I don't care whether you like it or not!"

Wiggins slumped his shoulders and dropped his tool bag on the scale.

"I'ma do it! Just to show all y'all why it won' work!"

I got sent upstairs to crack resin and run it through the crusher. Tuttle would be packing it out downstairs on the first floor. I hated cracking resin. It was a dirty job. Basically, it was the same stuff that you ran through the cutter, only the customer wanted into crushed instead of in cubes. I grabbed a pallet filled with about forty pans of the hot melt out of the freezer with an electric pallet jack and rode up the elevator with it, and parked the pallet by the crusher. I put one of the green Teflon pans on a table and hit the resin in it six or seven times with my hammer. The frozen resin cracked and broke into smaller pieces. I flipped the pan over, and the broken pieces fell out of the pan onto the table. These I pushed down the table into a shroud surrounding a hole at the table's end. The broken resin fell into the hole on top of a pair of cylinders with spiked teeth sticking out of them. I turned on the motor of the crusher, and the toothed cylinders began rotating inward toward each other. The broken pieces of resin were caught between the cylinder teeth and ground into smaller pieces that fell down into a big canvas hopper. Down below, Tuttle stood at a table directly beneath the crusher and filled cardboard boxes with the crushed resin as it fell down into the hopper.

I put another Teflon pan on my table and hit the resin until it was broken. Chips of resin flew everywhere. Some of them hit me in the face and neck. It was only the second pan, and I could already see resin dust settling on my arms. I flipped the pan over, emptied the pan on the table, then pushed the resin into the crusher. In total, there were five pallets of this stuff. We only had one hundred and ninety-eight pans of resin left to crush and pack out. Just like working the cutter, the trick was to make sure the resin didn't thaw out and gum up the crusher.

I worked quickly. I got the first forty pans done in less than half an hour. Tuttle kept pace. One pan equaled approximately one full box of crushed product. By the time the one o'clock break had rolled around, we'd crushed three entire pallets of resin. I was coated from head to foot with the stuff, though. I cleaned the resin off my arms, face, neck, and beard with corn oil. At least I'd been smart enough to wear a paper mask over my mouth and nose and a cheesecloth bag on my head. The first time I worked the crusher, I hadn't worn a mask and spent the next few days picking resin boogers out of my nose.

I went on break and listened to Wiggins give another blow-by-blow of all the problems he'd encountered with the new system for filling barrels on Tank 20.

"Lenny done called it th' future o' glue. Th' future o' glue! Can you imagine? I'd have me that whole tank empty by now without th' future o' glue. Past o' glue's good enough. I only got ten barrels done in two whole hours. Two! Lenny stood there watchin' me, too, that one eye muthafucker! Fill one barrel an' stand around for ten whole minutes waitin' for Red to come by with a forklif' so we could push it off'n the scale onto a pallet Red got on th' front of his lif'! Then he's got to drive one single barrel each time up to th' warehouse! One! The future o' glue! This ain't no future o' glue. It's th' reverse! Innit?"

When the break ended, I went up to the freezer and pulled another pallet of hot melt out with the pallet jack and went up the elevator with it. I cracked a couple of pans and threw the resin down the crusher. Tuttle still hadn't come back from break, so I turned off the crusher and waited for him. After ten minutes had passed, I went looking for him. He wasn't anywhere upstairs or downstairs. I went onto the bench, but Buda hadn't seen him either. He wasn't in the break room. I went into the locker room, but he wasn't by his locker. I eventually found him in one of the toilet stalls. He was seated on the toilet with his belt fastened around his left arm and a needle sticking out of it. He was still breathing, though.

The ambulance got there in less than five minutes and loaded him onto a stretcher. The rest of the crew stood by the open windows, looking out onto Front Street and watched them drive Tuttle away.

"Wonder if Tuttle counts as a lost time accident?" said Wiggins. "We at twen'y seven days now! Another few days be a department record since I been here!"

I went back upstairs. It took me until five o'clock to crack all the resin and pack it out myself. I'd run five or six pans through the crusher, then run downstairs and pack it out in boxes. Then I'd go back upstairs and run another five of six pans through the crusher. By the time the five o'clock break rolled around, I was exhausted.

I sat in the break room with Jerry instead of outside on the bench. I didn't want to hear Wiggins talk about the future of glue anymore that night. Jerry sat by himself reading his Bible. When I entered the break room, he put his Bible aside and invited me to sit at his table.

"How come you're not outside?" he said.

"Too much sound and fury, tonight. Wiggins and his craziness. Tuttle. Guess I just wanted a bit less bullshit."

"I know what you mean," Jerry said. "'Come to me, all of you who are weary and carry heavy burdens, and I will give you rest.' We're not so different, Strafe."

"How you figure?"

"I had a year of college. We're the only two here who can claim that. I was going to be a teacher. They interviewed me for the supervisor position, but the crew would never listen to me. You going to take the job?"

"Probably," I said.

"The kingdom of heaven is like treasure hidden in a field, which a man found and hid; and for joy over it he goes and sells all that he has and buys that field."

"I don't get it," I said.

"Just make sure whatever treasure you're seeking is worth everything you have to trade for it."

Jerry fell silent and went back to reading his Bible.

Break ended, and I went up to the weigh scale, the old one. The new scale had broken down. The pump had failed to shut down when the drum weight reached five hundred pounds, and about ten gallons of glue had overflowed the barrel and gotten down into the scale's mechanisms. Lenny and Wiggins stood by the tank, shouting at each other. It was a tale being told by an idiot. I went up on the roof, climbed the ladder of the water tower, and sat there for over an hour. I watched the sun come up over the rooftops of Majestic and hang in the chemical smoke and smog-filled sky like an enormous glowing iron egg. I put my hands in my lap and spent a few minutes counting my breaths. Then I sat and tried thinking of a story, but nothing came. And what a glorious thing that nothing was.

# Chapter 19 Ring

I wrote like crazy for the next couple of months. I started writing a book about two cowboys on a cattle drive who come across an abandoned lighthouse on the rim of the Grand Canyon. One of the cowboys decides to stay there and live in the lighthouse while the other continues on with his cows to a slaughterhouse in Texas. The cowboy in the lighthouse meets a woman wandering around in the Badlands who can see the future clearly when the events that are yet to occur are still distant. The closer the events get to the present, the less clearly she can see them. As soon as an event takes place, she doesn't remember it at all. As she is wandering the Badlands, she has a vision of the cowboy. He will find her wandering and take her back to the lighthouse. They will marry and have five children, and seventeen grandchildren, and eighty-two great-grandchildren, and a town will spring up around the lighthouse bearing the cowboy's name: Stone. When the cowboy finds her, she goes with him. They marry, and the future unfolds just as she had foreseen, though she has no recollection of having foreseen it at all. Meanwhile, the cowboy who has taken the cattle to Texas has become a sheriff in a frontier town. His name is Rivers. He befriends a Chinese railroad worker who teaches him the principles and precepts of Buddhism. He learns to meditate and resolves problems in the town without resorting to violence. Someone pulls a gun on him, and he uses the Precepts to convince the guy to drop the gun and come with him to jail. He marries a Mormon schoolmarm who was a former riverboat gambler, and the Rivers raise lots of children and grandchildren and great-grandchildren, nearly as many as the Stone family. Five or six generations later, in New Jersey, descendants of the Stone and Rivers families meet and fall in love. The guy descended from the Stone family is a writer working in a milk factory, and the girl descended from the Rivers family is a sculptor. That was my summation of chapter one. Basically, the novel meanders for five hundred pages from New Jersey to California with side trips to Arizona and Mars, where they farm wheat and have Martian children who are Buddhists and Mormons. Many generations later, two of the descendants meet while working together building a solar radio beacon that broadcasts a welcome message out to the universe. They fall in love, and the story continues.

When I wasn't writing *The Book of Stone,* I was spending lots of time with Mandy. She got off work from the art supply store at three in the afternoon, and we'd meet in the park across the river from New Brunswick. She'd bring sandwiches made from peanuts that she'd ground herself in a food processor. The peanut butter was mixed with sesame paste and bean sprouts, which was the only thing I didn't like. The bean sprouts looked like little sperm, so I'd take them off the sandwich and throw them away. One day in September, we were lying on a blanket eyeballing the sky.

"That cloud looks exactly like one I was writing about this morning," I said. "All high, white, and cottony. Funny how you can write something that ends up coming true."

Mandy raised herself up on an elbow and looked at me.

"Seriously," was all she said.

"Maybe it wasn't the best example," I said, "but things like that happen all the time."

"Well, I suppose some things happen you can't explain," said Mandy. "I don't know how many times I've looked at the clock and the time will be exactly 11:11 or 1:11. It's happened too many times to be just a random coincidence. I read about it in a book once. It said that when you see 11:11, it means that angels are nearby, and that Jesus and the other ascended masters are sending you a message that you're really a divine aspect of the Creator."

"I prefer the practical science of Zen," I said. "11:11 means nothing, not that it isn't important."

We both fell silent and looked at the cloud. It had kind of flattened out and seemed to be moving in a slow circle above us.

"I don't like the looks of that thing. It looks ominous."

"Spooky," said Mandy. "Do you think it's the start of a tornado?"

"I don't know," I said. "I've never seen one."

"Really, really spooky," said Mandy.

"What do the ascended masters have to say about that cloud?" I asked.

"Ha, ha! Very funny! I bet you didn't know that Buddha was an ascended master, too."

"Sure, I did! Buda and Jesús De Jesús ascend onto the bench between the small tanks every night."

"What do you mean?"

I had to spend the next ten minutes telling Mandy about the chemical operators and the bench and how I liked Buda from the start, but had only recently begun liking Jesús because he'd been a prick when I first met him. When I was done, I looked back at the sky. The cloud seemed to be spinning faster, and it was starting to get windy. A few drops of rain fell and hit me in the face. A drop hit Terra in the eye, and she blinked and sat up on the blanket.

"Let's get out of here," I said.

By the time we got to the car, it was starting to rain in earnest. Mandy and I sat in the front seat of the Bel Air and made out in the parking lot while the rain started coming down in buckets and the branches of the trees around the lot whipped back and forth. I put my hand under Mandy's blouse and felt her breasts while lightning zigzagged across the sky. I could even feel the silver cross that she wore around her neck dangling down around her bra. Then I reached under Mandy's skirt and fondled her for a couple of minutes before pulling down her underpants. Mandy fumbled with my belt buckle. We had sex while the rain came down like crazy, the wind tore branches of the trees, lightning flashed, and thunder boomed close by. It was like something you'd read in a book. Then it was over as soon as it started. The rain let up, and the wind died down. The lightning had moved on, and the flashes were farther to the west, over Bound Brook. Mandy sat up and put her underpants back on. I pulled up my pants and buckled my belt. We looked at each other and burst out laughing.

"That was crazy," I said.

"Crazy," said Mandy. "Wow!"

I looked in the backseat. Terra was sleeping. Men and women toil, but the world is unconcerned.

After I dropped Mandy off at her house, I stopped at a jeweler's in Middlesex and looked at rings. The man behind the jewelry counter had a moustache. He'd been looking at loose diamonds through a jeweler's loupe, and when he had the loupe to his eye, he looked like Mr Peanut. Most of the nice-looking rings were too expensive for my blood, some of them as much as six or seven hundred dollars. The cheaper ones just looked cheap. You could barely see the diamond. I wouldn't want my wife wearing one of the cheap ones, so everyone knew what a cheap bastard her husband was. I found a good-looking ring that was under one hundred dollars.

"Why's this one so cheap?" I asked.

Mr Peanut put down his loupe and came over to the counter. He looked at the ring I had pointed out.

"It's so reasonably priced because the stone isn't diamond. It's cubic zirconia."

Mr Peanut had an English accent that sounded fake. I hadn't met many Englishmen in New Jersey, so I was naturally sceptical.

"I like how it sparkles," I said.

"Indeed," said Mr Peanut. "It's a cubic zirconia. It's what they do."

I gave the man a check for $93.50, and he put it in a little velvet box for me. He wanted to charge me $.75 for the box, but I made up a story that my bride-to-be was sick with cancer and wanted more than anything to be married before she died. I was always pretty good at thinking on my feet. Mr Peanut handed me the box with the ring, and I put it in my pocket. When I got back to my car, there was a lady standing outside it looking at Terra through the window. For a second, I thought she was going to start sniffing about how I'd left my dog in the car. It wasn't even hot. The rain had cooled everything off, but she just wanted to tell me how cute she was.

"She's adorable, young man! What kind of breed is she?"

"I'm not certain. She's kind of a Heinz 57. Little of this and a little of that, I suppose."

"Well, whatever she is, she is certainly adorable!"

The lady walked off. Young or old, if you want to attract a woman, then having a dog is practically a necessity.

I went home and spent a couple of hours watching TV. The tornado was all over the news, and just not on the local cable news either. It even made the broadcast out of New York with pictures of it and everything. They even interviewed a man whose cat had gotten sucked away by the tornado and was found shivering in a tree about a quarter mile down the road about an hour later. The cat was expected to make a full recovery. Then they showed pictures of houses and cars that had been damaged when tree branches had fallen on them. It almost made me sad that the tornado hadn't happened over by the glue factory during one of our breaks. We would've talked about it for the next couple of days, the way we did when the big rig and the police cars had gone screaming by. The story was that the truck had run all the way to Westfield, but failed to make a curve and crashed all the way through a jewelry store and out the other side. It was too bad I hadn't been there. I might have been able to pick up a diamond ring for free. But there wasn't any use crying over spilled milk or glue or diamonds, that's for sure. What was done was done. I pulled the box out of my pocket and looked at the ring. It was certainly a sparkler. Someone doesn't give you a ring like that every day. I put the ring back in the box, then went downstairs with it. I opened one of my drawers and put it in there along with my stash of Playboy magazines. Then I went upstairs and worked on *The Book of Stone* until it was time to go to work. It might not have been a potboiler, but it was certainly interesting, to me anyway. A book like this could make me famous, I told myself. Maybe they'd make a movie out of it. Maybe they could get Jack Nicholson to play the writer. I'd seen him in "Five Easy Pieces" and "One Flew Over the Cuckoo's Nest." I liked the parts he'd played. If they got him to play the writer in *The Book of Stone,* he might really become famous. I went to the dryer and pulled out my glue pants. The legs were stuck to themselves because of all the glue on them. It was a hazard of the trade. I put them in a gym bag along with my glue

T-shirt and my steel-toed work boots. I even remembered to bring my hard hat, which we were all required to wear, but hardly anyone did. I didn't want anything to fall on my head and leave Mandy pre-widowed. On the drive over to the factory, the streets were full of downed branches and scattered debris. Things might fall apart around me, but everything in my life was holding together just fine.

# Chapter 20 Promotions

I proposed to Mandy in October. We'd been dating since June. I took her for dinner at HoJo's and popped the question while she was soaking a tea bag from her pocketbook in hot water. I'd given the waiter two bucks and asked him to bring the ring while he brought out dessert.

"Put it in the chocolate pudding," I said. "She won't eat it, but I will. I'll just kind of fish around in the pudding until I find the ring. Then I'll suck the ring clean and hand it to her."

"Romantic," the waiter said.

He rolled his eyes, and I stared at him.

"Maybe I should just take my two dollars back," I said.

"I've got something stuck under my contact lens," he said. So, I didn't have to take back my money.

The waiter brought the pudding in an ice cream sundae dish and set it down in front of me with a wink and a little flourish to let me know the ring was hidden in it. I poked around in it for a while but couldn't find it.

"Why are you poking at your pudding, Strafe?" Mandy said. "Is there something wrong with it?"

"I thought I saw a lump or two in it," I said.

I had to start eating the pudding, but I didn't come across the ring until I was two-thirds done. Then I put another spoonful of pudding in my mouth and felt it on my tongue. I nearly inhaled it by accident. It went all the way to the back of my throat and lodged there until I coughed a few times and got pudding all over the place, but the ring came out and bounced on the table in front of Mandy. She looked shocked.

"That's terrible," she said. "You should sue them for something like this. You could have choked to death on this thing."

I reached across the table and grabbed the ring, then I put it back in my mouth and sucked all the pudding off of it.

136

"Are you crazy? What are you doing?" said Mandy.

I spit the ring into my hand and held it up so Mandy could see the stone sparkle. Then I extended the ring across the table to her.

"I'm crazy," I said. "I'm crazy for you! Will you marry me?"

Mandy had gone all wide eyed when I began sucking the ring. Her expression hadn't changed even when I shoved the ring at her.

"Marry you?" she said. "But we've only been seeing each other since June!"

"That's over four months," I said. "That's plenty long."

"I don't know what to say or think," she said. "You make me laugh, sometimes not at what you say but how you are in the world. I've never met anyone even remotely like you. But marriage? Really?"

"Really," I said. "Just say 'yes' and make yourself the happiest woman in the world."

Mandy blinked a couple of times and shook her head, but then she extended her left hand to me.

"Yes," she said. "I'll marry you, my crazy poet. Yes!"

I put the ring on Mandy's finger.

"I can't believe I'm engaged!" she said. "We'll have a June wedding."

"June?" I said. "Why don't we get married this weekend. You can move out of your parents' house and move down into the basement with me."

"We'll need our own place," she said. "With a yard and a fence and a room for my spinning wheel and art supplies."

"Spinning wheel? You've got a spinning wheel?"

"Yes," she said. "I'm making everyone alpaca caps this year. I'm even spinning the wool. You can't spin it without a wheel."

Mandy got up to use the payphone at the back of the restaurant outside the restrooms to call her mom and tell her the good news. I followed her back and listened to her conversation with her mom. While they spoke, someone was groaning in the men's room. You could hear him farting and everything. It was really awful.

"Yes, mother, I thought it was a little premature, too. But we do love each other."

The man in the restroom farted a couple more times. Then you could hear the sound of him noisily emptying his bowels into the toilet.

"Jesus, that's fucking horrible," I said.

"No, mother. No…, no…, I am being serious."

The man in the restroom let rip with another salvo. Must be food poisoning, I thought.

"Okay, mother. Okay…, okay…, OKAY! I love you, too. Bye."

The toilet flushed in the restroom. His monologue had ended, too.

Mandy hung up the phone.

"What did she say?"

"She's thrilled," Mandy said. "We're going to start making the wedding arrangements right away. June will be here before you know it. Married!"

The restroom door opened, and a little skinny guy came sauntering out.

"You don't look like you sound," I said.

"What?"

"I didn't hear the sink running, pal. I hope you washed them hands of yours."

The skinny guy gave me a dirty look and walked away.

"What was that about?" asked Mandy.

"You don't want to know," I said. "Trust me."

I dropped Mandy off at her house and lit a cigarette after she got out of the car. I generally didn't smoke around her since she was probably the healthiest person I knew. She hardly ever drank and never smoked pot. I took a puff of the cigarette and was about to pull away from the curb, but I happened to glance at Mandy's house. You could see Mandy and her mom through the big picture window. Irene was shaking her finger at Mandy and talking a mile a minute. It was obvious they were talking about the wedding, and that made me happy.

When I got home, I called up my dad.

"I popped the question to Mandy," I said. "We're getting married in June. I'm pretty sure you'll be invited."

"Married? Seriously? Married? You've only known her for a few months. Are you sure this is a good idea?"

"We're in love," I said. "We're gonna get our own place with a yard, and a fence, and a spinning wheel."

"Well, okay," my dad said. "When do I get to meet your future bride?"

"Maybe we can go to HoJo's next week. Just don't use the restroom if you can help it."

"Married? Jesus! Sometimes I don't know what to make of you, but I guess congratulations are in order. Jesus! Well, congratulations! Have you told your mother yet?"

"I'll tell her when I get off work tomorrow," I said. "She likes Mandy."

"Well, thanks for giving me a call and telling me. Jesus Christ! Married!"

I said goodbye and hung up the phone. I called my brother.

"Hello," he said. "This is Derrick."

"It's me," I said. "Your brother."

"Hey, Pete, how ya doin'?"

"I hate that name!" I said.

"Yah, yah, I know, but I'm not calling yas by our last name."

"Let's not talk about my name," I said. "I'm trying to rise above it."

"Good luck, pahtnah," Derrick said. "You can nevah rise highah than all the bullshit that life will throw ya. The best thing to do is get wadahs. So, anyways, how ya doin'?"

"Glorious," I said. "I just wanted to let you know I'm getting married."

139

"Married? Jesus! Not that girl who wanted you to get a colonic, is it?"

"The very same," I said. "Her name is Mandy. We're getting hitched in June."

"Well, I got married right aftah law school, so who'm I to say anything except congrats, kid! Just make sure I'm in the wedding. I don't need to be best man or anything, but I'll be disappointed if I'm not a groomsman."

After I hung up the phone with my brother, I wrote five or six pages of *The Book of Stone*. It was pretty spectacular. I couldn't wait to read to Mandy what I'd written. The writer, descended from the Stones, and the sculptor, descended from the Rivers, had just gotten married and were going to honeymoon in the lighthouse overlooking the Grand Canyon. Someone had recently purchased it and turned it into a Bed & Breakfast. I was starting to pull out all the stops with my writing, now, dialogue, plot, character development, and use of symbols and imagery. I had gotten a book on writing out of the Majestic Public Library and was practicing the stuff in it the way I'd been practicing Zen. The results had been pretty impressive. I began putting hidden messages in books, too. Sometimes, if you read the first letter of every word in a paragraph, you'd find it spelled out some Zen message that was somewhat enigmatic. I put the handwritten pages in a big brown accordion file with an elastic band around it to keep it closed. Then I went to work.

The locker room was empty when I got there. The Locker Room Chief had put up a couple new signs in the shithouse. After I'd found Tuttle unconscious in the bathroom, a new sign had gotten stenciled on the wall:

## DO NOT OVERDOSE IN THE BATHROOM STALLS

I went up the ramp and punched in. Then I hung around the weigh scale until my shift began. It was a cool October evening, and I might even have to put on a sweatshirt later. I named the various circles of glue hell to myself: Cutter, refill, hot melt, crusher, latex, weigh scale, tank truck. Virgil came out of his office and walked over to me. He was in bad need of an alignment.

"Hey, Pete, good to see you."

"Same here, Captain. What's new?"

"I got a new hearing aid. Still working out the bugs. Picks up the intercom system out of the front office, and I hate the music they play up there. Classic rock. I'm country all the way. Wife died, too."

"Your wife died? Jesus, Virgil! What are you doing here?"

"Oh, we hadn't really spoken to each other in ten to twelve years. She did her thing. I did mine. She'd want me to keep working, though, you know. Keeping her memory alive."

"Anyway, Pete, what's new with you?"

"I popped the question to my girl," I said. "She said, 'Yes.' We're getting hitched in June."

"June, huh? Good on you! I hope your marriage is every bit as happy as mine!"

"Thanks, Virgil."

"By the way, management's made its decision. It's you by a landslide. You'll be the new midnight supervisor starting next week. There'll be a few days of training, then you're the boss! Exciting, huh?"

"Sure," I said. "I'm ecstatic."

"Ecstatic, huh? Well, notify your face."

Virgil walked off. I'd have a new circle of glue hell to conquer.

Graupner and Wiggins punched in and came over to the scale.

"There's the rat," said Graupner. "That's why they're making him the boss and giving him a bigger slice of cheese."

"Word's out," Wiggins said. "They makin' you the man! Gonna give yo' ass a clipboard an' keys to the office, keys to the supply room, an' keys to the suga' shack. Damn! They gimme all them keys I be unlockin' ever'thing, telling ever'body to take whatever they wanted! Damn!"

Willie staggered up to the scale. His eyes were bloodshot, and his face looked bloated. The skin grafts on his face and arms looked jaundiced.

141

"Goddamn! I'm tired…," Willie said. "Jesus Christ! Goddamn!"

Larry Edgerton stumbled down the stairs from the second floor. He didn't look as bad as Willie, but almost. Gresham walked up to the scale. For the past dozen years, fully one-third of his waking life had been devoted to walking around in a circle, pushing around heavy objects. Lenny came down from the bench and handed out the blue draw sheets. When he gave me my sheet, he looked me up and down with one eye while the other studied the clock on the wall above the scale.

"Congratulations, kid. I heard about your promotion. Gotta tank truck coming in. Go set up Tank 41."

I was the future o' glue.

Chapter 20 Klondike

My mom was awake when I got home the next morning. She was sitting at the dining room table, eating cold leftover rice like some peasant farmer in a Kurosawa movie. When I opened the door, she put down her bowl of rice and stood up. Then she bowed stiffly in my direction.

"Ah, Peter-san! Ilene call! Said you and Mandy get married!"

"Yeah, we are. What are you doing?"

"Paying my respect, Peter-san! You longer child!"

"Jesus, ma, cut it out. All this Japanese stuff is starting to creep me out!"

My mother sat back down at the table.

"Also, a friend called yesterday afternoon before I went to work."

"What friend?"

"From college, you know, funny one."

"What funny one?"

She tapped the side of her head twice with an index finger.

"Funny up here," she said. "Tetched!"

"All my friends from college were tetched, ma."

"Great big guy. Very tall."

"Klondike?" I said.

"Yes, that guy. He's a tetch!"

Klondike was the tallest guy I knew. He was six feet eight, and everyone at UConn thought he was a basketball player. The truth was, Klondike was pretty much terrible at anything involving physical exertion. He was studying math in its purity, free of any practical applications. When he spoke, it was always to say something entirely scathing and dismissive, like he was a division sign or a radical symbol whose job was to describe you in the least possible terms. I liked him. We had gotten in a fistfight down in the basement of the dorm during one of the bare-knuckle fights that someone in the dorm had organized my sophomore year as a break from studying for finals. He was from the fourth floor, so I didn't know him well. No one wanted to fight him because he was so big, but I volunteered. I was a lot quicker, and I'm super athletic, so I maneuvered him over to some pipes running across the basement wall where I pummeled him when he bent down to avoid the pipes. He pushed me away, then got out from under the pipes and hit me in the forehead with one massive fist. I saw cartoon stars and planets, then lay down and went to sleep. Later, when I woke up, we became friends. Well, maybe not exactly friends: Klondike didn't have any real friends. He just tolerated me more than others, probably because he'd knocked me unconscious, and he knew he could beat me physically as well as mentally if he had to.

He was a really great chess player. We mostly played chess together. He was really good. I could only beat him like one in every four or five games. When I did manage to win, he'd start hollering and swearing at me.

"How the hell does a moron like you even come close to beating me?" he'd shout. "You've no idea what you're doing! You pull moves out of your ass."

It was true. I pretty much didn't know what I was doing in chess. Sometimes he'd beat me in three or four moves, but if I could get through the first moves, I could start seeing the board clearly and begin pinning down his pieces with my bishop, rook, and pawns and start ripping through his ranks with my knight. Next thing you knew, I had his queen and a rook and would be chasing his king around the board. He just hated that. He'd resign by throwing the king at me. I thought it was hilarious. He'd also been the first person I knew who was a writer of sorts. He'd actually gotten me interested in reading enough to become an English major. He read a bunch of writers who incorporated math into fiction. I didn't understand any of it.

He wrote a story that takes place before the Big Bang. The universe is nothing but a tight stew-like soup of numbers and equations compacted into a size no larger than the head of a pin. Holding all of this together is something that may or may not be gravity, he doesn't say, but it's all held together somehow. Inside this pinprick, it is incredibly hot. A god lives inside this pinprick, too. He controls gravity or magnetism, or whatever force is holding the universe together. He's been making plans to expand the universe infinitely in all directions. Opposed to him is a group of radical gods who are looking to seize control of gravity or whatever it is and extend their influence throughout whatever happens the moment the first god says the word. Some other stuff happens that is unintelligible. Then the god that lives inside the pinprick shouts out the word, and all hell breaks loose. The story ends on a planet where a bunch of numbers crawl out of the sea and become birds and fish. Some prime numbers have become a man and a woman. They wake up in a garden where the number zero has become a tree bearing fruit. Inside the fruit are all the same numbers and equations contained in the universe before the Big Bang. The story ends when the man and woman eat the fruit of the zero tree, and the universe suddenly explodes in their heads. There isn't much dialogue except very stiff formulaic conversation between the prime god and some of the radicals. I really liked it, but didn't understand too much of it.

I called Klondike while drinking my normal morning sweet coffee. Klondike's mother answered the phone.

"Is Klondike there?" I asked.

"Jonah? Let me see if he's awake."

144

Jonah's mother dropped the phone on a table or something. Then there was silence for a couple of minutes. Finally, Klondike picked up the phone.

"Hello," he said. "This is Jonah."

"Klondike! This is Strafe," I said. "Just returning your call."

"Hey," he said. "I'm leaving for California and thought I'd stop by on my way. You're not that far off Interstate 80, are you?"

"Not too far. Just make sure you come around three or four. I'm working the midnight shift and don't get up until around then. When you coming?"

"Today, I've got a job in LA."

"Math?" I asked.

"No," he said. "Security for a grocery chain."

"How's the pay?"

"Terrible!" he said. "I only took the job to get away from my mother as far as possible."

"Mine annoys the hell out of me, too, but I'm moving out soon. I'm getting married to a girl who went to Amherst. She's a sculptor. Got a dog, too."

"That's great! A dog! I'm going to get a dog as soon as I get to California."

"OK, I'll see you at three," I said. "Swing by the house."

'Alright, see you this afternoon."

I hung around and watched the end of a movie on HBO with my mom. She sat on the sofa with my dog in her lap.

'You know that's my dog," I said. "Derrick told me you told him you have a new dog."

'This is so terrible dog," my mother said. "No one want such dog. Peter."

'Well, I do," I said.

"She'sa okay," my mother said. "Not so bad for terrible dog."

"Klondike's coming this afternoon," I said.

"I think he little bit tetched," my mother said.

"So, you said," I said. "He's got issues."

"Good thing I'm going work," she said. "Don't let him touch single knife."

"He's not THAT crazy," I said. "I'm going to bed, ma. See you tomorrow."

I went down to the basement, and Terra followed me. She hopped on my bed and stared at me as I climbed in under the covers. I was pretty tired. I didn't even put on a record. I fell asleep while a universe of words and letters sloshed back and forth in my head.

It was after four in the afternoon when I woke up. I sat up in bed, but was shocked to see an enormous figure sitting in a chair beside the bed. He had pushed the chair into a little square of sunlight filtering down through the only window in the basement room. The square of sunlight fell on half of his face. The rest of it was in the shadows. He looked pretty creepy, to be honest.

"Jesus, Klondike, you scared the hell out of me! How long were you watching me sleep?"

"Not long. An hour or two. I could've murdered you twenty or thirty times, dismembered you, and fed you to the dog. Then I would've driven to California and nobody would've known."

"I told my mom you were coming today. She would've known."

"I would've murdered her, too, then taken the dog. Get dressed," he said. "Let's play chess."

I didn't have a chess set, but we used a board from a game of checkers and fashioned pieces out of objects found in the kitchen utility drawer and on the shelves in the cabinets. He destroyed me in the first few games. In the fourth game, I managed to escape being checkmated in four moves and was able to take a bishop, then pin down his queen, king, and a rook simultaneously with my knight. He had to move the king. I captured the queen, and the rest of the game was pretty much me just trading pieces until there was nothing left but his king, my king, my queen, and a rook, chasing him around the board. I didn't know what I was doing, but still managed to checkmate him. He threw the pepper shaker at me. We'd been using that as his king. It hit me in the chest, and I laughed.

"Jesus, Klondike! You don't see me behaving like that when you beat me!"

"That's because you know you're inferior! You know it's how the games are supposed to go!"

"Hey, I've been writing stories," I said. "Want to read some?"

"Not really," he said. "But I will."

I went downstairs and got my accordion file and pulled out some of the stories. I watched him while he read. He had his finger up against the side of his temple and made chewing motions with his jaw, even though there wasn't anything in his mouth. He read the story about the conjoined twins and the one about Stella and scowled. When he finished, he threw the sheets onto the table.

"It's mostly crap," he said, "except the stuff you stole from me."

"What did I steal from you?" I asked. "You write stuff about math."

"C'mon, Strafe. "The Stars"? You know that you got that idea from the story I wrote about the galaxy where all the stars take human form."

"Stella's real," I said. "We had sex and everything."

"Uh-huh," Klondike said. "The stars in my story have sex, too. You don't remember that? Of course you do. I expected more from you, Strafe. Maybe I should've killed you in your sleep."

"I'm glad you didn't," I said glumly. I hadn't expected to be accused of thievery.

"Well, I've gotta go," Klondike said. "I'll send you some real stories as soon as I get situated in LA and have time to do some writing."

"Good luck!" I said. "Maybe I'll come visit sometime with Mandy."

147

"Sure," he said. "I didn't do much dating when I lived at my mom's. She kind of cramped my style. I'll probably have a girlfriend right away after I get there. There's millions of single girls in LA."

Klondike stood up. He had to duck to keep from getting hit in the head by the blades of the ceiling fan.

"Drive safe," I said.

He left without saying goodbye. I went out on the porch and watched him climb through the window of his VW Bug. He had a mattress tied to the top of the car with rope and bungee cords that he'd run through his windows so the doors wouldn't open. He settled into the driver's seat, and his knees came up nearly to his chest. I was sorry to see him go. He'd been one of my only friends in college.

# Chapter 21 Ship of Fools

I sat at my kitchen table and wrote for an hour or two, but it was slow going. I'd bought a typewriter at a secondhand store for a couple of bucks, and my hunt-and-peck method of typing was only good for ten words per minute maximum. I was way faster writing on lined paper with a pen or pencil. Plus, some of the characters didn't work. I had to type zero whenever I needed to type an O and 5 for the letter S. Mandy called while I was working on *The Book of Stone*. I had only managed to type out a page and a half in a couple of hours, and I needed a break.

"My parents went out for dinner and a movie," she said. "Maybe you can come over and we can talk, or we can…, you know."

"Sure," I said. "I can read you some of my book," I said.

"I was thinking of something else," Mandy said.

"Whatever," I said. "I'll see you in a little bit."

Mandy didn't like coming over to my house. It made her itchy just being there. There was dog hair everywhere, and my room wasn't the greatest place in the world. I had papers scattered all over and a ton of dirty dishes and empty pizza boxes. Not that I couldn't clean up after myself, but it wasn't the easiest thing to do when I was writing like crazy. As for me, I liked being at my place better than being at Mandy's. Her mom collected these expensive ceramic figures from Spain. They were all over the place. I was always afraid I'd knock one over and break it, or spill something on the carpet, or leave a watermark on the piano if I set my beer down on it. I didn't care that much if people accidentally broke my stuff or spilled something on it, but I'd learned that most people weren't as easygoing as me. People generally would get upset if you broke their stuff, accident or not, especially if it was expensive.

Mandy met me at the door when I got to her house and brought me right back to her bedroom. Fortunately, there wasn't a lot of breakable stuff in there. She lived pretty simply, which was one of the reasons I liked her so much. There was almost nothing in her room but a bed, her spinning wheel, a cross made of yellowed palm leaves on the wall, and a couple of sculptures she'd created in college. A family friend had a foundry in Weehawken, and he'd let her cast her iron and bronze pieces there for free just so long as she paid for the materials. Her closet was full of expensive clothes, mostly paid for by her parents, but I didn't hold that against her. I liked it that she dressed almost as nice as I did. Most of my clothes came from very upscale secondhand stores, and I never bought anything that had too many stains or scuffs on it. I was very particular about that. I didn't mind that much if my pants were too short or my jacket was too big, but just so long as the sweat stain under the armpits wasn't too noticeable, I was good to go.

She liked kissing more than I did. Mostly, I just liked getting right down to business, but she wanted to take her time. Normally, that wouldn't have been a problem, but it was already after ten pm, and I had to be at work in forty minutes in order to get dressed and punch in by eleven. I tapped on my watch to give Mandy the hint. We hurried up then and did the deed. I was very good in bed and able to last more than ten whole minutes. When I had finished, I rolled over.

"Are you okay?" Mandy asked. "The way you groaned and shivered at the end, I thought you were having a seizure."

"I'm fine," I said. "I didn't bite my tongue like last time."

I lay there with my hands behind my head. The room was dark. Mandy got out of bed to go to the bathroom and clean up, but tripped over the spinning wheel.

"Ow," she said.

"How can you trip over that?" I asked. "Your room is nearly empty."

Mandy turned on the light. She'd grabbed hold of the spindle when she tripped over the spinning wheel. Blood was running down her fingers and dripping on the floor. She was holding the spindle in her injured hand, and blood had stained some of the wool on it.

"It's too bad the yarn is ruined," I said. "You'll have to throw it away."

"No," she said. "I'll use it for your cap. It'll be stained with my blood. Isn't that romantic?"

"If you say so," I said, but I wasn't thrilled with the idea. Like I said before, I didn't like wearing anything that had stains on it unless I was wearing it to put glue in a barrel, and wearing a wool hat at work didn't appeal to me very much.

Mandy went into the bathroom to bandage her finger, and I got dressed. It was time for me to head to the factory. Mandy came back from the bathroom and put on a bathrobe. Then she kissed me goodbye.

"I'm crazy about you," she said. "I don't know why, but I'm madly in love with you."

"I know," I said. She'd never find anyone else like me, ever, and that made me happy.

I drove over to American Starch and got dressed. It was Friday, my last night on the floor as a process helper in Glue. Beginning Monday, I'd have a few days of supervisor training. Then I'd be given a clipboard and spend my nights preventing malingering and malfeasance while ensuring maximal effort. I wouldn't be able to meditate as much since I wouldn't be filling tank trucks anymore, but I would be making over twice what I was currently making, including overtime.

I walked up to the weigh scale alone. I was one of the last of the crew to arrive. We were shorthanded. Willie's drinking had progressed to the point that he was throwing up blood. The doctors had told him that if he didn't stop drinking, he would die. He'd sober up for a couple of days, then he'd start drinking again and wind up back in the hospital. That was where he currently was. Tuttle had gone to rehab but had relapsed shortly after he'd returned to work. The company had finally had enough and fired him. His replacement, as well as my replacement, will start on Monday.

I spent the entire evening loading tank trucks. All of them were fairly small jobs, although the filtration setups were different for each truck. I had to use micron filters inside a filter pump for the first truck. The batch was clean, and I only had to pump nine hundred gallons into the truck. I was done by midnight and spent the next half an hour setting up a filter press with organdy for that job. By the time the one o'clock break rolled around, I was about one-third done with the second truck. I went outside for a break. Grover Cleveland Winkler had stayed over from the second shift and was sitting on the bench. I sat down next to him.

"I heard this is your last night as a process helper," Winkler said. "I heard you're going to supervisor training next week."

"You heard correctly," I said.

"Word is that one of the people they hired to replace you, and Tuttle, is of the female persuasion."

"I don't know," I said. "They didn't tell me."

"I don't like it," said Winkler. "If God wanted women working, Glue it would be in the Bible," he said.

"I don't think the Bible says anything about anyone putting glue in barrels," I said. "I doubt that he cares."

"This job is trouble," said Winkler. "It says in Job that 'man is born to trouble as the sparks fly upward.' It doesn't say anything about women, i.e., a woman's place shouldn't be working hot melt. You want your mother working hot melt?"

"I don't think she wants to work hot melt," I said.

"Exactly," said Winkler.

"No one wants to work hot melt," I said.

"But we do it," said Winkler. "We're born to trouble as the sparks fly upward, i.e., hot melt is no place for women or children."

"As long as they get the job done, why do you care?"

"Seeing is believing," Winkler said. "I'll see it when I believe it."

The break ended, and I went back to filling my truck. I was done about two thirty, then I set up for the third truck. Of the three jobs, it was the simplest. I just ran a hose from the pump into the open lid at the top of the truck and tied the hose down with twine. I tied a cheesecloth bag on the end of the hose, turned on the pump, and let the glue fly. The tank truck was halfway filled by 3 a.m. I turned off the pump and went on break.

It was a chilly morning in late October, but with the exception of Jerry and Winkler, everyone shuffled outside and smoked cigarettes. Jerry was in the breakroom with his Bible, but Winkler's overtime shift was over, and he'd clocked out. We watched him walk across the street to the parking lot. He got in his car and drove off without turning on his headlights.

"That brother'll get pulled over by the police without no headlights on," said Wiggins. "You don't wanna be no black man gettin' pulled over by the police at three in the mornin'. Ain't that right?"

"Black?" said Graupner. "Winkler is white as me."

"Winkler? Are you guys blind?" said Larry Edgerton. "He's half Chinese like Strafe."

"Half Japanese," I said. "I'm half Japanese. Not Chinese."

"Winkler? Chinese?" said Wiggins. "Looky here, that brother might be high yella, but Chinaman? Chinaman my ass! That muthafucker be 100% brother or my name ain't Edward Percevius Wiggins!"

"Hey, Smoky," said Graupner. "Do you think Grover Cleveland Winkler is black, white, or Chinese?"

"Who?" said Smoky.

"Grover Cleveland," said Graupner. "You know, that second shift guy is working OT tonight. Sat out here on the one o'clock break. Just drove off a few minutes ago."

"I didn't see nobody," said Smoky.

"Me neither," said Gresham.

I stood up and went inside. Jerry was sitting at his usual table in the lunchroom. He was making notes in the margins of his Bible with a pen.

"What are you reading tonight?" I asked.

"Proverbs 13:20," Jerry said. "Whoever walks with the wise becomes wise, but the companion of fools will suffer harm."

The bell sounded to end the break, and I left the break room. I went into the restroom and washed the cigarette smoke from my face and hands. The Locker Room Chief had posted a new sign above the door:

## THIS IS YOUR FINAL WARNING

I went up to the tank pad and turned the pump back on. I finished loading the truck and cleaned up quickly, then I went up on the roof and climbed to the deck of the water tower. The stars were out. I recognized some of the constellations that Stella had taught me. Was there a constellation called Ship of Fools? I sat and focused on my breathing. While I was counting my breaths, Graupner climbed up the ladder.

"What are you doing up here, man?" Graupner asked.

"Becoming one," I said.

"Me, too, " Graupner said. He pulled a joint out of his pocket and lit it. "I won't be able to do this around you next week."

"Why?"

"The company will be paying you to make sure I'm not up here getting high. I'll have to find a new spot. You have to be a rat. It's in the job description. Just don't be a dick, too."

"I don't like rats," I said. "There's a really big one over by the tank pad. I've seen it a few times. I think it's got a nest over there."

"Yeah, that one's ginormous. There are some huge ones up in the warehouse. They feed on all the cornstarch and tapioca and get humongous. I don't like them either. I throw my hammer at them whenever I see them. Hopefully, I'll never hit one. Seeing a dead rat that's all bloody would be ten times worse than seeing a live one."

"Just don't throw your hammer at them."

"I try not to, but I can't help myself. It's a reflex. It's reflexive. I might as well tell myself not to breathe."

"Let me have a hit of that pot," I said. "My last night as a process helper."

Graupner handed me the joint. I took a couple of quick inhales and held the smoke in my lungs, then let it out slowly. I handed the joint back to Graupner. It was pretty potent. I started feeling high in just a few minutes.

"I'm getting married," I said. "June."

"Good for you, man. If I were getting married, I'd take a job as a rat, too. I believe in marriage. I got married right out of high school. We fought all the time. The best part was the divorce. She got everything I had, but I didn't care. I didn't have anything."

"No kids?"

"I don't think so. God, I'm high."

The bell sounded for break, and we climbed down the ladder. My legs felt rubbery and far away. We went up through the glue department and sat on the bench outside. Wiggins was standing on the sidewalk in front of the bench and held court.

"Five o'clock! It's all downhill, now! Innit? It done be your las' night as a donkey, Strafe! Nex' time we see yo' ass ain't nobody gon' be talkin' to you. Ain't that right? Ain't nobody don' talk to no boss! Never happen!"

"Nobody talks to rats," said Graupner. "Winkler said one of the new workers starting next week is a woman. Just so long as she's not my ex-wife, I'm okay with it."

"I heard 'bout that, too," said Wiggins. "Don' make no nevermind to me so long she good looking! Tired o' looking' at yo' ugly mugs ever' right! Like bein' back in prison. Innit? Damn!"

"I don't think most women could do this job as good as a man," said Larry. He'd been drinking and his words were slurred.

"Damn!" said Wiggins. "As slow as you work, a monkey could do this job better'n you."

When break ended, I went up on the bench. Buda was sitting on a step stool reading a newspaper written in Polish.

"*Siema*, Rocky, all done for the night?"

155

"Pretty much," I said. "Loaded three tank trucks tonight."

"Not too bad, heh? Your last night as a donkey, right?"

"Yeah," I said. "I'm getting married, too. In June."

"Congratulations!" Buda said. "Had many women but never married. Hope you have long marriage. Many children! That is my biggest regret as old bachelor. No kids."

"I heard a woman is replacing me in the department next week," I said. "What do you think about that?"

"Why not?" said Buda. "As many foolish women in the world as men. Why not a woman work here?"

I went down to the janitorial shed and got a broom and a dustpan. Then I wandered around the department pretending I was heading somewhere until my shift ended. My final warning had come and gone. I went down to the locker room and showered. Then I changed.

# Chapter 22 Terra

I drove to Sandy Hook with Mandy that weekend. I liked going there. The beach wasn't crowded, and there was always plenty of parking. There were trails leading down to the beach and the surrounding area. As we walked, I picked some sticky green cones from the cedar trees and some shriveled fruit from the beach plums and threw them at Mandy. She tried running away, but I caught her and pulled her down on the sand. We lay there for a bit, making out while Terra ran up and down the beach chasing other dogs, sniffing people's crotches as they were lying on their towels and blankets, and generally being a nuisance. It was a beautiful, clear day, warm for the end of October. I pointed out some osprey nests for Mandy, but they were all empty. The ospreys had all migrated south for the winter, as had the monarch butterflies. That was disappointing. Sometimes I'd been there and seen clouds of thousands of monarchs and watched the seahawks come and go from their nests carrying snakes, rodents, or ocean fish for their young.

I sat up and brushed the sand off me, and looked around. The sky was perfectly clear all the way to the horizon, the water sparkling blue and gray and green, the kind of day you wished every day would be, the perfect treasure at the end of a long drive, nirvana found at the end of the mind.

Mandy noticed me staring out into the distance and asked me what I was thinking.

"I'm not really thinking," I said. "I'm engaged in the process of being."

"That sounds deep," Mandy said. Her blue eyes sparkled with laughter.

"Absolutely!" I said. "I'm trying to see beyond the illusion of being and just be, if that makes any sense."

"Shut up and kiss me, you fool!"

I lay back down on the sand and kissed her on the mouth. She was a good kisser, not that I wasn't. I just didn't like using my mouth for anything other than talking or eating. I tried fondling her breast, but she kept pushing my hand away.

"Not on a public beach," she said.

"We had sex in a car during a tornado," I said.

"That was different! No one could see us!"

After a while, I gave up trying to grope Mandy. When she was all kissed out, we went for a walk down the beach. Terra chased after us. We walked for about a mile until we were at a section of beach that had hardly anyone on it. There were tide pools full of hermit crabs wearing periwinkle shells. I picked up a horseshoe crab nearly a foot across and chased Mandy with it, but she got away. We waded through the water picking up shells that we showed to each other before tossing them back into the water. Mandy splashed me with water from a tide pool, and I chased her across the beach and up a dune. When I caught up to her, I was too tired to knock her down, so I just sat down at her feet.

"You wore me out," I said.

"Serves you right!"

We sat on the dune and looked out over the water. Mandy was the one who noticed the people on the beach before I did.

"What are they doing?" she asked.

A couple of people were running back and forth at the water's edge. They were waving their arms frantically at something bobbing in the water. The current appeared to be pulling the object into deeper water. Mandy grabbed my arm.

"Strafe! I think that's a person in the water caught in the undertow!" she said.

I'm not sure why I did it, but I stripped off my shirt and pants and ran down to the water in my underpants. My parents had an above-ground pool when I was growing up, and I'd been a swimmer since I was three or four. I'd even been a Boy Scout for a while and gone to summer camp and everything. Before I got kicked out of the troop for lighting a scoutmaster's tent on fire because I was bored, I'd gotten merit badges for swimming and lifesaving as well as a special badge for swimming a whole mile. Anyway, I dove into the water, and when I reached the spot where the person should have been, there was no one there. I took a breath and dove a few times until I found the girl floating in the water. I brought her to the surface and started swimming to shore with her. The undercurrent was pretty strong, though, and after a minute, I hadn't made any real headway. For a second, I almost made a decision to let the girl go and swim back to the shore to save myself when I saw Terra's head bobbing in the water next to me. I grabbed her collar, and she began paddling back to the shore. In a couple of minutes, we were in shallow water, and I was able to stand up and carry the girl onto the beach. I gave the girl mouth-to-mouth resuscitation and probably broke some of her ribs giving her CPR, but after a little bit, she puked up seawater all over the place as well as half her lunch. I had puke all over me that Terra tried licking off, but I jumped in the water then and cleaned it all off.

The girl's parents couldn't thank me enough and tried hugging me while I was standing there in my tighty whities, but I put my pants on first and then let them shake my hand. I'm not really a hugging person unless we're having sex. Then you can touch me all you want. The girl was shivering and lying on the sand, wrapped in a blanket, moaning. She still had puke and snot all over her face that was beginning to dry. I really probably broke half her ribs. Terra went over to the girl and licked some of the puke off her, then came over to me and tried licking me, too.

"Cut it out, Terra!" I said.

The girl's parents spent a lot of time patting Terra and thanking her, too, which they should have. Without her, I would've dropped their kid back in the water and just swum back to shore. Then they thanked Mandy up and down for being the one who spotted their kid in the water.

Finally, I stopped all the slobbering "thank yous" and told them to take their kid to the nearest hospital to get her ribs checked. I had pushed her chest nearly out of her back, jump-starting her heart. Then the father carried his daughter up the beach to the parking lot while the mother walked beside them, blubbering tears. They had left all their possessions on the beach. Umbrella, beach chairs, a cooler full of sandwiches and beer, even a large portable radio with the football game on. The Giants were playing the Eagles. I wanted to sit down in one of the chairs, eat a sandwich, drink a beer, and listen to the rest of the game, but Mandy wouldn't let me.

"It's not right," she said.

"We just saved their kid's life. They won't care," I said.

"It's not right," said Mandy.

In the end, she let me listen to the game and sit in a chair under their umbrella, but she wouldn't let me raid their cooler.

The game ended. I wanted to leave, but Mandy wanted to stay.

"We need to wait here until they get back. We don't want anyone to steal their stuff."

"What kind of irresponsible people let their daughter drown, then just leave their stuff around?" I asked. "What do they expect?"

Finally, around 5 o'clock, the park closed, and a ranger drove up in a green Jeep and told us to leave. We told him what happened, and he agreed to take their stuff back to the Ranger Station. Then he gave me a ticket for having an unleashed dog on the beach.

"No good deed ever goes unpunished," I told the ranger. "My dog rescues a girl, and this is the thanks we get?"

The ranger handed me the citation and smiled.

"The State of New Jersey thanks all of you for your service above and beyond the call of duty."

On our way back to the car, I complained about the citation while Mandy laughed.

"I'm never saving anyone from drowning again," I said. "There's no percentage in it so far as I can tell."

"You just need to keep getting out of the way of yourself," Mandy said.

We reached the car. I opened it, and Terra jumped in the back and began licking herself.

"You should be more like your dog, Strafe. She's already forgotten everything that's happened today."

I looked at Terra.

"If I could lick my own balls, I'd do it," I said. "Then I wouldn't need a girlfriend, would I?"

"Ughhh," Mandy said. "That's gross!"

"You're a terrible dog, aren't you, Terra? That's what I like about you."

On the way back to Majestic, I pointed out the trees we passed as the sunlight was filtering down through their branches. The leaves had all changed color, and the light made the leaves glow as though from within. I knew the names of nearly all the trees. My time in the Boy Scouts had taught me all sorts of useful stuff.

"Elm, silver maple, black oak, sycamore, red oak, sugar maple, birch."

"I love this time of year," said Mandy.

"Poplar, pin oak, red maple, ironwood, ginkgo, tulip tree, beech."

"I'd like to make a few bronze sculptures of those little seed pods that twirl down off the maples," Mandy said.

"Pitch pine, dogwood, white oak, sassafras, silver bell, black spruce, ash."

"You know everything and nothing, don't you?" Mandy said.

She cuddled up next to me and felt my beard.

"Everything about you is a contradiction," she said.

"I've been eradicating the contradictions in my life," I said.

"Sure, you have," Mandy said. "There'd be nothing left."

It was nearly six when we got back to Majestic. It had been a good day in spite of the citation. I hoped the girl didn't have too many broken ribs, but the alternative was not very pleasant to contemplate. I would've kept mashing that girl's chest for the next twenty minutes. They would've had to drag me away from her. I dropped Mandy off at her house, and she kissed me, then hopped out of the car. Terra watched her go, then climbed into the front seat with me. She lay down and put her head in my lap.

"I got a ticket today on account of you," I said.

Terra yawned and settled into sleep. You can learn a lot about dogs if you watch them long enough. If you love them long enough, you'll learn a couple of things about yourself.

# Chapter 23 Training

I spent the next few days in a company-run training class called Supervisory Management. There were three of us in the class. One guy was going to be a supervisor in the Refinery Department. They processed and filtered raw starch milk down there in big vats. Then they cooked all the water off in a fairly complicated vacuum and cyclone drying process to keep the starch from gelatinizing until all that was left was a punch of white or yellow floury material that they bagged and sent up to Glue and Solvents to make adhesives. The new supervisor in the Refinery was older than me. His name was Bob Roberts. He was a former Marine who was a burly, no-nonsense type. He'd worked at American Starch for six or seven years and was the kind of guy who demanded respect. Unfortunately, he was nearly completely deaf. A mortar round had landed near him in Vietnam and blown out both his eardrums. He had hearing aids in both ears, but still couldn't hear. Every few minutes, he'd interrupt the training and demand the instructor repeat what he'd just said. It was annoying as hell, but I wasn't dumb enough to say anything to him. He looked like he could mash me as thoroughly as I'd mashed that girl giving her CPR.

The other guy was close to my age. He was going to be a supervisor in SAD, Solid Adhesives. His name was Prana Jyoshi. His family was from India. He wore khaki pants and a long-sleeved shirt that was buttoned all the way up to his neck. When I first walked into the room, he stood up and greeted me by extending both his hands to me with his palms together. He clasped my hands in his and held them for longer than was comfortable for me. Then he bowed slightly and let go of my hands. He had an English accent, too, and spoke in a thoughtful manner, like he was actually thinking about what he was saying. All in all, it was kind of weird, but not in a creepy way. He was polite and respectful, like he was not just representing himself but all Hindus everywhere.

The instructor was from Arkansas and spoke like he had a mouthful of shit coated marbles. His name was Ward Montgomery, and as much as I hated the name Peter, it would've been worse going through life being teased for being named after a mail order catalog  I couldn't understand

163

half of what he said, but I wasn't going to ask him to repeat himself. After five minutes, it was pretty apparent that the instructor knew nothing about being a supervisor. His job was to read us material from a book for three days and have us follow along in a workbook that had blank spaces for us to fill in. When we'd successfully filled in all the spaces and passed a quiz at the end of the three days, we were certified to supervise people in an environment of equipment and chemicals that could kill you dead or maim you in nothing flat.

Basically, the gist of the class was how to handle situations we were likely to encounter as supervisors. First, we learned to identify incidents involving malingering and malfeasance. We also learned to identify incidents of insubordination.

"Can anyone gimme a 'xample of insubord'nation," mumbled Mr Marble Mouth.

"That's easy," I said. "If you tell someone to do something and they say, 'Fuck you, I'm not doing it', that's insubordination."

Monty turned red.

"Well, I s'ppose," he mumbled, "but we try to adop' a less 'thoritative and p'sitional att'tude with 'mployees. We ask 'em or make r'quests of 'em. We try not to tell 'em what t'do."

We were not supposed to berate, fight, reprimand, or even discipline employees who were engaging in malfeasance, malingering, insubordination, or giving less than maximal effort. Our primary recourse was to request that the employee immediately cease their offending behavior. It was then the supervisor's responsibility to submit a report on each incident he'd witnessed. There were separate forms that needed to be filled out depending on whether the offending party had committed an act of malfeasance, malingering, insubordination, or failure to give maximal effort. Reports would then be submitted to our immediate supervisor, who would submit them to his immediate supervisor, who would relay the proper course of action back to our immediate supervisor after consulting with the management team behind closed doors. Our immediate supervisor would report the proper course of action back to us, and we would inform the offending party of this course of action for their

164

malfeasance, malingering, insubordination, or failure to give maximal effort. The clipboard was a necessary tool for the completion of these incident reports. Without our clipboards, we were defenseless in the halls of the enemy.

I was pretty well done with the training by the first break of the day. I went down to the management break room outside the refinery and sat down with Bob Roberts and Prana Jyoshi.

"Great training," said Roberts. "Don't you think?"

"They probably could've boiled this down to fifteen minutes and sent us back to our departments with our clipboards," I said.

"I didn't catch all of that," said Roberts. "You'll have to speak up."

"I said it's pretty worthless!" I shouted. "It pretty much sucks!"

"That's a pretty cavalier attitude," Roberts said.

"We fill out incident reports. Each form has the word 'Malfeasance' or 'Malingering' or 'Insubordination' or 'Failure to Give Maximal Effort' printed across the top of it. What else do we need to know?"

"Do you know the proper form to complete and submit for property damage, work injury, or sick time?"

"Yeah, only twenty-two hours left to find out which forms we need to fill out for those! Be still, my heart!"

"It is our destiny to remain dedicated and persevere in this as in all things," said Jyoshi. "It is our karma, otherwise we would not be here at this moment in space and time."

"Oh, for Chrissake," said Roberts.

"When we put flowers on the spinning wheel of karma, we get bouquets in our lives. When we put knives on the wheel, we get daggers to tear our flesh."

The break ended, and we went back to the training room. Monty had set up a TV monitor and VCR and showed us a half-hour video on how to recognize appropriate and inappropriate behavior in the workplace. We weren't allowed to solicit sexual favors from anyone in exchange for promises of promotions or preferential treatment. We weren't allowed to sexually harass others in the workplace, either physically or verbally, and we weren't allowed to physically or verbally intimidate others.

"This only applies to the workplace, right? I mean, we're free to do whatever we want when we're not here. Or am I reading this wrong?" I asked.

"Well, we 'spect all our 'mployees to abide by our rules o' conduct outside th' workplace, but fo' the purp'ses o' this d'scussion we'll confine the conv'sation to the workplace only."

The instructor then showed us the various forms that we needed to fill out and submit in the event we came across incidents of harassment and intimidation in all of their splendid physical and verbal manifestations.

The lunch break rolled around, and we were given an hour to do whatever we wanted. I drove down to a deli in Dunellen and ordered a capicola sandwich on a roll with oil and vinegar. While I waited, I sat down at a table and read the sports page. The Pistols had lost again. I put the paper down and looked up just as Sonia from the lab opened the deli door and walked inside. I hadn't seen or thought about her in months, but it was hard to ignore her when she was standing in front of me. She looked at me and smiled. I turned around to see if anyone was behind me.

"Hello," she said. "I've never seen you without your glue clothes. You're pretty cute."

"I got these pants at the Salvation Army Thrift Shop in Westfield. They have the best clothes. They're almost my exact size. I don't need a belt 'cause the waist is elastic."

"They look good on you," she said. "I heard you were in the new supervisor training. I bet it's a relief that you don't have to worry about blow jobs anymore."

"Well, I'm engaged," I said. "To someone else."

"Oh, who's the lucky girl?"

"She went to Amherst," I said. "She's a sculptor. She makes her own yogurt and spins wool. Her name's Mandy."

My sandwich arrived, and I picked it up at the counter and paid for it.

"See you around," I said.

"Yes," she said. "I'd like that.

I sat in my car and ate my sandwich. Maybe I'd let Sonia read some of my stories. There wouldn't be any harm in that. I'd told her I was engaged, and that was the end of it. But I couldn't blame her for flirting with me. I was quite a catch. Anyone would be lucky to have me, especially since I was undoubtedly the greatest unknown writer in America. Plus, I was now a supervisor making $25,000 per year at a Fortune 1000 Company. People like me didn't just grow on trees. No, sir, a person would have to stumble through a thousand cabbage patches before they'd trip over anything remotely like me.

After I finished my sandwich, I drove back to the factory and parked my car in the lot across the street. I didn't like parking on the street outside the refinery. If you left your car there too long, it would be covered with powdery starch. Once I'd made the mistake of parking there during one of my shifts. When I came out eight hours later, it looked like my car was blanketed by snow.

I walked into the training room about twenty minutes early and started writing the opening lines of a new book. I had finished writing *The Book of Stone* longhand and was planning to buy a new typewriter with my first supervisor's paycheck. Then I'd type out *The Book of Stone* and send it out to publishers looking for exciting new talent to fatten their bottom line with incredible guaranteed profits. I took the notepad that the instructor had given each of us and began writing the first sentence:

"Call me Strafe. My full name is Peter Caldwell Strafe."

The book was going to be the fascinating account of a young protagonist who happens to share my name. He gets a job in a glue factory and has a bunch of very interesting and entertaining experiences and adventures culminating in his meeting a girl named Mandy and getting married. It would be a potboiler. I managed to get a couple of pages written while waiting for the training class to restart. With any luck, I'd manage to finish it in a week or two.

Monty came in and sat on the desk while waiting for Roberts and Jyoshi to return from lunch. He tried starting a conversation with me, but I was too engrossed in what I was writing to pay him any attention. Unfortunately, just when I'd begun writing about Strafe's conversation with his father about stick-to-it-ness and gumption, Roberts and Jyoshi walked into the room together, and I had to stop writing.

Monty came over to my desk and tried looking at what I'd been writing, but I had the good sense to cover my papers with my arms so he couldn't really see it; although, he had his suspicions that what I'd been doing wasn't work-related.

"As supervis'ry personnel, y'all ah held to higher standards o' conduct. Y'all ah 'spected to be focused solely on comp'ny goals an' metrics," he said. Monty looked me right in the eyes. "Make sure that when y'all ah on comp'ny property, y'all ah only engagin' in comp'ny business."

Then, for the next two hours, I had to sit and listen to the instructor show us how to fill out a lost time accident form. The form had a picture of a man on it. Whenever someone was involved in any incident potentially resulting in time off from work we had to circle the area of the body on the picture of the man's body and fill out a detailed report that included the name of the injured party, the nature of the injury, the location in the factory that the injury occurred, the severity of the injury, etc. Mr Monty Marble Mouth's voice drifted to me from the edges of the room as he discussed the importance of filling out the form accurately. His voice seemed to be made of the same kind of white powdery flour that covered my car when I'd parked outside of the refinery. Fortunately, I woke up just in time for our afternoon break.

While Roberts called his wife during break, Jyoshi and I sat down in the refinery break room and got to know each other. His parents were from Punjab and had come to America in the 1960s. His father had been an engineer and had worked for NASA briefly on the moon mission. Jyoshi, however, had flunked all his math classes in high school. He just wasn't engineer material. Nor was he doctor or lawyer material. His parents had tried to set him up as the owner of a convenience store, but he'd failed at that, too.

' That was not actually my fault, Mr Strafe. Some thieves came to the store one evening while the store was closed. When we arrived in the morning, we discovered the store had been robbed. I tell you there was nothing left but a hole in the ground, Mr Strafe. Not even one single coffee cup, Mr Strafe. The next day, I tell you, I came to American Starch and applied for a job in Solid Adhesives. It is a terrible job, but that is how it is, Mr Strafe. I have a wife and child to support. We live with my parents, but I plan on using the pay increase to rent our own place in Majestic. Please come visit after we've moved into our new home."

Roberts came into the break room and sat down. He put his elbows on the table and put his hands to the side of his face.

"Is everything okay, Mr Roberts?" Jyoshi asked.

"It's my son," Roberts said. "He's thirteen. My wife took him to the doctor recently because he'd been having abdominal cramping."

"It's not serious, is it?"

"It's serious as hell," said Roberts. "The doctors did a bunch of tests and discovered that he's got…, he's got…."

"Well, what's he got?" I asked.

"He's got a uterus and ovaries inside him. I mean, how can this be? He's got a dick and balls, so he's a boy, but the doctor's say he's actually a girl. He's actually been ovulating every month for the past year."

"Wow!" I said.

"Yeah, wow!" said Roberts. "Doctors want to know if they should remove the uterus and ovaries or his penis and testicles."

"Why can't they leave everything the way it is?" I asked.

'They say it's not really an option," Roberts said.

'I'd get a second opinion before the doctors start whipping out their scalpels," I said.

169

"Yeah, second opinion. Right, right."

"This condition is very prevalent in India, Mr Roberts. These individuals are worshipped as Gods. I tell you, Mr Roberts, everything is for the best!"

The break ended, and we went back to our last supervisor training session of the day. Even though I wasn't particularly fond of Monty's comments about only working on company business while on company time, Bob's revelation about his son was making the training worthwhile after all.

# Chapter 24 Halloween

I went to dinner with my father that evening. I was in the mood for pizza, so we went to Dominico's, a little pizzeria down the street and around the corner from my house, next to the coffee shop and the dry cleaners, and the corner drugstore where I used to buy my dad cigarettes. He'd give me a note explaining that the Lucky Strikes were for him, and the guy behind the counter would take my thirty cents and hand me a pack. Then I'd run home and hand him the cigarettes. Sometimes he'd give me as much as a dime when I picked up his cigarettes or his dry cleaning.

I'd mailed him some sections of *The House of Stone*, not all of it, just a couple of chapters. I'd been writing so much, I just hadn't had the time to copy more than that. My father read it while we waited for our pizza. Every so often, he'd laugh out loud and shake his head. When he was done, he tossed the chapters on the table and stared at me as though seeing me for the first time.

"Jesus, Pete! This is great stuff! Really great stuff. You're a real writer! It's got everything! Plot, narrative, dialogue, character development. It's funny as hell, and you're struggling with the same big ideas that humans have struggled with since the beginning of time. Life, death, love, sex. It's all in here, and it's just the first two chapters!"

"I just put down what I think," I said.

"You're like a fountain gushing stories. I still don't know what the market is for this, but just keep at it. Keep knocking at the door of genius, and eventually someone will answer."

"Thanks, Dad. I just started a potboiler, too."

"Potboiler, huh. Terrific! Thriller, mystery? What?"

"It's sort of autobiographical," I said. "I'm using a character that has my own name. Only I'm making him a better-looking version of me. He goes to work in a glue factory so he can get a dog. Plus, he gets a girlfriend named Mandy, the same name as my real girlfriend. The name of the book will be *Unglued: The Book of Strafe*."

"I thought you said it was a potboiler."

"Everything's a potboiler the way I write," I said.

"Speaking of Mandy, where is she? I thought you were going to introduce her to me."

"I forgot," I said. "I'll take you to dinner when I get my first supervisor check. You can meet her then."

The pizza came. It was thin and covered in mozzarella and tomato sauce, and flopped over in my hand when I picked up a slice. Olive oil dripped down my arm, and the mootz burned my mouth when I took a bite. It really was the best pizza in America, maybe even New Jersey, which is a joke about Jersey. I'd used that line before and always got a big laugh. I made a mental note to include it in a book someday.

"Speaking of supervisor's checks, how's your training going? Learning anything new?"

"You bet," I said. "Other than the company not wanting me to write any stories on company time, I learned that one of the guys in the training found out during a break that his son has a uterus and ovaries inside him. He's got a vagina behind his penis and scrotum, and the doctors want to operate. He's been menstruating inside himself for the past year. It's complicated because he's got a testicle that actually produces sperm, too. Apparently, it's pretty rare. The doctors want to operate and turn him into a full man or a full woman. Pretty interesting, huh?"

"This isn't one of your stories, Pete? Is it?"

"I swear," I said. "The other guy heard it too. The other guy's family's from India and set him up in a convenience store. He showed up at the store one day, and thieves stole the building right out of the parking lot in the middle of the night."

"How's that even happen?" my dad asked.

"It wasn't a really big store. Only a few hundred square feet. Maybe not much larger than a trailer," I said. "Someone obviously figured out a way to do it. Nothing that happens is ever really too weird as long as you're willing to think about it long enough."

172

We ate pizza and had some beer. I probably had three or four since I didn't have to worry about stumbling into a batch of hot melt that night or falling headlong into a vat of latex and getting mangled by the mixing blades.

"What about you, Dad? How's everything in your life?" I asked.

"Things are pretty good. Work's great. The Defense Department is working on a new generation of weaponry that they've been testing at Picatinny. Lots of new hires. I've been busy reviewing their work and assigning their pay scales."

My father worked at Picatinny, a military arsenal about forty miles away from Majestic in Dover. A few years earlier, a truck carrying nitroglycerin in solvent had blown up when it backed into a loading dock. The driver was killed, and a bunch of people were injured. Fortunately, my father wasn't around that area of the plant when it happened. I was just glad I worked in a factory where stuff generally didn't explode when you made a mistake. You generally had to make contact with the stuff at American Starch in order for it to kill you decades down the line.

"How's your girlfriend?" I asked.

"Good," my father said. I could tell the question made him uncomfortable, so I dropped it. I'm fairly empathetic when it comes to crap like that.

When we were done eating and drinking, we went outside. I pointed to the coffee shop.

"This was where the blind guy told me the story about the girl with the Bible verses written on her in Braille."

"Keep writing, Pete. I'm proud of all the progress you've made, and not just with your writing either. You're like a freight train that just keeps barreling forward in all areas of your life."

"Thanks," I said. "I'm proud of you, too."

We shook hands, and my father got in his car and drove off. He had a new car, a sporty little Fiat that looked good on him. I walked down the street to my mom's place. I tried to write a bit, but after a few beers, it wasn't very productive. Drinking beer is really only good for peeing and drinking more beer. I hung around in the living room and watched TV with Terra. I had a few more beers and even let Terra drink from one of the bottles. We hardly spilled any of it. Somewhere around midnight, I heard a noise outside. Terra sat up and began barking. I went to the kitchen and got a steak knife. Then I went to the front door and turned on the porch light. When I opened the door, some guy hiding in the bushes to the right of the porch went running off like a bat out of hell. I watch him scoot across the lawn in the moonlight and down the street that ran beside the house. I'd heard there'd been a series of robberies in the neighborhood, though he'd probably picked the wrong house to rob if that's what he was doing. There wasn't anything very valuable in my house except for my dog. He'd have been better off trying to rob one of the houses in Mandy's neighborhood. I thought about stenciling a sign over the front door like Shitty Smitty was always stenciling around the locker room at American Starch:

NO VALUABLES HERE

But that was just one of those stupid ideas a person gets when they're drunk. Smitty was nearly always drunk, hence his ridiculous signs. The first thing I was going to do, I told myself, was to cut down on the drunkenness in the department, though that was probably just the beer talking, too. I looked out over the moonlit lawn and the street and told myself that someday I'd live in a neighborhood that someone would be proud to be a burglar in. Then I went back into the house and locked the door. I went down into the basement and put on a Simon and Garfunkel record and got undressed while moonlight spilled through the basement window and fell in a little square on the floor. I got into bed, and Terra hopped up next to me. I sang along with the words to "Fakin' It." I didn't really know the lyrics, I just kept repeating "I'm only fakin' it" over and over until I dropped off to sleep.

I woke up early and went upstairs to take a shower. The house was still and cool. It was autumn, my favorite time of the year, when everything turned brown and died. After my shower, I got dressed and went down to the coffee shop before heading to American Starch for my second day of supervisor training. I was a bit hungover from the six or seven beers I had the previous night. I sat down at the counter and ordered coffee and a couple of cinnamon rolls that I ate like pancakes. I poured a bunch of fake maple syrup on them and scarfed them down in like a minute, then I sat and drank my coffee and read the Star-Ledger, the big paper out of Newark. While I was reading the paper, the door opened, and Sonia walked in. She saw me and sat down next to me. She had a couple of scratches on her face.

"Are you following me?" I asked.

"Why would I follow you?" she scoffed.

"I was making a joke," I said.

"I come here all the time," she said. "I was dropping off my dry-cleaning next door."

"Uh-huh," I said.

"I go to the pizza place next door, too," she said. "All the time. I even saw you there last night talking to an older man, but I didn't want to interrupt you. It looked like you were having quite the conversation from what I could hear of it."

When she said all that, the hairs on the back of my neck prickled.

"Yeah," I said. "That was my dad. He's been reading some of the stories I've been writing before I send them off to magazines and whatnot."

"A writer, too," she said. "Interesting."

"Some weirdo was hiding outside my house in the bushes last night," I said. "If I'd caught them, I probably would've stabbed them."

"Really," she said.

I looked at her arms. There were scratches on them, too.

"Yeah, I would've torn them a new asshole, that's for sure."

Sonia laughed nervously and ordered a cup of coffee.

"I'd love to read some of your stories sometime," she said. "I bet they're fascinating."

"No doubt," I said. I threw three dollars on the counter for the cinnamon rolls, coffee, and tip. "Gotta head over to my training now."

175

"Stop by the lab sometime," she said. "I don't get many visitors."

"Sure," I said.

I walked outside and got into my car. I wondered why Sonia had been hiding in my bushes. She didn't seem like the kind of person who'd be a thief. It's possible she suffered from some disorder like kleptomania or something. I decided that I'd better watch out for her, which was weird. A few months earlier, I'd really wanted to get into her pants. Now that it was fairly obvious she was interested in me, I wanted nothing to do with her. Still, I was flattered by the attention. On the drive to the supervisor training, I passed some kids wearing different costumes. There were a couple of princesses, a hobo, and mostly the boys looked like monsters with scary makeup on their faces. It was Halloween. I'd forgotten all about it. I'd make sure to pick up some candy to hand out when the kids came trick or treating.

The supervisor training was more of the same, though Swifty did stop by and give us all a pep talk about how important our jobs were, and that we were the vanguard for bringing American Starch into the forefront of the adhesives industry. All in all, it was a pretty good speech, the kind you might see some military dictator in a uniform and funny hat make to a group of soldiers just before sending them to their deaths. After he left, we all sat around and talked about how fortunate we were to be part of the vanguard. Even Roberts looked glad to be part of the vanguard despite having a kid whose fully functional penis and testicle or ovaries and uterus were about to get destroyed. I wondered what would prevent someone like that from getting pregnant, other than the obvious mechanical difficulties. I couldn't see why not. I wondered if someone who took their own virginity would technically still be a virgin since they'd never had sex with anyone else, but I didn't really come to any definitive conclusions about that. Maybe I'd write a story about it or include it in *Unglued: The Book of Strafe*. Anyway, while I was ruminating about human self-fertilization, the instructor had been asking me for examples of appropriate responses to unwanted sexual advances made by co-workers.

"Mr Strafe, ah you payin' attention or ah we g'n have to fill out a fo'm on you?"

"Well, obviously the correct response is to fill out an incident report and submit it to our immediate supervisor."

"An' what'd be the name o' th't fo'm, Mr Strafe."

"That would be the 'Unwanted Sexual Advance Form'," I said.

"That is corr'ct, Mr Strafe. We won' have to be fill'n out no fo'm on you t'day."

Lunchtime came, and I hung around the management break room and bought some chips and a soft drink out of the vending machine. I didn't want Sonia tracking me around Dunellen if I left the plant for a sandwich. I sat down at a table with Jyoshi and Roberts. Roberts still didn't know what they were going to do. They were going to pray about it with their pastor later in the week, and I was pretty certain how that would end up. One perfectly good uterus and a couple of ovaries would go to waste, though maybe they could be transplanted into a woman who wanted a baby but whose own plumbing didn't work. Jyoshi told us all about his uncle who'd been born with a foot growing out of his head and another Indian woman who'd had surgery to remove a growth that contained an eyeball, a couple of teeth, and something that looked like an ear.

"The woman and her husband kept the growth in a jar and prayed to it every day," Jyoshi said. "India is full of such gods."

Day two finally ended, and I drove down to the Shop Rite and picked up some Smarties and Mars Bars. I'd give out all the Smarties first and save the Mars Bars for later in the evening just to ensure there'd be some left. I liked Mars Bars and could never get enough of them. By the time I left the grocery store, it was already starting to get dark, and the streets were filling up with kids dressed like witches, vampires, zombies, and monsters. Majestic was full of such gods.

177

# Chapter 25 Sonia

Other than the Fourth of July, Halloween was probably my favorite holiday, not named Christmas or Thanksgiving. Free candy ranked right up there with getting a bunch of presents, eating until you puked, and blowing stuff up with fireworks, both legal and illegal. I probably went trick or treating until I was nearly ready to graduate from high school. I'd get stoned with friends, then go door to door without even a costume when I got the munchies, so I didn't really mind when the older kids came to my door. They usually didn't start showing up until it was much later in the evening. The really little kids would start knocking on my door around five or five thirty while their parents watched from the sidewalk or stood on the doorstep behind them, making sure I wasn't a pervert. The unchaperoned kids generally showed up from six to eight, the younger ones earlier, the twelve and thirteen-year-olds, later. After eight thirty, it was usually just the scroungy high school kids with pimples and wispy chin hairs who knocked on the door because they were high. Sometimes they wore costumes, which was weirder than if they didn't. I mean, what normal seventeen-year-old actually plans on going trick or treating if they aren't high? Mostly, I liked messing with the older kids who weren't wearing a costume when they came to the door.

"Hey, man! Nice costume," I'd say. "You must be a pirate!"

"What? I'm not wearing a costume!"

"Well, if you're not wearing a costume, you don't get any candy."

"Yeah, okay."

"Dude, just say 'I'm a pirate!' and I'll give you some candy,"

"Okay, I'm a pirate."

"No, man. You gotta say it with enthusiasm. 'I'm a pirate!!!' Otherwise, no candy."

"I'm a pirate!"

"What?"

"I'm a pirate!!"

"C'mon, man, one more time!"

"I'm a pirate!!!"

"Okay, dude. Here's your Mars Bar. Don't go next door. They only give out that candy corn crap."

This particular Halloween went pretty much according to script for most of the evening, though it was a bit bizarre, too. Most years, half the kids dressed up like Superman or Batman or Luke Skywalker or the latest superhero. This year, the kids all dressed like John Travolta in Saturday Night Fever. It was a bit concerning to me as a citizen. I mean, what did it bode for the future of the free world if the kids of the USA were dressing up like Tony Manero instead of Rocky Balboa? I had to count my breaths for a couple of days afterward just to get my head around it.

There were probably only a couple of hundred kids who'd shown up that night, which was fine with me. By eight forty-five, I'd hardly given out any Mars Bars and would have darn near the whole bowl for myself, though I did have to give out a couple more when two stoners without costumes rang the doorbell. They stood giggling on the porch when I opened the door.

"Trick or treat, man!" The first one said.

"Yeah, man, like trick or treat!"

"Ok, guys, do a trick!"

"Huh?"

"What?"

"You said 'trick or treat', so I'm asking for a trick."

"No, wait! We're supposed to get a treat!"

"I think you do the trick, man!"

"You wanna see me pull a rabbit out of my hat?" I asked.

"Cool!"

"You got a real hat?"

"Tricked you!" I said. "I don't know any magic tricks."

"That's lame."

"No, wait! Where's your hat!"

"Ok, guys, here's your Mars Bars. I'm just glad you guys weren't dressed up as Tony Manero."

"Who?"

"I don't think you even have a hat, man!"

"Get out of here," I said.

I went inside and looked at the clock. It was after nine. No one was likely to show up now, though I kept the front porch light on just in case. I went into the kitchen and grabbed a beer out of the refrigerator, then I went and sat down in the living room with Terra and watched "Three's Company" for a while. It was kind of a dumb show. Two women and a guy try living together platonically. If I were the guy, I would've been trying to nail both women. The episode that was on was about a serial womanizer named Larry who gets engaged to a woman who only wants his money. She makes a pass at Jack, the guy living with the two women. Jack turns her down, then tries to convince Larry that she's not really the woman for him. It was completely unbelievable. If it had been me, I would've completely had sex with her since she was hot. When that show ended, "Taxi" came on. It was fairly new. It had only been on for a couple of months. The show revolved around a taxi company that had a bunch of weird drivers, and a mechanic named Latke who hardly spoke English. They had a really crude dispatcher who's played by a guy who was basically a midget. He clomped around and threatened the drivers with termination and withholding their pay. It was funny as hell. The episode that came on featured another wedding engagement. INS agents descended on the taxi company and tried to deport Latke for being an alien. The drivers set Latke up to marry a hooker so he won't get deported. I had just gotten to the point in the show where the hooker comes down a flight of stairs wearing a bridal dress when the doorbell rang. It was nine forty-five. The stoners were out late tonight, I told myself. I went to the door and opened it, then took a step back. I'd been expecting to find another pot-smoking teen or two that I could mess with before giving them their Mars Bars and sending them on their way, but I discovered a woman standing on my doorstep dressed in a sexy nun's outfit. She wore a wimple that covered her hair and a black mask over her face. Her dress was tight, low-cut, and exposed most of her cleavage. it came down to the top of her thighs and exposed virtually all of her legs, which ended in a pair of red stiletto pumps.

"Hello, Strafe," she said. "Trick or treat!"

I opened the screen door, and the woman extended her arms to embrace me, and I noticed there were scratch marks on them.

"Sonia?"

"In the flesh," she said. "Aren't you going to invite me in?"

"Okay," I said, "but you can't stay too long. I'm heading to bed in a little bit."

"Me, too," said Sonia.

Sonia took off the black mask. She came into the living room and sat down on the sofa in her sexy nun's outfit. On the TV, Latke and Vivian, the hooker, were getting married by Reverend Jim. He was giving a crazy, rambling discourse on love.

"Aren't you going to offer me something to drink?" Sonia asked.

"I've got beer," I said.

"Don't you have anything harder?" Sonia said. "The harder the better."

"It's beer or nothing," I said.

"When in Rome," Sonia said.

I went to the kitchen and got a beer. I put it in a semi-clean glass that I'd used earlier to measure out rice into a saucepan. I handed the glass to Sonia, and she sipped at it and made a sour face.

"I'm not much of a beer drinker," she said. "I prefer my drinks the way I prefer my men, strong and neat, or maybe with a little twist to keep it interesting."

"Look around," I said. "You're in the wrong place if you're looking for something neat."

"I've been a very naughty nun," Sonia said. "Aren't you going to spank me?"

"Look, Sonia, a few months ago I would've happily carried you downstairs and done the dirty with you until 'Starsky and Hutch' came on. But I told you I was engaged, and I'm not going to do anything to screw that up."

"Are you sure you can't be persuaded?" Sonia said.

She pulled off her nun's wimple and shook out her hair. It was long and cascaded down around her shoulders. She pulled her blouse down below her breasts and reached behind her back, then she unclasped her bra and took it off. Her breasts were large, firm, and beautiful, although she did have a fairly large birthmark on the left one that looked somewhat geographical.

"I appreciate the offer, Sonia. I really do. Under different circumstances, we'd already be in bed together. It kills me to say it, but I just can't. By the way, has anyone ever told you that the birthmark on your left boob resembles the Italian peninsula?"

"A lot of guys have told me that before," Sonia said. "Maybe all of them."

"Well, it's appropriate given that you're Italian and everything."

"My last name is Papadapolous," Sonia said. "I'm Greek."

"Close enough," I said. "When I was in college, one of the guys in my dorm had a mole on his stomach that looked like Abraham Lincoln. It even had six or seven hairs coming out of the part that looked like Lincoln's beard. Whenever he got drunk, he'd take his shirt off and recite the Gettysburg Address, which wasn't as interesting as you'd think it would be. Not after the third or fourth time, anyway."

Sonia put her bra back on and pulled up her blouse. I was somewhat relieved, though not entirely happy. It would've been alright with me if she'd just sat there for the rest of the night and let me stare at her boot-shaped birthmark. After she'd finished putting her breasts away, she put her hands to her face and began sobbing. I was used to women crying. When my dad left a couple of years back, my mom cried all the time, so I knew exactly what to do. Nothing. You let them cry until they cry themselves out. Then you gave them a tissue so they could wipe their eyes and blow their nose, preferably in that order. Finally, you said as little as possible, or they'd think you actually cared and talk to you all night.

"I don't know what's wrong with me," she said. "I do this all the time. I'll stalk some guy for a while who might even start dating me. After a couple of months, the guy leaves because I tried seducing his best friend or his father. Then I'll go weeks rejecting every guy who's even remotely interested in me. I'll be nasty to guys who just say, 'hello.' After about six months, I started thinking that maybe I'll begin dating again. That's when I turn back into a stalker."

"Uh-huh," I said.

I handed her a tissue that she used on her nose. I had to give her a clean one, so she didn't wipe her eyes with snot.

"Maybe you should become a real nun and practice chemistry in a monastery in France that makes wine or something."

"I was a real nun!" she cried, "Where do you think I got this from?"

She picked up her wimple and threw it across the room, and started blubbering all over again. The wimple had hit Terra sleeping in the dining room. She yawned and sat up. Fortunately, she stayed in the dining room. If she'd come over, Sonia would've started petting her and would've really wanted me. Such was the power of dog ownership. I got up and picked up the wimple and handed it back to Sonia with a couple more tissues.

"I got kicked out after sleeping with one of the priests," she said. "That's when I went back to school to study chemistry."

Sonia put her wimple back on and stood up.

"I won't bother you again," she said. "Thanks for listening to me."

She left, and I went to the door, locked it, and turned off the porch light. Then I went back to the sofa and called Terra. She came over and climbed onto the sofa with me. Together, we watched the rest of Starsky and Hutch. Starsky gets involved with a woman whose previous lovers have all died at the hands of one of her other boyfriends, who's a psychopathic killer. When the episode ended, I was pretty glad that I'd never done the deed with Sonia. I didn't need some psychopathic ex-lover of hers stalking me. I picked up the beer I'd given her. She'd hardly touched it. I polished it off, then went into the kitchen for another. By the time midnight rolled around, the beer was all gone, and I was pretty hammered. From a writing standpoint, the evening was a complete disaster, but at least I'd gotten some material I could write about. I had to admit my interaction with the teenagers who were high when they knocked on my door was just classic.

# Chapter 26 Drink

I went to my last training supervisor training session and slept through most of it, but I passed the test at the end of the training and got a certificate that I could frame and hang on my basement wall along with my black light posters. I threw it in the trash can on my way out the door. I didn't need that. I was officially the midnight shift supervisor for American Starch. I went down to the glue department to see who was around, but I didn't really know many of the guys on the second shift except Cenkghis Uk. He saw me and came to the weigh scale.

"Hey, cousin, how come you never teach my cousin English? Company fire him! Now he in New York working as busboy in gay bar."

"Hey," I said. "I never said I'd teach him English. I said I'd think about it. So, Guney's working in a gay bar? He's gay?"

"No, not gay, cousin. Just work there. Sometimes pick up little spending money letting gay men play with penis but never play with theirs. Not what Turkish men do."

"Uh-huh," I said.

"Is not bad money," Cenkghis said. "I work there when first come America. Americans willing to pay good money for putting mouth on penis. Much better than when I live Germany."

"Well, nice talking with you," I said.

"Okay, cousin. I'll tell Guney you say 'hello'."

Cenkghis left, and I walked up to the lab. Sonia was getting ready to leave for the day.

"Hi," I said.

"Hello."

"I just wanted to stop and tell you not to worry about last night. I've done my share of stalking in my day."

"You have?" Sonia asked.

185

"Sure! Sometimes I'd see an attractive woman in a grocery store and follow her up and down the aisles, trying to get the nerve to say something to her, but it's never led anywhere. I never had much success using 'nice tomatoes' as an opening line. Of course, I never hid in their bushes or followed them home, either, though I've thought about it."

"Well, thanks for telling me that," said Sonia. "It makes me feel better."

Sonia gave me a hug, and I left the lab. I felt good about how I handled the situation with her. I'd honored a bunch of the Grave Precepts of Zen. I had taken refuge in the Dharma and was one with the universe. I left the factory and went down to Coconuts. I hadn't been there much since I'd started dating Mandy. I had a beer and watched a few of the girls dance. Charity was up first. She was a bit too chunky for me. After ten or fifteen minutes, she was replaced by a dancer named Faith. She had a nice, tight athletic body and swung around the pole like an Olympic gymnast. Her face was a bit of a mess, though. After a while she left and was replaced by a girl named Hope who couldn't dance worth a damn. She just kind of stood there shuffling her feet back and forth, but she had a nice body, and her smile looked genuine. I tossed Hope a couple of bucks, then went to the phone and called Mandy.

"Where are you?" she said. "It sounds like you're standing inside a jukebox."

"I stopped for a beer," I said. "What are you doing?"

"Oh, I've been sketching out some ideas for sculptures," she said. "The church that commissioned the one you saw is thinking about hiring me to do another. They'd like one about the concept of love. It still has to get final approval from the church board, but it's got me thinking about how much I love you."

"I love you, too," I said. "Wanna go out for a burger and fries?"

"No," she said. "You know I'm a vegetarian, but I'd love to sit with you while you eat."

"I knew you'd say that. That's why I asked. I'll be over in a little bit to pick you up."

186

I drove over to Mandy's and parked on the street. Her parents' cars were both in the driveway, so there'd be no fooling around at her place that evening. Her dad was in the living room reading the paper and listening to Beethoven or Bach, or Mozart. It all sounded pretty much the same to me. Not like rock 'n roll, where all the bands sounded different.

"Hello, Mr Victor, how are you tonight?" I asked.

Mr Victor put aside his newspaper and picked up his scotch from a little table next to him. His eyes were red and glassy.

"Fine, Peter. Amanda tells me you got a promotion at work."

"Yeah," I said.

I was about to tell him about Bob Robert's son, who was an honest-to-goodness hermaphrodite, but Mandy came down the stairs. I'd have to tell Mr Victor about it another time.

"We'll be back in a couple of hours, Dad."

I looked at the clock. It was almost six.

"Don't wait up," I said.

Mr Victor looked at me with a scowl and took a sip of his scotch. He picked up his newspaper and opened it in front of his face, so we didn't have to look at each other. Mandy and I went outside and walked to my car.

"I don't think your dad likes me very much," I said.

"Oh, that's just the way he is, Strafe. Don't take it personal."

"Maybe I should let him read some of my stories, you know. Give him a chance to get to know me."

"You be better off just buying him a bottle of scotch."

"Yeah, he likes scotch better'n I like beer," I said. "And I like beer pretty good."

"I've noticed," said Mandy.

We got in the car and drove over to HoJo's. I didn't want to go to Dominico's and risk running into Sonia just in case she wasn't completely over stalking me. The same waiter who served us the night I'd proposed to Mandy waited on us again. He looked at the ring on Mandy's finger.

"It looks better without pudding on it," he said.

I ordered a beer and a burger with fries for myself. Mandy got a salad and a cup of hot water for the tea bag she had wrapped in a napkin in her pocketbook. She'd only used it once before, and it had another use or two in it. While we waited for the waiter to bring us our orders, Mandy talked about the wedding.

"My parents want to keep the guest list to under one hundred," she said. "Is that okay with you?"

"One hundred?" I said. "It'll be a stretch to have fifteen people on my side of the family show up. Where am I gonna find another thirty-five people?"

"Well, that's fine," she said. "Just make a list of people you want at the wedding with their addresses so invitations can get sent out. Plus, you'll need to take some classes at the church before we can get married. You have to get confirmed and baptised or the church won't marry us."

"Confirmed? Baptised? Really? How much is this gonna cost me?"

"I don't know that it costs much, if anything," Mandy said. "You're okay with it?"

"Sure," I said. "I don't have to believe it. I just have to do it."

"Well, it's better if you believe it, too."

"Why?" I asked. "Just so I behave like I believe it, what's it matter if I think it's a load of crap?"

"That's a terrible thing to say!"

"Action trumps thinking in my book," I said. "People say all sorts of nonsense, but if you want to see what people believe, just watch their feet. The feet don't lie. You can talk about being a sculptor, but what makes you a sculptor is actually making a sculpture. 'Talk is cheap when the fat's in the fire'."

188

I heard that somewhere and wasn't really sure exactly what it meant, but it sounded appropriate, under the circumstances. Mandy mulled over what I'd said for a few seconds, then nodded her head.

"Okay," she said. "Okay. Just don't get into any theological discussions with the priests about Zen or Emptiness or anything. Just get confirmed and baptised so we can get married."

"We can go down to the county offices and get married tomorrow," I said. "We don't need the church and Jesus or Zoroaster and Ishtar of Mesopotamia in order to marry."

"I would like a marriage that is sanctified by God," Mandy said. "Don't you want a marriage that's holy in the eyes of God?"

"Well, if you're asking me if I want an unholy marriage, then the answer is 'no.' Mainly, I want you to be happy, and I'll do whatever you want, Mandy. I'm that crazy about you."

The waiter brought our orders, and I began eating right away. Mandy said a little grace over the sad-looking leaves of her salad before digging into it, but from where I sat, the grace didn't do anything to make the lettuce leaves perk up. When I pointed that out to her, she laughed.

"That isn't the point," she said. "Every once in a while, I just like to express gratitude to God for every good thing in my life."

"You should've ordered a milkshake instead of the salad," I said. "Those are way better here than that sorry-looking thing you're eating. Though I wouldn't recommend the pudding."

"You're a good person," Mandy said. "Sometimes I just wish you'd see yourself the way I see you."

"How's that? How do you see me?"

"I try to hold the image of Christ in front of you and see you from that perspective. 'We are God's children now, and what we will be has not yet appeared; but we know that when He appears we shall be like Him because we shall see Him as He is. And everyone who thus hopes in Him purifies himself as He is pure'."

"Big shoes to fill," I said. "But you might want to hold an image of the Buddha in front of me. I'm trying to reach an ideal state of oneness with everything, including this hamburger."

"A lot of Buddhists don't eat meat," Mandy said. "Why don't you become a vegetarian, too?"

"Well, I can give up ham," I said.

The capicola sandwich I'd had a couple of days ago hadn't sat well with me. I'd passed gas nearly all afternoon in the supervisor training class.

"It's a start," said Mandy. "Now, let's talk about your drinking."

"I don't drink that much," I said. "Less than just about everyone I work with."

"I don't want you ending up like my father," Mandy said. "He drinks every night and just passes out in his chair. I don't want you ending up like that."

"I hate scotch," I said.

"It's not what you drink. It's just that you drink."

"You drink wine," I said.

"I have an occasional glass," Mandy said. "Maybe once every two weeks. I don't get drunk."

"I don't get drunk every night."

"Well, lately it seems like you've been getting drunk just about every night."

"Okay," I said. "I won't give up drinking completely, but it does get in the way of my writing. I'll make sure I keep it under control."

"Promise?"

"Sure," I said. "Easy."

I drove Mandy back to her house and walked her up to the door. I could see her father through the living room window. He was still sitting in his chair with the newspaper covering his face and head. An empty bottle of scotch sat on the table next to him, next to an empty glass.

190

"It's like this every night," Mandy said. "It's sad and a waste of life."

"Did you know the word 'alcohol' comes from the Arabic word 'al-kuhl', which means body eating spirit?" I asked.

"You know everything and nothing," Mandy said. "Talk is cheap when the fat's in the fire."

She kissed me and went into the house. I watched her take the newspaper off her father's head and help him to his feet.

I drove home and thought about what Mandy had said about my drinking and about holding the image of Jesus in front of me. At least she hadn't gotten on me about my dog. I probably would have called off the marriage if she'd said anything bad about Terra.

When I got back home, I wrote a chapter in my book about the character named after me. Strafe had gone to work in a glue factory and had his first blow job while working there on his first night. When I was done writing, I read what I'd written. It was good stuff. I couldn't wait to get a real typewriter and make it look professional enough to send to a publisher. A story like that typed out on unlined paper was sure to get the notice of dozens of publishers who'd no doubt fight over the right to publish my work. I had another beer, then went to bed. The world swirled round and around like the lines of a Van Gogh painting as I drifted off to sleep.

# Chapter 27 Frogs

I went to the Pistols game before my first night in the glue department as a supervisor. It was Safe Sex Night at the arena, and all paying customers received a free Trojan with the face of the Pistol's starting point guard printed on the wrapper. Underneath his picture, these words were printed:

Because You Always Dribble Before You Shoot

It was really pretty clever. I wish I'd come up with that slogan myself. The free condom promotion was way better than the free toilet bowl plunger giveaway I'd gone to a couple of weeks earlier. After the game, I was pretty sure that a bunch of people were using their promotional item in the parking lot, though I didn't go up to any parked cars and peer into them for confirmation, but it did appear that the customers were scoring more than the Pistols had that evening.

I only had one beer around halftime. I wanted to be sober for my first night as a supervisor. I got to the factory early and parked in a spot reserved for the supervisors, and went into the factory. I didn't have to change into my glue pants or even punch in. I just walked down to the office in my street clothes and opened the door. Virgil was sitting behind his desk, adding and subtracting numbers on his calculator. He looked up when I walked through the door.

"Hey, Pete. How's the hammer hanging?" he said.

"My hammer's hanging just dandy," I said.

"I like that, Pete. I like your hammer's hanging dandy. I'll have to remember that. I should write it down before I forget."

Virgil pulled a little notepad from his shirt pocket and scribbled something in it with a pencil, then returned the notepad to his pocket. After he put it away, he grabbed a clipboard from the top of his desk and handed it to me. There was a stack of forms clipped to the board. I flipped through them all. Everything I needed to report incidents of malingering, malfeasance, insubordination, failure to give maximal effort, sickness, lost time injury accident, and various types of physical and/or verbal harassment and intimidation was on the board.

"Boy, there certainly are a lot of forms for us to fill out," I said.

"Fill out?" said Virgil. "Don't worry about filling any of those out except for the lost time injury accident form. That one's important. The rest of them? Forget it. If you see the crew doing something you don't like, just threaten to fill out a form. That generally brings them back into line. Nobody has time to fill out those forms, let alone read them."

"Well, that's a relief."

"Ok," Virgil said. "Now get out there and supervise the hell out of those guys."

I left the office and walked over to the weigh scale. On the way, I passed the sign showing how many days the glue department had gone without a lost time accident. That number stood at two. One of the donkeys on the day shift had smashed his hand with a hammer while banging down lids to some five-gallon buckets of latex-based adhesive heading to a paint company. As far as injuries went, it was pretty minor. Just a few broken bones in his hand. He'd be back to work with a cast on his hand, and they'd put him on light duty. All in all, an injury like that was a godsend to the injured person. You got paid the same as everybody else, but hardly had to do anything. There was only so much anyone could do with a busted hand.

Lenny was handing out blue sheets at the scale when I walked up. Everyone ignored me. Now that I was a supervisor, I was no longer welcome in the fraternity of glue. I'd been disbonded and no longer adhered to the substrate comprised of the midnight shift workers. It was disorienting. There were two new members of the crew who had started earlier in the week. One was the woman everyone had been talking about the previous week. She was a short, stocky black woman with short hair that looked like it had been pasted to her head. She had a crude tattoo on her arm that looked suspiciously like one of the prison tattoos some of the other workers in the glue department sported. She also had a single teardrop tattooed on her face beneath her right eye. Everything about her flashed "Don't Fuck with Me."

The other new process helper was a guy about my age. His name was Dawkley. He was a bit slack-jawed and had a bad, short haircut that looked like he'd given himself with one of those haircutting attachments that came with a Kirby vacuum. There were bald spots all over his head. He stood slightly apart from everyone else and scratched himself. It made me itchy just watching him. Lenny put Dawkley with Wiggins and set them to work cutting and packing out resin for the soup company. Wiggins would be doing the cutting. Dawkley would stand on the back side of the cutter and pack out the resin after the pieces fell into a tray on his side. I walked down to the cutter with them.

"Whatever you do, make sure you follow the safety protocols posted here on the wall," I said. "Under no circumstances are you ever to put your hand under the cutter blades. If the blades get gooey, then get a can of Insta-Freeze and spray it on the blades. Then scrape the resin off with a chisel. Trust me. I've put my fingers under that blade before, and I'll never do it again. No one told me about the Insta-Freeze until after I'd already cleaned off the blades by hand, but I'm telling you now."

"You done?" Wiggins said. "Or we gonna stand here all muthafuckin' night with you be jibber jabberin' at us?"

"I'm done," I said. "Just keep your hands out of the cutter."

I went up to the weigh scale and looked at the pink sheets in Lenny's box. The pink sheets were duplicate copies of the blue sheets and had the work assignments of everyone in the department. When I was done reviewing them, I stuck them back in Lenny's box, then wandered around the department and supervised the hell out of the place. Graupner was working on a tank truck. He had torn a cheesecloth bag into strips and wore them around his head like a sweatband. When he saw me coming, he put his hammer and a crowbar together and held them up like a cross.

"Don't get any closer or I'll put a fucking stake through your heart," he said.

"Fuck you, Graupner. I just came over to see if you needed any help setting up the filter press for your tank truck."

194

"Naw," he said. "I got it. I don't want to get done any quicker than two o'clock. There's another tank truck due at three, and I don't need to be put on hot melt or sent up to the crusher while I'm waiting for the next truck to come in."

"Suit yourself," I said. "I'm supposed to threaten you with filling out one of these Malingering Forms on my clipboard, but I'm not gonna do that."

"Good," said Graupner. "Just because they give you a whistle doesn't mean you have to call a foul. I like that. You're not bad for a fucking rat."

I went upstairs and found the new woman dumping bags of tapioca in Tank 6. Her name was Shirley. I introduced myself and watched her for a couple of minutes. She was quick and efficient. She picked up fifty-pound bags, sliced them open with her box cutter, and dumped the tapioca in the tank in quick fluid motions. I could've watched her work all night. After a while, I left her alone to work and went downstairs. Larry Edgerton was slopping around in a puddle of latex and water by Tank 24. He was half ass drunk and wouldn't start sobering up until two or three in the morning. He looked pretty terrible. His face was all grayish yellow and saggy like old wet dough. It was fairly ghastly, like one of those rubber Halloween masks that some of the kids had worn earlier in the week when they'd knocked on my door. He was struggling with a three-inch hose that he was trying to attach to a fitting on the tank. It wouldn't go on, so I grabbed a heavy metal pipe and pounded it into place for him. The brass fitting on the hose would have to be swapped out with a new one soon. Once they got to the point that you couldn't attach them to a tank without pounding the hell out of them with a metal pipe, they were pretty well shot. The ears on the hose fitting wouldn't stay down by themselves, and I had to tie them down with strips of cheesecloth so that the hose wouldn't come off the tank. When I'd finished tying down the ears on the fitting, Larry grunted. It was like working with a pig. I walked away and left him to fumble around in the water and latex some more.

One o'clock came, and I went up on the roof and sat by myself on the water tower deck while the crew all went on break. The air was chilly, and I could see my breath come out in short, visible shrouds of mist.

You could feel winter lurking around the corner. I sat in the dark and counted my breaths and only counted my breaths. My mind was an empty circle wrapped around a rock, sitting by itself in the darkness. I could hear all the noise of the factory and the traffic passing by on Front Street. I could even hear the sound of Wiggins shouting and laughing in front of the bench, but it was just another form of silence that meant nothing. I had answered another riddle. Then I stopped counting my breaths, and the bell ending break echoed throughout the glue department. I was and was not the sound of a bell ringing across a vacant sky.

I climbed down from the ladder and then walked over to the bench. Buda was adding caustic soda to a tank. I kept my distance until he was done. He took off his safety goggles and removed his long rubber gloves.

"You supervising all the donkeys?" he said.

"Supervising the hell out of them," I said.

Buda laughed.

"Who's supervising the supervisor? Eh? You?"

"I'm pretty well self-contained," I said. "I don't need anyone watching me."

"Self-contained? What's that mean, Rocky?"

"It means I'm accountable for myself," I said. "That's the way it should be."

"Should be, could be, would be. Everybody tink they are accountable to self. Then boss come and tell them to do this some tink or that some tink. Then they jump like little frog. You little frog, Rocky?"

"I'm not a frog," I said. "I'm the thing that watches the little frogs."

"Don't kid yourself. Everybody is little frog. Even the ones who watch the ones who watch the ones who watch the frogs. Must never forget that. You forget that and next tink you know you are marching people to gas chamber, wondering how you came to be marching them to gas chamber. Stay little frog, always in your head. Do that and everybody wins."

"Got it," I said.

I left the bench and went down to the weigh scale. Shirley had finished dumping Tank 6 and was getting another blue sheet from Lenny.

"What you got?" I asked.

"Tank 8," she said.

I took the sheet and looked at it.

"Cigarette glue," I said.

It was going into a single 750-gallon stainless steel tote bin.

"This is your lucky night," I said. "This job is a piece of cake."

I helped Shirley put organdy in the filter basket and hook it up to the pump. Then we pushed the funnel of the pump up to the tank and positioned the filter basket over the tote. When everything was ready, I told her to open the gate on the tank and turn on the pump.

"Let 'er rip!" I said.

Just before she turned on the pump, someone let out the worst blood-curdling scream I'd ever heard. I banged the gate on Tank 8 closed with my hammer. The first scream had been followed by several more. I ran down the ramp to the cutter. Dawkley had blood all over the front of his t-shirt and down his pants. He was holding his left fingers in his right hand. Wiggins was standing next to him.

"I done tol' him not to put his muthafuckin' hand un'neath that blade while he was packin' out on t'other side of the cutter. Think he listen to me? Hell no! Now look what he done! Cut them goddamn fingers off like they was made o' butter!"

"You stay with him," I shouted at Wiggins.

I ran up to the office and dialed 911. An ambulance got there in six or seven minutes. Then they loaded Dawkley into an ambulance. He was still clutching his fingers to his chest when he left. The paramedics had tried to take them from him and put them on ice, but he wouldn't let them go. After the ambulance left, everyone stood around the weigh scale, talking about what they'd seen or where they were when they'd heard Dawkley scream.

"Save it for break," I said. "Go back to work. The tanks aren't gonna empty themselves."

I walked over to the office with my clipboard.

"Good job, kid," Virgil said. "Make sure you fill out that Lost Time Accident Report Form before the end of the shift and get it to me. I've got to submit it to my boss, Terry Donahue. Terry'll review it and get it over to Swifty. Okay? Don't forget."

"I'll get it done," I said.

I went outside and took the number two off the lost time accident board and replaced it with a zero. With any luck, Dawkley would get his fingers sewn back on if he was willing to let go of them. He probably wouldn't be returning for light duty any time soon. The problem with little frogs is that they're easy to overlook and easy to squish. Then you end up wondering how they managed to get squished while you were supposed to be watching them.

# Chapter 28 Refinery

The refinery department was a series of wooden, steel, and brick structures that seemed both dilapidated and labyrinthine. I'd walked through it several times by myself and had always gotten lost. I'd end up in an enormous room full of huge stainless-steel tanks with rotating blades that were twenty feet across, or stumble into some silent, decrepit warehouse in the heart of the refinery filled with a pharaonic treasure of tapioca flour, sago, and cornmeal. Bags of potato, wheat, and rice starch would be piled to the ceiling, which was stained, here and there, with water that had dripped through the roof during the last passing storm.

It would be a good place to hide if you were an employee. It seemed twice as big as the glue department, but the circles of hell were fewer in the refinery. The sign outside the refinery office door served notice that the department had gone 622 days without a lost time accident. Upon closer inspection, that accident was due to the improper lifting of a fifty-pound bag of tapioca. The employee was sent home with a sore back and returned to work after a long weekend at home, soaking in a bathtub and applying bags of ice to the affected area. So far as I knew, no one had lost so much as a fingernail in the refinery, let alone a finger.

I didn't like going down to the refinery, even though it was obviously safer than working in Glue. The rats were even bigger than those in the warehouse. I'd seen a couple when I'd gotten lost in the refinery, trying to take a shortcut from the management office to the glue department. A couple of them were sitting on a bag of rice flour they'd torn open. They looked to be the size of the raccoons I'd seen in the woods by a creek near my house when I was a kid. One of the workers down in the refinery told me that the rats arrived at the factory in shipments of raw tapioca from the Philippines, which was why they were twice as large as normal rats. A second shift refinery hand found a dead one after it had eaten a bunch of chicken laced with arsenic that he'd put out for it. He claimed it measured thirty-two inches from its nose to the tip of its tail and weighed close to five pounds. From what I saw of them, it looked like a fairly accurate estimate.

Mostly, I didn't think about the refinery much. I had no reason, too. Virgil handled the material ordering for the department, and Red, the forklift driver, brought pallets of flour and starch from the refinery on a daily basis. He stacked them near the tanks as needed so the workers had easy access to them as well as the drums of chemicals that arrived at the factory and were unloaded every day or two.

I saw all of the supervisors once a week at the Monday afternoon staff meeting held at 4 p.m. in the supervisor's trailer next to the refinery. That was the best time for all of the first, second, and third shift supervisors to meet. The first shift supervisors had just gotten off work, the second shift supervisors were just beginning work, and the third shift supervisors were awake and present if nothing else. We'd go over production schedules and production targets. Someone would organize a committee to look into whether it was better to hire new employees or just pay more overtime. The safety committee would issue its weekly report on lost time accidents, and the immediate supervisor of any worker injured in a lost time accident would read his Lost Time Accident Report Form verbatim and give a short summation of how the accident could have been avoided. There had been two lost time accidents in the glue department that week. Billy Blake had been on duty during the first shift when Jason Ergot had broken his hand by hitting it with a hammer. Billy read his incident report, then gave a quick summation of how the accident could have been best avoided.

"Request was made of employee not to hit self with hammer."

"Maybe we should collect all hammers from the employees," opined Bob Roberts. "Maybe that would eliminate incidents of this nature."

"That idea was floated several months back when Dukey Edwards mashed his thumb with a hammer down in Solvents," said Hyman Semenowitz. "At the time, the management committee deemed it a non-starter. The major concern was that it would have a negative impact on productivity since a number of processes could not and would not be affected without direct force, most efficiently applied by the force amplification derived by converting mechanical work into kinetic energy. Of course, you had no way of knowing that since this is your first meeting, Bob."

Hyman had a BS in Mechanical Engineering and took every opportunity possible to impress the rest of the supervisors with how smart he was.

"Would you repeat that louder?" said Bob. "I only heard about half of what you said."

After Hyman repeated his observation for Robert's benefit, it was my turn to read my report on Dawkley's fingers. When I'd finished reading my report, one of the second shift supervisors from the off-site chemical warehouse asked how the accident could have been avoided.

"Well, I'm sure the cutter could have fitted with a simple device like you find in just about every grocery store door in the country," I said. "As soon as a worker reaches into the cutter, his hand breaks an electrical or infrared beam of some sort, and the cutter blade immediately stops its descent and the cutter's hydraulics retract the blade to its original position."

When I was done talking, there were several seconds of uncomfortable silence. Soupy Blackman, a second shift supervisor in the Maintenance Department, finally spoke while all the other supervisors shot me glances out of the corners of their eyes.

"From a mechanical standpoint, the idea has merit, but from a liability standpoint, any alteration to the cutter ex post facto is an admission of culpability on the company's part. Kid, the question is 'what could the employee have done differently not to cut off his fucking fingers?'"

"He could have followed company safety protocol as posted on the wall beside the cutter as well as a direct statement from me issued at the onset of his shift to never under any circumstances stick his fucking hand into the cutter," I said.

"Excellent!" said Soupy. "Well done, kid."

"And on a positive note, surgeons at St Elmo's were able to successfully reattach Dawkley's fingers. Estimated return to light duty is eight to twelve weeks. Estimated return to full duty is sixteen to twenty-four weeks."

"Let's get him back to full duty in fourteen weeks," said Virgil's boss, Terry Donahue. "Let's not forget, if the doctors had been unable to

201

reattach his fingers, he'd have been able to return to full duty in six to ten weeks. If he's not ready for full duty in ten weeks, we'll just let him go and replace him with someone else. The guys down in Glue have always been expendable."

I wanted to say something after Terry spoke, but I didn't want to rock the boat. I mean, I'd only been a supervisor for a couple weeks and wasn't sure how much I could or should say about the horrific working conditions in the Glue Department that people had been complaining about for weeks, and months, and years, without anything being done by the company to correct any of the problems. So, I kept my mouth shut. When I published my thinly veiled fictional autobiography whose main character had the same name as me, then the entire world would know what crappy conditions the donkeys in Glue had to work under. Until then, I would just go along to get along, and I wouldn't use company time to write my stories either. I'd just carry around a little notepad like Virgil did and jot down ideas for stories and poems when they struck me as I was supervising the hell out of people.

After the meeting Jyoshi and I went down to Coconuts for a beer. Jyoshi had never been in Coconuts before, but he did drink alcoholic beverages, once in a while, since there was no Hindu religious prohibition against their consumption. Jyoshi drank his beer very slowly and deliberately while watching the stripper's dance. He seemed curiously detached. After five or ten minutes, Jyoshi looked at me and smiled.

"In Hinduism, erotic dancing is part of our religious tradition, Mr Strafe. In India, there were snake dancers who danced in the temples. Their job was to guide the souls of men away from the suffering of this world. It is believed that suffering can be eliminated through prayer, meditation, or through sensual enjoyment, where the pleasure of sex frees men from desire. The *apsaras*, the female spirits of the clouds and waters, are superb in the art of dancing. The erotic dance between Krishna and the goddess Radha represents the unity of masculine and feminine energy. Sex is sacred in Hinduism, Mr Strafe. Thank you very much for showing me the American version of sacred eroticism."

"I don't know how sacred this is, Jyoshi. They pretty much just want you to throw money at them."

202

"Oh, no, Mr Strafe. The dharma does not allow this! Nor would my wife understand!"

"Yeah, my fiancée wouldn't understand, either. Fortunately, I gave up throwing my money away on the strippers last year, right after I started working in Glue. I pretty much gave away my first couple of paychecks down here for nothing. Now I just come down here to look and grab a quick beer."

"Well, Mr Strafe, I thank you for my beer and the pleasant time spent in your company. Now I must return to my duties at home."

I stood up, and Jyoshi clasped both my hands in his. Then we walked outside and spoke for a moment. I looked down the street towards American Starch. As I watched, the outer wall of the refinery bowed outward, and a great cloud of smoke and debris was hurled into the street. An enormous boom followed, and the ground shook under our feet. Debris began raining down around us a few seconds later.

"Jesus!" I said. "I think the refinery just blew up!"

Jyoshi and I ran down the street toward the refinery. As we got closer, we could see people staggering out of the ruins onto the pavement in front of the building. Some of the workers were bleeding, and many had their clothes shredded by the blast. I recognized Whitey Black. He was sitting in a pile of brick, wood, and twisted strands of rebar in the middle of Front Street. His left hand had been severed in the blast and was sitting in his lap. I took of my jacket and tied it around Whitey's arm as best I could. The funny thing was that Whitey just sat there calm as pie, as though nothing had happened. He even asked me for a cigarette. I handed him one and gave him a light. He took a long drag. Then he smiled and transferred the cigarette to the fingers of the hand that was sitting in his lap while the long, loud wail of an emergency alarm from somewhere inside the refinery sounded continuously for the next twenty minutes.

Jyoshi and I helped as many of the dazed and injured as we could, but there wasn't a whole lot we could do. We had nothing to cover the injured with to keep them warm. I stripped off my outer shirt and gave it to a worker who was covered in blood and seemed to be missing an eye. Fortunately, fire trucks, ambulances, and police vehicles began arriving on the scene after a few minutes, and the injured began receiving the medical attention they needed. I looked inside the hole in the outer wall of the refinery. It looked like the explosion had ripped through a couple of the refinery buildings. There was nothing but a pile of sticks and rubble where the trailer housing the supervisor's office had been ten minutes earlier. I caught myself wondering who was going to fill out the Property Damage Form. I hung around for a half hour or so assisting as best I could. When it started getting dark, I went home and sat in the living room without turning on the light. Terra came over and sat beside me.

Around seven o'clock, I turned on the local news. The main story, of course, was the explosion at the refinery. There were a bunch of pictures of the devastation and film of fire trucks and ambulances with their emergency lights flashing. The Chief of the Fire Department was interviewed and informed everyone that an investigation as to the cause of the explosion was underway. Three workers were confirmed dead, and two were still missing. Eleven people had been transported to St Elmo's with head, arm, or leg trauma. Swifty was interviewed by a man in an overcoat and a knit cap.

"We're still investigating the cause of the explosion," said Swifty.

Some of the residents, a few blocks from the refinery, were interviewed.

"We heard the explosion and went outside. That's when debris began coming down from the sky," one nearby resident said.

"We heard the explosion, went outside, and then a brick hit the windshield of our car and shattered it," said another.

"We heard the explosion, went outside, and there was a man's arm hanging from the limb of a tree," said a third.

After about ten minutes, I turned off the TV. Then I went downstairs and put on a record. Jimi Hendrix was asking Joe where he was going with that gun in his hand. I climbed into bed and took a nap before heading back to work. I had the feeling that the guy who'd lost his arm would not be returning to full or light duty ever.

# Chapter 29 Nosmo

The investigation into the explosion lasted nearly two months and was conducted by local and state regulatory agencies as well as the US Chemical Safety Board and OSHA. Based on the evidence gathered at the point of the explosion, it appeared that the ventilation system in the refinery had failed. Starch dust and flour had quickly saturated the air in one of the drying rooms, and a spark of static electricity from one of the belts driving the huge tank blades had caused the powder explosion that ripped apart the drying room and killed Johnny Gottfried, who was in the room when the explosion occurred. The initial rumor was that Johnny had literally gotten blown out of his boots, but this was completely false. His boots were found with his feet still in them. It was his arm that had been discovered hanging from the tree several blocks away. His other arm was never found, but his head and legs were located a few days later in Chicago. Apparently, they had gotten blown up into the air and landed in the uncovered hopper of a railway coke car that had been passing behind the refinery when the explosion occurred. All in all, this was fortunate since Johnny originally hailed from the Windy City. The rest of his remains had already been shipped back to his parents in Union Park for his funeral. By the time Johnny's head and legs were identified as belonging to the victim of an industrial accident as opposed to the victim of a serial killer, the funeral had already taken place. Johnny's torso and arm had already been buried. A separate casket was prepared for Johnny's legs and head, and he was buried                             beside                             himself.
The investigation also concluded that the supervisor trailer had been destroyed by shrapnel from the initial blast. It had been literally torn to pieces, as was the trailer's sole occupant at the time, Bob Roberts. American Starch had finished the job that the mortar in Vietnam had been unable to complete. According to the Fire Chief of the Majestic Fire Department, Bob had been "blown to smithereens." Some of the smithereens were never found, but among those that were recovered was a piece of forearm with the words "Semper Fi" tattooed beneath an eagle sitting atop a world globe that was superimposed in front of

an anchor. It was from this tattoo that Bob's identity was confirmed by the coroner's office.

I sometimes wondered if Bob and his wife had ever prayed with the pastor of his church about the subsequent disposition of their son's sexual orientation. Had he been castrated, and had a penectomy been performed? Or had his uterus been surgically removed along with his ovaries? My own personal opinion was that the child should have been allowed to make the decision himself as to whether to live as a man or a woman or both, but I had little faith that anyone had allowed him, her, or them to make that decision himself, herself, or themself. I never found out what happened with the son or daughter or them, but I do know what happened to Bob. They collected his pieces, and he was buried with his Silver Star. A squadron of Marines fired a twenty-one-gun salute while his widow grieved.

The explosion had also destroyed the refinery locker room while Shitty Smitty, The Locker Room Chief, had been standing on a ladder stenciling a message above the door:

PLEASE NOSMO KING

For a brief period, FBI agents converged on the factory in an attempt to determine if a Mr Nosmo King was connected in any way to the refinery explosion. They left after a few days, but not before they'd interviewed just about everyone in the glue department. They'd even interviewed me. An FBI agent came to the glue department around midnight and asked each of us if we knew a Mr Nosmo King.

"You're kidding? This is a joke, right?"

"Do I look like I'm kidding?"

"Nosmo King? You know it means 'no smoking', right? The guy who posted this was an alcoholic who did stuff like this all the time."

"So, you do or don't know a Nosmo King?"

"No! No one else in Glue knows him either."

"We'll be the judge of that."

The only worse investigation into the cause of the explosion was conducted by American Starch itself. It concluded that the explosion was caused by Johnny Gottfried, who violated all safety protocols by lighting a cigarette inside the drying room while the air was filled with tapioca dust and cornstarch. As evidence, they produced a Zippo cigarette lighter with Johnny's initials engraved in the metal. In front of a state investigatory board, they pulled out the lighter and introduced the testimony of several workers who all claimed that Johnny was a heavy smoker, though under questioning, none could recall any incident where they'd ever actually seen him smoking while working inside the refinery.

In the end, American Starch was found to be responsible for the explosion, and a judgment in the amount of one hundred and thirty million dollars was levied against them. On appeal, the amount of the judgment was reduced to two hundred and fifty thousand dollars. Similarly, the class action lawsuit brought against the company by former employees who'd been maimed, disfigured, or disabled while working at the factory was settled out of court. American Starch agreed to pay the plaintiffs a total of ten million dollars. In exchange, the plaintiffs agreed to drop their lawsuit against the company for maintaining a hazardous workplace, and plaintiffs' demands that the company admit guilt and/or responsibility for the injuries workers sustained while working at American Starch were dropped as well. Dawkley and others were given six-figure settlements for three-finger losses. Non-disclosure agreements were signed by all parties, the clouds parted, and the sun shone on American Starch brighter than it had before the refinery had gone up in a cloud of smoke.

All in all, the judgment against American Starch, as well as the out-of-court settlement with those former employees who'd been injured, represented a huge victory for the company. The company invested the money they should have lost, had justice actually been served and the original judgment been allowed to stand, in upgrades to the equipment in terms of safety and efficiency. The future o' glue had actually arrived. But it arrived without my approval or blessing. Ultimately, no one in management lost their job. No one went to jail for criminal negligence. The parts of the refinery that were damaged in the explosion were repaired within three months, and everyone was happy, except for the families of the workers who'd been killed and replaced by other expendable pieces of human machinery.

207

In the weeks and months following the deaths and injuries in the refinery, my heart wasn't in working. I couldn't reconcile my growth as a person with my responsibility as a supervisor in the glue department for a company that put profits before people. I went to work, but I refused to supervise the hell out of people. If I found someone sleeping on the job, I walked past them and let them sleep. I caught Graupner peeing in the hot melt tank and joined him in adjusting the pH with my own pint of uric acid. I hung around with the crew during breaks and listened to Wiggins discourse on the death and destruction that had occurred in the refinery. The midnight shift still wasn't talking to me, but they let me sit on the bench with them while Wiggins walked back and forth in front of us, gesturing wildly.

"Company claim that white dude Gottfried done blowed up the refinery smokin' in the dry room in all that starch dust and powder. I don't b'lieve that fo' a minute. Not one goddamn minute! Ain' that right? He been 'round that refinery ten year. Ten whole muthafuckin' year! That white muthafucka gone smoke in all that damn dust and powder? Hell no! That sonofabitch might be dumb, but nobody that damn dumb! OSHA say it was static electric. CSB say it static electric. State reg'lation board say static electric. Ever'body say static electric but this muthafuckin' company! Wanna blame a dead man who got blowed out his shoes! That's a goddamn shame! Innit? I don't believe it fo' one muthafuckin' minute!"

I walked back up to Glue with the midnight crew. Virgil was waiting for me at the top of the ramp.

"Let's take a walk, Pete," Virgil said. We went up to the second floor and I sat on a drum of corn oil. Virgil stood on a pallet next to a drum of trichlorethylene.

"I've noticed you've been taking your breaks with the midnight crew," Virgil said.

"I have been," I admitted.

"Officially, there's no real policy against fraternizing. But there's an unwritten rule about it, Pete. The unwritten rule is unwritten for a reason. The company can't legally force you not to take your break outside, but birds of a feather and all that. People are watching, Pete.

208

People are watching, and they talk. I hear the talk. Believe me when I tell you I'd rather not hear it, but there it is. Word gets around. I don't want to hear it, but it's definitely there."

"Word gets around," I said.

"Exactly! In the beginning, there were a bunch of words. People notice, and there's idle chatter. People are watching you. Now, I don't give much stock to rumors, but there's an unconfirmed rumor going around that you've been using company time to do some type of non-company work. Now, it's just an unconfirmed rumor from an anonymous source, but if upper management sees you fraternizing with the hourlies and doing non-company work on company time, it might not be good for you. People want to know that you're a company man, Pete. Are you a company man?"

"I don't know," I said. "The explosion in the refinery messed me up. I have questions I haven't been able to reconcile about myself and the company."

"The explosion?" Virgil said. "No one believes for a second that poor bastard Gottfried was smoking. What kind of dumb bastard lights a cigarette in a blizzard of starch? Gottfried was a smart man. He ran Bingo Night at the Knights of Columbus. He didn't deserve to get blown out of his shoes. No one does! But all that's immaterial. Are you going to be a company man or go on break with people you're better off leaving behind? Are you going to do non-company work on company time? What's it going to be?"

"Can I think about it?"

"Sure, Pete. Take your time. Think it over. Just remember that people are looking at you, which means they're looking at us, which means they're looking at me. I went to bat for you, Pete. When the fat's in the fire, just remember who went to the plate for you with the lumber in his hands."

Virgil walked off. He walked like his shoes were attached to his pants, not his feet. He moved like a ghost over the grounds of a graveyard and then disappeared down on the bench. I hopped down off the barrel of corn oil, then turned around and looked at it. Someone had taken the large bung out of the top of the drum and had replaced it with a screw-in hand pump. I looked at my hands. They were clean and free of glue or latex. I pumped some corn oil onto my hands and rubbed it all over my hands and face. I worked it into my hair and beard like I was anointing myself into some priesthood I didn't understand. I took my shirt off and rubbed the oil all over my chest. Then I dropped my pants and coated my legs and thighs with it.

I sat out with the midnight crew on the three o'clock break and again at five. I'd made my decision. Seven o'clock rolled around, and I left as quickly as I could. When I got home, my mother was in the dining room. There was fresh coffee in the percolator. I poured myself a cup and then sat down at the table across from my mother.

"Hi, ma. How are you?"

"Fine, Peter, you know. How are you?"

"Okay," I said. "I'm thinking about leaving American Starch. Ever since the accident in the refinery, my heart's not in it. It's bad enough they don't want me writing on company time, but now I'm supposed to ignore the crap the company does that gets people injured and killed."

"What you do then? Where you work? You can't have wife and live under bridge!"

"I'm not gonna live under a bridge. I'll find something. I'm just wondering if the glue factory is really the place for me. I mean, I like the money, but people lose fingers and get killed, and I'm supposed to be a company man. I'm supposed to let the company piss on my head and tell me it's raining."

"Someone try make piss on you?"

"Ma, no, no one's pissing on me literally. The company wants me to believe that a worker named Gottfried blew up the refinery while smoking a cigarette. Everyone knows that the explosion was caused by an equipment failure that filled the dry room with explosive powder that got ignited by a static electricity spark."

"Not right, they tell you a lie."

"No," I said.

"You good person, Peter. You do the right thing. Okay?"

"Okay," I said.

"How come you smell like corn oil?"

"I anointed myself with it."

"Oh, really? Why you annoyed?"

"Work, " I said.

I went outside and brought in the newspaper. Then I read my mother her horoscope and the comics and explained them to her. When I'd finished my coffee, I tossed the newspaper on the table and went downstairs. I'd bought a new typewriter, an electric one, and I sat and wrote a chapter in *Unglued: The Book of Strafe*. Strafe goes to work one night in the glue factory, and one of the other workers kicks over a bucket of boiling petrochemical resin and waxes and falls in it. When I was done writing, I reread the chapter a couple of times. It was absurd and tragic, pretty much how everything was at American Starch. I put the chapter in my accordion file. Then I put on one of the few jazz albums I owned, *Time Out* by Dave Brubeck. I put it on and climbed into bed. I listened to "Blue Rondo a la Turk," "Strange Meadowlark," and then my favorite song on the album came on, "Take Five," It was quirky and odd with its 5/4 time that sounded like a tire going flat beautifully while the alto sax floats through the song like a giant blue butterfly. If I were a musician, that's how I'd do it, I told myself. That's how I'd do it. That's how.

I was awakened at about two o'clock by the ringing of the phone. I went upstairs and answered it. My mother was sitting in the living room watching TV with Terra.

"Ma, how come you didn't get the phone?" I asked.

"What?"

"Never mind," I said.

I picked up the phone.

"Hello?"

211

"Yeah, I'm back."

"Who is this?" I asked.

"Who do you think?"

"Klondike?"

"Bingo!"

"What do you mean you're back?"

"California sucks!" Klondike said. "Everything's costs three times more than it should. I'm moving back to my mother's place. LA's a toilet!"

"Where are you now?" I asked.

"Somewhere near the Delaware Water Gap. I'll see you in a couple of hours. Bye."

"Bye," I said.

"Who call?" asked my mother.

"Klondike," I said.

"Oh, crazy person. *Kichigai*!"

"He's not that bad," I said. "He'll be here in a couple of hours."

"Good thing I go work. Not be here. Tetched."

I went back upstairs and showered. Then I went downstairs and got dressed. It was late December, just a couple of days before Christmas. After I finished dressing, I went upstairs to call Mandy. She'd been sick the last few days and had gone to the doctor, but wasn't getting better. I was a bit concerned. I'd bought two tickets to see the Pistols, and I was concerned that Mandy would be too sick to go. She'd never been to a pro basketball game before. I hadn't been to a game since Safe Sex Night, and was really looking forward to seeing them play. They were playing the Buffalo Buffaloes. The Buffaloes were terrible, almost as bad as the Pistols, but their coach was into Zen, and I wanted to see how he coached his team. I dialed Mandy, and her mother answered.

"Hi, Irene," I said. "Is Mandy there?"

"No, she went back to the doctor. Do you want her to call you?"

"Absolutely," I said.

"Okay, I'll tell her. Goodbye."

"Okay," I said.

I hung around the basement writing until my mother left for work, then I went upstairs and ate a couple of cans of sardines and some French toast that I made with some saltine crackers since we were out of bread. I hadn't eaten anything made from pork in over a month and had really cut back on my drinking, and felt transcendent and spiritual. I'd gone to all the confirmation classes that I was supposed to and was nearly at the end of them. I hadn't argued with the priest at all. I was doing this for Mandy, I told myself, not me. The fact that I was doing something for someone else, in spite of how I personally felt about it, made me feel pretty warm inside. Then I thought about work and felt kind of sick and depressed. I just couldn't get enthused about it. I went downstairs and put on a record of Nat King Cole singing Christmas songs. That cheered me up. Wiggins really did look like him.

The Christmas Song came on. The song ended, and I put it on again. After I'd played it about four times, the doorbell rang. I went upstairs and opened the door. It was Klondike. He looked half frozen. The heater didn't work in his Volkswagen, and he couldn't close the windows all the way because he'd put his mattress on his roof again and tied it down with rope and bungee cords that he'd run through the windows.

"You want some coffee so you'll warm up?"

"Is it fresh?" he asked. "Don't give me any crappy coffee."

"I can make a fresh pot," I said.

"Let's play chess," he said. "I'm looking forward to smashing you!"

We scrounged around in my mom's sewing kit for buttons and bobbins and spools and things we could use for pieces. After the board was all set up, Klondike got the first move. He destroyed me in the first game, which was par for the course. He beat me in the next games easily. Somewhere around the fifth or sixth game, I managed to take one of his rooks with a bishop. Then I took a knight with the bishop. Then I called to check with my rook. Then I took his queen. Then he was furious. He was the worst loser of just about anyone I knew.

"The problem is you're too attached to the result," I said.

"So?"

"It prevents you from appreciating the process," I said. "From being in the present."

"Sounds like you've been doing that est training. California is full of those phonies. Those assholes are everywhere. Some chick invited me to an est evening, and the whole thing is a cult."

"I'm into Zen," I said.

"Same bullshit, different toilet paper."

The phone rang and I went into the kitchen and answered it. It was Mandy. Her voice sounded weird. It was like she was laughing and crying at the same time.

"Are you okay?" I asked.

"I'm not sure," she said. "I went back to the doctor today."

"What did he say. You're not dying, are you?"

"No, I'm not dying."

"Well, what did he say? Jesus!"

"He said you're going to be a father?"

"What?!"

"I'm pregnant! We're going to have a baby!"

"Jesus! You're kidding. A baby!"

"The doctor thinks sometime in September."

"No kidding?"

"No kidding!"

"Okay, I said. Are you feeling good enough to go watch the basketball game tonight?"

"I think so."

"I'll pick you up at six thirty. It's free puck night tonight. Everyone gets a free hockey puck with a Pistols logo on it."

"It's a basketball game. Why aren't they giving away basketballs?"

"It's probably way too expensive to give away basketballs. Pucks are cheap."

"Okay, I need to tell my mom I'm pregnant," Mandy said. "You're not mad, are you?"

"About what?"

"About being a father."

"That, no that's great. I've got a dog. Pretty soon I'll have a wife and a kid! I'm really happy!"

"I was a little nervous about how you'd react," she said.

"I'm thinking about quitting my job," I said.

"Wait! What?"

"My job. I'm thinking about quitting."

"We've a baby on the way!"

"Yeah, you said that."

"Let's talk it over before you do anything crazy."

"Okay," I said. "I'll see you at six thirty. I don't want to be late. Only the first five thousand people get hockey pucks. There's usually only about two thousand five hundred people who show up to the games, but the Pistols have a chance to win tonight. The Buffalo Buffaloes are terrible. Probably a lot of people will be there."

"Okay, bye."

"Bye!"

I hung up the phone and sat down at the table across from Klondike.

"So, are you gonna be a father or what?"

"Yeah," I said. "I'm gonna be the best father in America."

215

"I hate kids," said Klondike.

"Is there anything you don't hate?" I asked. "Is there one thing in the world you absolutely love?"

"I don't think so," he said.

"You need to love something," I said. "A dog or a cat or a woman. Even yourself."

"Don't get started with the est crap. The next thing you know, you'll be selling Amway door-to-door. If that's not a cult, I don't know what is!"

We played a couple more games of chess. Klondike smashed me in both games. He stood up and put on his jacket. I gave him a cup of coffee in a Styrofoam cup and went outside with him. I held his coffee while he snaked his six-foot-eight-inch frame through the Volkswagen's open window. Then I gave him his coffee. He backed out of the driveway and headed toward the highway. It was good to see him, but this time it was easier to watch him go. I was going to be a father, and it was free hockey puck night at a pro basketball game. What could be better?

# Chapter 30 Circle

The Pistols won, which was really good. If they'd lost, people would've probably started tossing pucks onto the court and at the opposing players and referees. I think that might have been on the backs of the minds of the refs when they were calling fouls. It was pretty interesting watching the Zen Master coach the Buffaloes. Most coaches drew up plays during timeouts, not the Buffaloes' coach. He just sat quietly while the team crowded around him, looking lost. They just needed to find their inner playmakers, I thought. They probably would have beaten the Pistols if some of the Buffaloes had discovered their inner playmakers.

Afterward, we went to an all-night diner and had a cup of coffee, though Mandy just ordered her regular cup of hot water and a slice of lemon and used her own tea bag.

"My mother decided to push the wedding up to March from June," Mandy said.

"Your mother? Why did she decide?"

"Well, they're paying for it. She doesn't want everyone to know I'm pregnant. I won't be showing that much in March."

"Okay," I said. "I guess the sooner the better."

"We need to send out the invitations in the next week or two, so you need to get me the list of everyone you want invited."

"I can do that right now," I said. I was about to start naming people off, but Mandy stopped me.

"Write it down," she said. "On paper."

"Okay."

"I know you hate working at the glue factory, so I was thinking. I have a sister who lives in California."

"LA is a toilet," I said.

217

"It's north of San Francisco. It's beautiful there. I've visited. They've got wineries and dairies and redwood trees and the ocean. I think you'd like it there. With your background pumping glue from tanks into barrels, you should be able to get a job in a winery putting wine into bottles."

"Do they have breweries, too?"

"I don't know, but my sister sends her kids to this school, that based on the writings of some mystic Christian anthroposophist who wrote a lot of books about the astral plane. I read some of it and would like to study it more. There's a whole community of anthroposophists who built a school in Santa Rosa and are educating their kids as spiritual beings, not just as machines to be chewed up and spit out like that factory you work in."

"It sounds like a cult," I said. "Will we have to sell Amway?"

"What are you talking about?"

"I just want to make sure I don't have to go door to door selling anything. If I'm going to join a cult, I want it to be a good one."

"It's not a cult."

"I can still be Zen?"

"As much as you want."

"Okay," I said. "It's a deal."

I spent the next couple of months getting prepped for the wedding. I got confirmed so that we could get married by the church. I even got baptised. A priest poured water on my head out of a chalice. I went to church and took communion and everything. After services, people would come up to me and shake my hand. Old guys were always patting me on the shoulder and telling me I needed to be one of the Crusaders of Seville, a church-based fraternal organization, because of all the good work they did in the US and around the world.

"We do a lot of work in the peripheries," one of the old guys said.

"Peripheries?"

"You know, around the globe. The peripheries."

"Oh, yeah, the peripheries, right?"

"We collected $65,000 last year for children in need of prosthetic legs in the Lesser Antilles."

"Wow, how many of these children in the peripheries need artificial legs?"

"You'd be surprised, young man!"

"You bet!" I spoke.

"We need a bingo caller, too! Ever pull balls out of a basket?"

"I got them caught in a drawer once. Hurt like hell."

"What?"

"Maybe after Mandy and I are hitched and get all moved to California," I said.

"Oh, the Crusaders of Seville are everywhere in the world. Wherever there's a need, we rush right in and fill it. Our brothers in California are doing fine work with the poor and indigent."

"I work with the indignant, too!" I said.

"A fellow like you could fit right in! A strong back and a willing spirit!"

"Sounds great," I said. "They don't go door-to-door selling Amway, do they?"

"What?"

"Amway, they don't sell it, do they?"

"Well, I happen to be an Amway Ruby Direct Distributor," he said. "Why? Do you happen to need some liquid organic cleaner?"

"Does it work on glue?"

"Absolutely," he said. "Let me go get you a bottle. I've got some in the car."

The old guy left, and Mandy came over.

"I like that you're talking to people," Mandy said.

219

"I'm pretty sure it's a cult, but it seems like a good one. They give legs to kids in the Lesser Antilles. Plus, I just bought a bottle of organic cleaning fluid from somebody. He said it works with glue. Probably not bumper sticker glue, but it's worth a try."

The old guy came back and gave me a bottle.

"Here's your LOC," he said.

"Yep, this is the LOC, alright. How much do I owe?"

"Nothing! That's a gift for your wedding! If you ever want to become a distributor, look me up, young fella. I'm Arsenius Pepper. I used to be a doctor too, so everybody calls me Dr Pepper, but my friends call me Arsy."

"Arsy," I said. Stacked up next to Arsy, I'd probably choose Peter any day of the week.

"Like the cola," he said. He drew some imaginary letters in the air. "R C, Arsy. This your bride to be?"

"Yeah. This is Mandy. She's a sculptor. She made those hands and the globe out in the courtyard."

"Oh, yes! Yes! Lovely to meet you! My wife and I have admired that sculpture so much."

"I'm a writer," I said. "I wrote a book that starts at the Grand Canyon, goes to New Jersey then to California. Finally, the book ends up on Mars. It's pretty good."

"I've no doubt. Mars, eh? Hmmm."

Arsy left, and Mandy and I went to her house. Her parents were out of town for the weekend, visiting friends in Connecticut. It was the first time I'd ever had sex with a pregnant woman. It didn't feel any different. Not then anyway. It was only the beginning of February, and you couldn't tell she was pregnant or anything.

When we were finished, Mandy lay her head on my chest and ran her fingers through my beard. Then she sneezed a couple of times.

"You might have to shave it off," she said. "I think I'm allergic to the food in it or something."

"It's probably the shrimp," I said. I'd had fried shrimp recently, and when I ran out of napkins, I wiped my hands on my beard.

"I think I got pregnant the night I cut my hand on the spindle," Mandy said. "That's the only date that makes any sense."

"It's symbolic," I said. "The spinning wheel is a symbol of the cycles of life."

"And the spindle?"

I put my hand on Mandy's belly.

"The spindle? The thing that pricked you? The thing you put in that whorl in the spinning wheel? The thing that gets fatter as you wind the wool around it? No idea." I said.

Mandy laughed.

"I think you'll be a good father," she said.

"The best," I said.

Mandy and I spent most of the day in bed. Late in the afternoon, we got up and dressed. Her parents were due back in a couple of hours. She made me some baked tofu with brown rice. I choked it down and had a second helping, just to prove I could.

"I haven't eaten ham or pork in a couple of months," I said. "I'm mostly on a fried shrimp and fried clam diet."

"Fried food is bad for you. It clogs your arteries," she said. "I want you to live a long life so you can see your grandchildren and great-grandchildren."

"On the planet Mars," I said.

"California's far enough," she said. "Aren't you excited?"

"I don't know," I said. "It sounds good, but I've never been farther west than Pennsylvania. What if we both hate it?"

"Then we'll go somewhere else, but I think you'll like it. My sister says it never snows. There are mountains and rivers. Oyster farms and cheese factories. She says once you live there, you never want to leave. It's like nirvana, a land flowing with lotus flowers and honey."

221

"When do you want to go?" I asked.

"Why don't we leave after the wedding. Our children will all be natives of the Golden State."

"You don't want to stick around here for a few years? Maybe leave after I save up a bunch of money?"

"I think we just need to do it. We can stay at my sister's in Forestville for a little bit. She lives in an apple orchard."

"Sounds like a fairy tale," I said. "Okay, let's do it."

I went out to dinner with my dad a couple of days later. He looked at me over the tops of his glasses when I told him that I planned to leave for California in a month.

"What are you going to do for money?" he said.

"I've put glue in barrels for the past year and a half. I can probably figure out how to put wine in barrels, too. I'll write a bunch of books and make millions of dollars off them, too."

"Uh-huh," he said. "What about Mandy? She doesn't have a problem with this idea?"

"She's the one who suggested it. Her sister lives out there already and will put us up until we get our own place."

"Well, okay. I don't understand you at all, Pete, but I suppose this is something you feel you really have to do."

"Yeah," I said. "I've thought about this long and hard for the past two days. I even wrote out a list of the pros and cons."

I pulled a folded-up sheet of lined yellow paper out of my pocket and handed it to my dad. He unfolded it and read it aloud.

"'Pros: wineries, cheeseries, ocean, mountains, no snow, orchards, oyster farms.' 'Cons: You've got nothing written under cons'," he said.

"I couldn't think of any," I said.

"It's far away," my dad said. "You won't see me or your mother very much."

"Maybe I can take up bike riding," I said. "I'll ride across the country every few years on a vacation and come visit."

"Why not just walk?" my father said.

"C'mon, Dad. Be serious. That would take forever."

"Okay, California, huh. That's quite an adventure. I'll miss these dinners of ours. Make sure you call."

"You bet," I said.

After dinner, we went out to the parking lot. The sun had gone down, and the moon and planets were out. It was a clear, cold night in early February, and hard knots of snow and ice rutted the parking lot like dirty broken dishware.

"In a way, I'm glad you'll be getting away from that factory. It's a death trap. I worry about you every night."

"I'm glad, too," I said. "But I'll certainly miss it. It's certainly been interesting being there the last year and a half. Short of being in prison, I can't imagine a more interesting thing I could've been doing."

"If I live to be one hundred, I'll never understand you, Pete."

We shook hands, and I watched my father stumble across the parking lot to his car. He'd been wounded in Korea and walked a little bit like Virgil. I'd miss him. Terribly.

I drove back home, and Terra greeted me at the front door. I'd have to buy my mother her own dog to keep her company now that Terra would be leaving. I flopped on the sofa and watched another episode of Taxi. Louie, the crude short dispatcher for the Taxi company, goes to the hospital for surgery and promises God he'll turn over a new leaf when he's afraid he might die. It was really a great show. It reminded me of all the funny, dumb stuff that happened in Glue. Maybe someday I'd write a screenplay and turn Unglued: The Book of Strafe into a funny TV series about people getting drunk or high in this glue factory and making really costly mistakes called blow jobs then getting their fingers cut off or their faces and arms burnt so bad they'd have to have skin grafts. If they didn't turn it into a TV show or at least a movie, then that would be a terrible loss. Nearly every comedy makes you laugh at things in people's lives that are pretty much tragedies when they're going through them.

When the show ended, I went to the factory early. The second shift was winding down, and I went up to the weigh scale. John Motley, the one who'd claimed he'd had a stable of women in Detroit when he was a pimp came over to me.

"Brother Strafe!"

"Hey, John."

"My man!"

"Indeed."

"Scuttlebutt is you gon' be leaving for the wes' coast."

I'd told a couple of the guys on Monday night that Mandy and I would be heading to California right after we got married. The word was already circulating through the department.

"Scuttlebutt is correct," I said.

"Where'bouts?"

"North of Frisco," I said.

"They got all sorts o' wine up there," Motley said. "Grape wine, cherry wine, plum wine, pear wine, make it out o' beet root, taters, yin yong, an' cantatious marrow, too."

"I'm gonna try to hook up with a winery," I said. "They put it in bottles, though. I don't think they put it in drums."

"Ima big wine fan. You heard that song 'There's Nothing Like the Rose'? Oh, yeah. That's the jingle jangle for one of my favorites, Wild Irish Rose wine. I like to mix it with vodka and Seven-Up. You may even call me a conno'sir of wine as well as women. Wished I were a younger man. I'd come out there wid you. We'd drive all the way to the Spacific and chase pussy till the sun rise up over Mexico! Get ourselves some Tijuana ladies an' pimp 'em out. Big John Motley back on the scene! Wes' coast, bes' coast, allus was my motto! There's nothing like the rose!"

Motley wandered away from the scale and into whatever crazed paradise he saw in his head. I went upstairs to the roof and climbed up to the deck of the water tower. It was freezing up there. I had to scrape a bunch of ice off the deck so I could sit down. I counted my breaths for ten minutes with my eyes closed. Thoughts rose up in me like bubbles that I let drift into the silence. Everything was empty and meaningless, and it was empty and meaningless that it was empty and meaningless. I opened my eyes. My pants were stuck briefly to the frozen deck. It was an easy matter to extricate myself. I just had to stand up. Then I climbed down the frozen ladder and went down into the glue department. One of the big Philippine rats stopped and watched me warily as I moved past him. They no longer scared me. I went up on the deck and said 'hello' to Jesús and Buda. I told them that I'd be leaving the factory and moving on to California, where I'd put wine in barrels instead of glue and make millions of dollars publishing books, and they both shook my hand. Buda even took the glove off his right hand, the one without the fingers. I could feel the stubs of his fingers pressing into my palm.

"Congratulations, Rocky. You make a wise decision."

"I don't know what the future holds, but it's going to be better than this," I said.

"Different. That much is certain."

I walked down the stairs to the first floor. The midnight shift was gathered in a halo of light shining down from a hooded ceiling lamp above the weigh scale. Lenny was handing out blue sheets, and the crew began shuffling off to their various locations throughout the department: Hot melt, tank truck, perfume glue, latex, jelly gum, cigarette glue, and cutter. In a little while, the area around the weigh scale was empty, and I just stood and watched Gresham circle round and round and round, weighing out the drums. My own circle of life was just beginning.

# Epilogue

Mandy and I got married on March 10th, 1979. She was three months pregnant and just starting to show. Her three sisters were the bridesmaids. Each of them was pregnant, too, not one of them under five months. I felt like a participant in a weird fertility ritual. I had wanted to do something special for the wedding, like walk down the aisle on my hands. I'd even practiced it and could have probably done it too, without falling more than once or twice, but Mandy wouldn't allow it. Against her better judgment, she did allow me to read my own vows, which were very mystical and full of Zen riddles. She even pre-read and approved them, except the part where I pulled out a piece of paper and read off a list of the pros and cons about marrying Mandy. There were lots of good reasons, including sex and the fact that she was going to be the mother of our child. I hardly listed anything in the negative column, just a couple of minor things like her being a vegetarian. When I was done reading the wedding vows and the list, you could've heard a pin drop in the church. People were so blown away by the list. One woman even said, "I never!" which obviously meant she'd never heard anything as fantastic at a wedding before.

My brother was my best man, which pissed Klondike off. He stood next to my brother on the right side of the altar and glared at him. Next to Klondike was Fillmore Graupner. He'd gotten a new headband for the wedding, one that matched our purple crushed velvet tuxedos. We definitely looked bitchin'. I hadn't wanted to steal all the attention away from Mandy since it was really her big day, but I could tell everyone was staring at our tuxedos. Klondike's had to be special ordered because he was so tall, and it almost didn't arrive in time. We almost had to get him a white one and spray paint it purple, which would've been okay. It just might not have dried in time.

The reception was the best! Everyone danced and had a really great time. The whole midnight shift crew from the glue department showed up and behaved like baboons. They drank all their champagne before the toast, and were all drunk before the food was served. I'd even invited Sonia from the lab. She probably had one glass of wine too many, too. While everyone was eating cake, she and Wiggins had gone out to her car in the parking lot and had sex. One of Mandy's sisters saw her hands and face pressed up against the passenger window in the backseat while Wiggins spanked her from behind with his belt. Virgil came and danced with my mom. They stayed together for many years afterwards and were happy and content until death separated them. My dad showed up with his girlfriend. She was pretty and witty, and they seemed perfectly suited for each other. Around ten o'clock, the party wound down. Everyone left and got home safely. Mandy and I went home to my basement and celebrated our first night as a married couple while Terra lay on the end of the bed and watched. All in all, everyone got what they'd come for.

We left for California at first light the next morning. It rained a little bit, which was supposed to be good luck, according to Mandy, anyway. We'd loaded everything in the Chevy for the trip west, but we hardly had anything. Some winter clothes and some books, my typewriter, a couple of Mandy's sculptures, and a bunch of wedding gifts. Mostly, they were boring things: toasters, food processors, oven mittens, and a frying pan with our names engraved on the cast iron handle. My favorite gift was a hand-carved wooden box with nothing in it. Klondike gave it to us. I have the box to this day and have kept it full of nothing continuously. Every so often, I open it up to remind myself just who and what I am. I kissed my mother goodbye, and she cried and kissed me back. Mandy's spinning wheel wouldn't fit in the backseat, so I tied it to the roof of the Bel Air and climbed into the driver's seat. Mandy climbed into the passenger door, and Terra sat between us. Then we left. On the way out of Majestic, we passed the blind man on his way to the coffee shop.

"Who was that man with the cane?" asked Mandy. "He waved to us as we passed him."

We pretty much drove straight through. When I got tired of driving, Mandy took over. When she got tired, we pulled over and napped. Somewhere around the third day, we passed through Reno and came down through the snowy mountain passes into California. The lower in elevation we got, the greener it became until the snow was far behind us, and it was warm and like finding ourselves in a green quilt of farms and almond trees, and walnut groves. We came down through

227

Sacramento then up through Napa and the quilt changed to vineyards and more vineyards and fields of yellow mustard and orange poppies all the way through Calistoga to roads lined with 300-foot redwood trees at the edge of more vineyards and dairy farms and orchards of pear and apple so beautiful we missed the turn and just kept driving out along a river than ran through hills covered with vineyards and cattle and sheep until we arrived at the Pacific Ocean with enormous gray green waves that crashed and surged against the great cliffs and rocks and listened to the barking of seals and the roaring of sea lions then stopped up on a headland jutting high above the water to watch a gray whale and calf pass silently down below us then doubled back through little towns and farms until finally we reached a little house in an apple orchard, the wooden circle of the spinning wheel going around and around and around as we pulled into the gravel driveway. We were home.

www.ingramcontent.com/pod-product-compliance
Lightning Source LLC
Chambersburg PA
CBHW070103260626
47160CB00004B/1295

* 9 7 9 8 8 9 3 9 7 5 5 5 0 *